MERCILESS KING

A DARK, MAFIA ROMANCE

DYNASTY OF DECEPTION

AJME WILLIAMS

ABOUT THE AUTHOR

Ajme Williams writes emotional, angsty contemporary romance. All her books can be enjoyed as full length, standalone romances and are FREE to read in Kindle Unlimited .

Dynasty of Deception (Dark, Mafia Romance Series)
Merciless King | Ice Princess

Mafia Mysteries (Dark, Mafia Romance Series)
Tangled Loyalties | Savage Devotion | Bulletproof Baby

Shadows of Redemption Series (Dark, Mafia Romance Series)
Soldier of Death | Queen of Misfortune | Prince of Darkness | Angel of Mercy

The Why Choose Haremland
Protecting Their Princess | Protecting Her Secret | Unwrapping their Christmas Present | Cupid Strikes... 3 Times | Their Easter Bunny | SEAL Daddies Next Door | Naughty Lessons | See Me After Class | Blurred Lines | Nanny for the Firefighters

High Stakes
Bet On It | A Friendly Wager | Triple or Nothing | Press Your Luck

Heart of Hope Series
Our Last Chance | An Irish Affair | So Wrong | Imperfect Love | Eight Long Years | Friends to Lovers | The One and Only | Best Friend's Brother | Maybe It's Fate | Gone Too Far | Christmas with Brother's Best Friend | Fighting for US | Against All Odds | Hoping to Score | Thankful for Us | The Vegas Bluff | 365 Days | Meant to Be | Mile High Baby | Silver Fox's Secret Baby | Snowed In with Best Friend's Dad | Secret Triplets for Christmas | Off-Limits Daddy

Billionaire Secrets
Twin Secrets | Just A Sham | Let's Start Over | The Baby Contract | Too Complicated

Dominant Bosses
His Rules | His Desires | His Needs | His Punishments | His Secret

Strong Brothers
Say Yes to Love | Giving In to Love | Wrong to Love You | Hate to Love You

Fake Marriage Series
Accidental Love | Accidental Baby | Accidental Affair | Accidental Meeting

Irresistible Billionaires
Admit You Miss Me | Admit You Love Me | Admit You Want Me | Admit You Need Me

Check out Ajme's full Amazon catalogue here.

Join her VIP NL here.

DESCRIPTION

I was born to rule an empire. She was born to shatter it.
Now, the girl who vanished a decade ago is back—with a secret
that could destroy us both.

I just broke an alliance with the most powerful crime family in
Chicago.
All for Piper Collins—the only woman who's ever brought the
mighty Don D'Amato to his knees.

She's not the same girl I fell for in high school.
She's stronger. Colder.
And married to a man who doesn't deserve to breathe the same air
as her.

I'll tear apart heaven and earth to protect her.
Even if it means war with the Rinellas.
Even if it means blood on my hands.

But when her daughter calls me "Daddy," my world implodes.
Suddenly, I'm not just saving Piper from her abusive husband.

I'm fighting for a family I never knew I had.

Now, as enemies close in from all sides, I'm faced with an impossible choice: My empire or my heart?

And when the dust settles, will Piper ever forgive me for the sins of our past?
Or will the secrets we've both buried become the bullets that tear us apart for good?

MERCILESS KING is book one in the **DYNASTY OF DECEPTION** series. Step into Chicago's treacherous underworld, where alliances crumble and forbidden desires ignite. This pulse-pounding story is the first of four interconnected standalones, each delivering its own guaranteed happily ever after. Brace yourself for scorching passion, heart-stopping suspense, and the raw power of love triumphing against impossible odds.

PROLOGUE

Elio - Eight Years Ago

L ife is fucking awesome. I drive my Porsche, bought with my own money I earned working in the family business, through the streets of Chicago to pick up Piper for our date. Tonight is a special night. The first night of the rest of our lives.

I grin as I remember the day Piper Sanderson walked into my English class at Ashwood Prep last year. She was quiet, unassuming, and not at all impressed with me or anyone else. It rubbed my friends the wrong way, but something about her had me wanting to know what made her tick. It wasn't just that she was pretty because she clearly didn't work as hard in that area as other girls did. Her long blonde hair was always up in a ponytail or braid. She didn't wear makeup as far as I could tell. She didn't try to make changes to her uniform to make her tits or ass stand out. Yet, she was the prettiest girl there. At least I thought so. But more than that, she was her own person.

"You should go out with me," I'd said to her with bravado. I was following her up the hall toward her locker.

She arched a brow. "I can't imagine why."

My friends snickered. I didn't love it, but I wasn't one to give up. "I'm Elio D'Amato."

"I know."

"So go out with me."

She stopped, her deep blue eyes looking at me with wariness. "Or what? You'll kill me?"

So she knew my family. Most girls found my family reputation exciting. A few were afraid of me.

"Does my family's business bother you?"

She snorted and continued to her locker. "All businesses are corrupt, organized or not."

That intrigued me. "You think so?"

"I know so. They all lie, cheat, steal, commit fraud, and take advantage of people. The only difference is the so-called legit businesses don't murder so many people."

I laughed. I liked this girl. "So go out with me."

She shook her head. "So far, I haven't found anything interesting about you."

I grin. "I'm Elio D'Amato."

She stops again. "You're rich?"

"Yep."

"Powerful?"

"Of course." I ruled the school.

"That's it?"

My cocky grin faltered. What else was there?

"I mean, you take away your family's money and power, what's left?" Her gaze scraped over me again, and I felt like a fraud. It wasn't a good feeling. I think anyone else would have told her to fuck off. But deep down, I wanted her to see me. The real Elio.

"Go out with me and you'll see."

She didn't agree to a date then, but within a week, she'd given in.

We've been together ever since.

We still have a few months before we graduate from high school, and then we need to get through college, but I have no doubt that Piper and I will be together forever. I once overheard my father express concern about my "infatuation" with Piper, but my mother assured him that once I went to college, I'd sow my oats. Oh, how wrong they are. Piper is it for me, and I plan to let her know that tonight.

I pull up in front of her home. It's modest. The only reason Piper can attend Ashwood Prep is a scholarship. Someday, when she's my wife, she'll live in the lap of luxury.

She exits her house so I don't come up to the door. Her parents don't love me. I suppose they're afraid of me and my family.

I open the car door, giving her a kiss before she gets in.

"Are you feeling better?" I ask, remembering she hadn't been feeling well at school that morning.

"Yep. Must have been something I ate."

I'm psyched. It would suck if she canceled. I drive us to town to one of the buildings my father owns. The roof has a terrace that overlooks Lake Michigan. It's still cool out for spring, but I've arranged heaters along with all the lights and other décor.

"What have you planned?" she asks as we ride the elevator up.

"It's a surprise."

She shakes her head in amusement. "You look very pleased with yourself."

"I am. Hopefully, you'll be pleased too." I pull her into my arms. "Perhaps we can both be pleased." My dick hardens at the thought, and I'm sure to let her feel it. We've only started having sex within the last month. Before that, there was kissing and touching. I'd finger her and she'd rub my cock or suck it. But it wasn't until last month that I was able to sink my dick inside her. It was fucking fantastic.

Her cheeks flush. "That's all you think about."

"I'm a horny teenager."

The elevator opens and we step out onto the terrace. I've arranged for dinner and privacy in this rooftop paradise.

"Elio," she breathes, her blue eyes shining as she takes in the lights and flowers and a table set for two. "You did all this? It's so beautiful."

I drink in the sight of her. She feels so important to me. Like breathing. It's scary sometimes. "Only the best for you."

Once dinner is served, we're left alone and no one will bother us. It's a perk of being Antonio D'Amato's son. No one would dare upset him or his family.

Dinner is filled with laughter and conversation, sometimes about deep stuff and sometimes about nothing at all. When we finish eating, I guide her to a double chaise lounge. We sit, nestled together.

"I have something for you." My heart rate is going a million miles a minute from nerves. I don't normally get nervous, but I'm damn near shaking.

"Oh? It's not my birthday."

I pull out the blue sapphire ring.

She gasps. "Elio?"

"I know we're young and still have college and stuff, but we'll always be together. This is a promise of that."

Her eyes fill with awe. I love it when she looks at me like I'm a superhero. "A promise ring?"

I nod. "Will you wear it?"

"Of course."

I slip it on. "Never take it off, okay? You're mine now."

She gives me her signature smirk and head shake that tells me she thinks I'm being a sexist, macho guy. "I am my own—"

"You're mine. And I'm yours."

She shrugs, apparently okay with that. I kiss her then. I don't wait too long before I slide my hand under the skirt of her dress.

"Elio... we're outside. Anyone can come."

It's always a surprise to me when she's modest. She's usually so outspoken.

"No one will bother us. I've made sure of it. Only God can watch, and I'm sure he's okay with it. After all, he made us into sexual beings."

She laughs. "You have an answer for everything."

I unzip her dress. "It's romantic. You like romantic, don't you?" I pull the bodice of her dress down and rub my palm over her bra-covered nipple. It's hard and I want to suck it.

She sighs and settles into me, giving herself over to me. "Yes."

I'm impatient. My hands are everywhere. On her tits. Squeezing her ass. Fingering her pussy. She takes a turn, stroking my cock, but I need to fuck her.

"Get on top, Piper." I tug her until she's straddling my thighs. We haven't done it like this yet. I love the position. Her tits are right there. I can bury my face in them while she rides me.

With her hands on my shoulders, she lowers over me. The most excellent sensations electrify my dick. She rocks and slowly starts to ride me. I stick my tongue out, licking then sucking her nipples.

"More," I growl as need coils in my balls. "Faster, baby." My hands grip her hips and urge her on.

She's breathing hard. Her head is back, her long hair cascading around her like she's a goddess. Her tits bounce in front of me. Yep, life is fucking awesome.

"Elio... I'm... Oh..." Her pussy squeezes my cock, hard.

"Fuck yeah..." My orgasm rocks through me, my hips bucking under her as pleasure radiates to every cell in my body.

Afterward, we lie under the stars and talk about our future. My father is adamant that successful Dons are smart in business and in understanding people, so I'll be studying business and psychology. I can see my life so clearly. I'll be more successful than my father. I'll have Piper as my queen. Yes, life is fucking awesome.

Later, I drop Piper at her house. She blows me a kiss from her bedroom window and I finally drive home. The next morning, I wake up late and shuffle down for breakfast. I find my father at the door, my mother fussing with his tie.

"What's going on?" I ask. My father doesn't have usual work hours, but Saturday is usually his golf day. He doesn't golf in a Brioni suit so something must be up in the business.

He looks at me, his lips pursed in that way that tells me he's irritated by me. "I—"

"He's going to clean up a mess," my mother interrupts him, patting him on the chest.

I frown, wondering again what's up and if it has to do with me. If so, why is my mother intervening? My parents can be assholes sometimes. They never pull a punch when it comes to me.

My father sniffs. "I want you with Joey today."

"I was going to—"

"I said, with Joey." My father's voice booms.

Fucker. But I nod and can't wait until I'm the one in charge. My father leaves, and my mother stares at me for a moment with that same disappointment my father has.

"What'd I do?"

"Nothing. Get dressed." She leaves me alone wondering what the fuck is going on.

I shrug and head back up to my room. I shower and dress in a suit thinking I'll be working as a bagman today since that's what Joey does. It feels a bit like a demotion. I was a bagman for my father starting at fourteen. The last few years, I've been more on the business side with my father, learning the ropes.

I message Piper to let her know I'll be busy today. Bummer. I was hoping to see her again.

I get home that evening and try to contact Piper, but she's not answering. I'm thinking about driving over to her house when my mother insists that the family eat together tonight. That normally happens during holidays. Today is not a holiday.

So I have dinner with my parents, my brother, Lazaro, and sister, Lana. Lazaro was suspended from school again. I swear my little brother has a screw loose somewhere. He's a bit feral, which can be good or bad for the future of my father's business.

Lana is grilling my father on business shit. She's bound and determined to be a significant part of the business, which is no easy feat considering the Mafia holds archaic views of women.

After dinner, my mother insists that us three kids spend time together. We all roll our eyes but make our way to the home theater to watch a movie. By the time it's done, it's too late for me to go over to

Piper's. She hasn't responded to any of my texts. A part of me is pissed. Another part of me is worried. Is she mad at me? I rack my brain, trying to think of anything I might have done to upset her, but I come up empty. Our dinner on Friday night had been perfect—the promise ring and the way she melted into my arms.

On Sunday, my father puts me to work again. I want to sneak away to see Piper, but Joey is watching me like a hawk. I don't have any authority to tell him to go fuck off, so I do my duty. I'll see Piper at school Monday and find out what's going on.

Monday morning, I pull my Porsche in front of Piper's home ready to pick her up for school. The house is dark, which is unusual. I knock on the door. No answer.

I look through the window. The room is bare. What the fuck? Where are Piper and her family? Confusion and dread wash over me as I retreat back to my car, my eyes scanning the street for any clue as to what might have happened.

There's no one to ask. I get in my car and drive to school. I'll see her there and find out what the fuck is going on.

I pull into the school parking lot, my eyes already scanning for Piper. I don't see her. Not on the way to homeroom. Not in English.

After English, I head to the office. "Mrs. Sawyer, have you seen Piper?"

The secretary glances up from her computer, her brows drawn together. "She didn't tell you?"

"Tell me what?" I feel like I'm on a precipice and about to fall.

"Her family moved."

"What? Moved where?"

"I can't believe she didn't tell you. I know you're close—"

"Where?" I demand.

"England. Her father got an inheritance or something."

What the fuck? Surely, I'm having a nightmare. This doesn't make sense. Why didn't she tell me they were moving? Why did she take my ring if she knew she was leaving?

I leave the office, my mind reeling. I'd had everything. My life was plotted out, planned to perfection. And now it was all blown apart.

I sulk for days, weeks even, until my father threatens to kick my ass.

"You'll end up dead if you let a woman turn you into a pussy, Elio," he says. "Get your fucking head straight. Once you do, I've got work for you."

It's another day before I realize he's right. I'm a pussy for wallowing. I become laser focused on business. By the time I head to college, I'm already my father's right-hand man and trusted advisor. By his side, I learn everything I need to know. I follow my father's lead, growing more powerful the more merciless I become. There's no room for sentiment or love. I've outgrown those childish ideas. The only things that matter are money and power.

1

PIPER

Present Day

I take a deep breath as I stand at the kitchen counter, preparing breakfast for my husband and daughter. The kitchen is bright and airy, with large windows that let in the morning sunlight. Anyone looking in would think this is a happy home, a happy family. It is not, and being back in Chicago after my parents took D'Amato money and moved us to England isn't helping. Yes, I'm in a nicer home and have more money, but money doesn't buy happiness.

I scoop eggs from the pan onto a plate and bring it to my seven-year-old daughter, Elysse.

"Eat up, baby." My tone is filled with sunshine, hiding the darkness within. As I turn to go back to the stove, I catch a glimpse of my reflection in the window. The woman staring back at me is a stranger. The life is gone from her eyes. The fight in her is gone except in the protection of her daughter. I'm a shell of the woman I once was.

"Is breakfast ready?" Gabriel's gruff voice cuts through the silence, and I flinch involuntarily.

"Yes." I hurry back to the stove and put the remaining eggs on a plate. I set it on the table at his seat.

Gabriel sits down, his brow furrowed in a perpetual scowl. Elysse looks up at him nervously, her fork poking at her eggs.

"These eggs are overcooked," Gabriel snaps, his gaze fixed on me. "Can't you do anything right?"

I feel the familiar sting of shame and humiliation as his words cut through me. Over the years, I've become accustomed to his constant criticism and belittling, but it never gets easier. Still, it's better than pushing or slapping.

"I can remake—"

"Don't bother."

I glance at Elysse, who is looking down at her plate, her shoulders hunched. This isn't the life I imagined for myself. I used to be strong, independent, and full of dreams. But that Piper is long gone, buried beneath the weight of Gabriel's cruelty and my own fear. I can hardly remember the carefree girl who fell in love with Elio, the boy who promised me the world.

Why am I thinking of him again? It must be because I'm back in Chicago.

A surge of anger at Gabriel rises within me, but it's quickly extinguished by the overwhelming sense of dread. I know better than to challenge Gabriel's temper. The last time I stood up to him, he shoved me against the wall, his hands wrapped around my throat. I can't risk Elysse witnessing that again, can't bear the thought of her being afraid of her own father.

Elysse looks up at me, her dark eyes filled with confusion and concern. I force a smile, hoping to reassure her, but the ache in my heart is too heavy to hide.

I watch in silence as Gabriel finishes his breakfast and stands up, his chair scraping against the hardwood floor. The tense atmosphere in the room is palpable, and I can feel Elysse's eyes on me, searching for reassurance.

"I'm heading to the office," Gabriel says gruffly, grabbing his briefcase.

"Have a good day." I say it by rote. It no longer has any feeling behind it.

As soon as the front door slams shut, Elysse jumps down from her chair and hurries to me for a hug. I tell myself she wants reassurance, but I can't help but think she's the one feeling like she needs to reassure me. God, what sort of damage am I doing to her psyche?

"Why is he always so mad?"

I blink back tears, feeling a surge of gratitude for my daughter's kindness and a deep well of guilt for exposing her to this toxic environment.

"Some people are just grumpy in the morning." More guilt builds at defending him. "Everything's going to be okay."

The lie tastes bitter on my tongue, but I can't bear to shatter Elysse's innocent belief that everything will work out. The truth is, I'm trapped, and Gabriel has made it clear that if I try to leave, he'll hurt Elysse. The thought of my daughter being in danger is the only thing that keeps me from running.

After a few moments, I pull back and give Elysse a reassuring smile. "Come on, let's get you to school."

As we walk hand in hand through the quiet streets, I reflect on how different my life is here now compared to when I was a child growing up. I grew up in a modest neighborhood. Bookish and studious, I earned a scholarship to a private academy that should have set me up to attend a prestigious university. Just because I tended to mind my own business and have my head in the books, some thought I was shy or timid, but when provoked, I had no problem speaking my mind. That part of me didn't die until Gabriel.

Memories of those carefree days flood my mind, and I can't help but think of Elio. The way he used to look at me, the way he made me feel... it all seems like a lifetime ago. I can't forget the sweet innocence of love we had, and yet, the anger and resentment for sending me away are too strong to ignore.

Living in England wasn't so bad. I had free healthcare, and my mother helped me with my pregnancy and early years with Elysse. I'd been able to take university courses and eventually get my degree. My life was moving on. I never overcame my resentment toward Elio, but now I recognize how young we were. Too young to make promises.

When Gabriel entered my life, he seemed like the perfect man. Polite. Smart. Successful. He said and did all the right things, including saying he wanted to be Elysse's father. Less than six months after marrying, his true colors were revealed. It started with him encouraging me to quit my job teaching. Then it was alienating me from my parents. Irritation turned to anger. Anger turned to violence. The last four years have been a nightmare, one I can't seem to escape.

When we reach Elysse's school, I kneel down and pull her into a tight hug. "I love you, sweetheart. Have a wonderful day, okay?"

Elysse nods, her eyes shining with a mixture of excitement and concern. "I love you too, Mommy. Don't be sad."

I watch as she scurries into the building, my heart heavy with the weight of how much I'm hurting her.

Taking a deep breath, I turn and head toward the bank, determined to keep up the façade of normalcy. Gabriel keeps me on a tight budget, so I only withdraw the money I'm allowed for groceries. As I step out of the bank, I walk into a wall of man.

"Excuse—" My heart nearly stops when I see a familiar face. Elio D'Amato. A rush of emotions floods through me—anger, hurt, and an involuntary flicker of love that I thought I had long buried.

Elio's dark eyes meet mine, and when recognition forms in them, a warm smile spreads across his face. "Piper. Wow... you're here. You look great."

The compliment stings, reminding me of the carefree girl I used to be, the one who had fallen so deeply in love with him. Memories of our past come rushing back, and with them, bitterness and pain. It was because of him, him and his parents, that my family was pushed out of town, although it wasn't a hardship for my father to take D'Amato money. I never understood why Elio was so sweet, making promises one night, and the next day supporting his family's effort to send me away. The only answer is that he didn't want the baby... Elysse.

There's a moment when I look at him and see a way out. But I dismiss that notion. I know who he is, what he does. Chances are he treats his women worse than Gabriel treats me.

"I guess you never thought you'd see me again," I say bitterly.

Elio's brow furrows slightly. "Why would you say—"

"I don't have time for this." I cut him off, my voice dripping with venom. "Just do us all a favor and drop dead, will you?"

Without waiting for a response, I turn and hurry away, my heart aching, betraying the anger I want to feel.

As I walk, my mind is a chaotic storm of emotions. After all these years, after everything that's happened, a part of me still yearns for his touch, his kiss, the way he used to look at me. The promise he made to love me forever. It's a shameful, agonizing truth that I've buried so deeply, I'd almost convinced myself it wasn't there.

But seeing him standing before me with that familiar warm smile, for a moment, the last eight years melted away. In that moment, I was a naive, love-struck girl again, the one who thought she and Elio could defy the odds and build a life together.

I can't deny a curiosity about his life now. Is he the head of his family yet? Is he married? Does he ever think of me?

I shake my head of those thoughts. I can't let him back into my life, not now, not ever. The risk is too great. I've built a fragile existence here, a life that, while not perfect, at least keeps my daughter safe. If Elio were to reenter it, the consequences could be devastating. Gabriel's jealousy and possessiveness would know no bounds, and I can't bear the thought of Elysse being caught in the crossfire.

Resolved, I quicken my pace, desperate to put as much distance between myself and Elio as possible. I need to get home, to retreat into the relative safety of my own four walls, where I can try to pull myself together before Elysse returns from school.

By the time I unlock the front door, I'm emotionally drained, my nerves frayed. I sink down onto the couch, burying my face in my hands as the tears finally come. It's a release, a catharsis, but it's also a reminder of just how much I've sacrificed to keep my family safe.

Elysse. I have to be strong for her. She's the only thing that matters now, the only light in this dark, twisted existence. I can't let my past, my unresolved feelings for Elio, jeopardize her future. I have to be the mother she deserves, even if it means continuing to bury a part of myself.

With a deep, shuddering breath, I wipe away the tears and pull myself together. I have chores to do before Gabriel returns home. I have a home to keep and a family to take care of. For Elysse, I'll do whatever it takes.

2

ELIO

I watch, stunned, as Piper storms away, her golden hair swaying with each furious step. Her cold greeting has taken me completely by surprise, leaving me grappling with a whirlwind of emotions.

I replay our brief encounter in my mind, trying to make sense of her hostility. Why is she so mad at me? I wasn't the one who disappeared without a word. How had I wronged her so deeply that she could barely stand to look at me?

For a long time after she left, I held a great deal of anger and resentment that I buried beneath my focus on the family business. But now, seeing her again, those aren't the feelings that come first and foremost in my chest. No, I feel longing, an ache to restore what we lost.

Nostalgia floods my senses as I drink in the sight of her. She's stunning, although there's a tiredness or wariness to her that has me wondering about her life. She'd always been willing to speak her mind, but the coolness, the vitriol of today, that's new and I can't deny that it stings.

As she disappears into the crowd, the longing tugs at my heart. Eight years have passed, yet the connection between us is still palpable, like an invisible thread that refuses to be severed. I desperately want to understand what happened, to find a way to make amends for whatever pain I caused her.

It's clear she doesn't want anything to do with me, but the questions swirl. I'm a man who likes answers. I stride down the sidewalk, Piper's stinging words echoing in my mind and igniting my determination to find out why. I can't stop the image of finally getting the life I'd desired, the one I'd mapped out for us, from blooming in full technicolor in my head. I can see her in my home. In my bed. In my life. Fuck. I can practically taste it.

There's just one problem. Not long after Piper left, my father arranged an alliance with the Rinella family, cemented by my marriage to Ava Rinella. At the time, she was barely ten years old, which is fucking creepy. But now, she's eighteen, and while my father is dead, I have honored all his alliances so far. I've been planning to go through with the marriage. I don't love Ava. Hell, I've never met her. But I'll treat her well. Occasionally, we'll fuck to produce an heir. It's not the life I'd imagined with Piper, but the love of my life disappeared. Until today.

A sense of unease settles in the pit of my stomach. The alliance with the Rinellas had been a carefully calculated move, one that would solidify our family's power. But now, with Piper back, the decision feels more like a shackle than an opportunity.

How can I marry Ava when Piper is here? If there is any chance of true happiness, she's it for me. I curse under my breath, remembering the way Piper looked at me with such disdain, and yet there'd been a moment when I thought I saw something more... like hope.

I know I'm risking fucking up business, but I have no choice. I have to find Piper and learn what happened all those years ago. And I can't let my impending marriage to Ava stand in my way.

I trail Piper at a discreet distance, my eyes never leaving her as she navigates the familiar streets. After a few blocks, she makes her way up the walk of a large two-story home. She's come up in the world, and I smile thinking of the success she has achieved.

She unlocks the door and enters the home. I hesitate for a

moment, wondering if I'm really going to risk everything my father and I've worked for with the Rinella family. Of course, there is no real debate. It's selfish of me, but there's been only one real thing I've ever wanted in life, and that was Piper.

I move quietly, careful not to draw her attention as I peer through a window, watching her unpack a few boxes. Inwardly, I laugh at my actions. I'm like a fucking peeping Tom. A neighbor will likely call the police. What a story that would be. The police can't take down Elio D'Amato for corruption or murder, but he's jailed for trespassing and peeping on a woman.

The house is warm and inviting, a far cry from the modest home her family lived in when I knew her. I'm filled with a mixture of happiness and frustration—happiness that she has found a sense of stability, but frustration that our reunion had been so strained.

As I watch her set up what looks like a home office, a plan takes shape in my mind. I have to find out what happened all those years ago and then break down the wall she's built regarding me. I need to convince her that she and I are meant to be.

With a renewed sense of determination, I leave her property and head back to my car, my mind racing as I work out the best way to approach Piper. Back at my car, I find my men glaring at me.

"We can't protect you when you run off—"

I wave their concern away. "I'm fine. Take me home."

When I arrive home, my sister, Lana, greets me with the same cold irritation I just experienced with Piper. "There you are. You're late. The Rinellas have been waiting for you."

Normally, I'd feel more chagrined by this, but I don't have any guilt or regret for being late.

"Matteo has been entertaining them in your absence," Lana continues, her sharp eyes studying me. "You'd do well not to keep them waiting any longer."

I want to remind her who is the boss in this family, but now isn't the time. Straightening my posture, I push the lingering thoughts of Piper to the back of my mind. This is no time for distractions. I must present a composed and charismatic front to the Rinellas. I have to maintain the delicate balance of power between our families.

With a deep breath, I stride into the living room, where I'm met by the expectant gazes of Ava and her family. Matteo, my cousin and most trusted lieutenant, stands nearby, a subtle nod of acknowledgment passing between us.

I plaster on a charming smile, greeting the Rinellas with the poise and confidence they expect. Ava's father, the formidable Vincenzo Rinella, a fellow boss in The Outfit, extends his hand, and I shake it firmly.

"I'm sorry I'm late." I turn to Ava. Admittedly, she's beautiful with thick raven hair and gray eyes. There's an innocence to her, likely due to her young age. But I also see a flicker in her eyes suggesting there's more spirit to her than she reveals. "Ava, it's lovely to meet you."

"You too, Mr. D'Amato."

"Please, call me Elio."

As the conversation flows, I navigate the social dynamics, carefully balancing the needs of our families and not betraying the conflict raging in my heart. Ava engages me in polite discourse, and I find myself impressed by her intelligence and poise. She'll make a good wife. And yet... I can't rid my mind of Piper. Her face, her voice, the raw emotion that had flickered in her eyes.

I steal a glance at Matteo, wondering if he senses the turmoil brewing beneath the surface. But he gives no outward sign of concern, his attention focused solely on the task at hand.

I curse my own weakness, my inability to compartmentalize the past and the present. I am the heir to the D'Amato legacy, and I cannot afford to be distracted, not when so much is at stake. I redirect my focus to the Rinellas, determined to make a lasting impression and solidify the alliance that will shape the future of our families. But fuck me, deep down, I want to end this engagement because I can't not seek out Piper and try to fix whatever broke between us.

3

PIPER

I can't get Elio D'Amato out of my mind. Here I am setting up Gabriel's office, but I'm thinking about another man. Elio's face, his voice, his touch... they haunt me. I thought I'd buried those feelings, locked them away where they could never hurt me again. But seeing him today has cracked that door wide open, and the memories have come rushing back, overwhelming me.

He was the same but different. Bigger. Not taller, but broader in the shoulders. He wore an expensive suit that had to be tailored to him the way it fit like a glove. His boyish face is now one of a man. But his eyes... those dark eyes that were always so kind, sometimes mischievous. Those were the same. His voice was a bit deeper, but my name on his lips still felt like a caress.

I hate that I'm still so affected by him. After all these years, I should be over it. I should be able to look at him without feeling the old familiar ache. At the very least, all I should feel is anger and betrayal. But the moment I saw him today, it was like being transported back in time.

I remember the way he used to look at me, like I was the only girl in the world. The way his fingers would trail along my skin, setting it afire. The way his lips would curve into that devastating smile that always made my knees go weak. I can hear his voice whispering sweet nothings in my ear, promising me a future together. A future that was snatched away from me in the cruelest of ways.

Even now, I can't help but wonder what would have happened if his family hadn't intervened. If they hadn't paid my parents to take me and leave town. Would we have made it? Would we have been able to build a life together, despite the odds? But then I remember that he had to have known about it. Otherwise, he'd have tried to stop it. Or he'd have found me. But he didn't.

I squeeze my eyes shut, trying to push those thoughts away. It doesn't matter now. What's done is done. I have a daughter to raise, a husband to support. I can't afford to get lost in the past. A past filled with silly, school girl thoughts of fairy tale love.

I'm so lost in memories, I've forgotten the time. I'm late to start dinner. I rush from Gabriel's office and hurry to get dinner on the table, my heart pounding as I hear the front door slam shut. Gabriel is home having picked up Elysse from her afterschool art program.

The pressure builds as I rush to plate the food, knowing Gabriel expects everything to be ready the moment he walks through that door. I can already hear the frustration in his voice as he calls out, "Piper! Where's dinner?"

"It'll be right there," I call back, trying to keep the tremor out of my voice.

He enters the kitchen, Elysse trailing behind him carrying a large piece of paper. I'm sure she wants to share her art for the day, but Gabriel has her trained as well. She lives in fear and I can't do anything to stop it.

Gabriel's brow is furrowed, his lips pressed into a thin, angry line. "It's past six o'clock. Why isn't dinner ready?"

"I'm sorry, I was just finishing up," I stammer, avoiding his eyes. I serve the plates, ready to take dinner to the dining room where he likes to eat.

"That's not good enough," he snaps, his hand lashing out and knocking the plates out of my hands to the floor. Porcelain shatters, food splattering across the hardwood.

Elysse jumps, her eyes wide with fear, and I instinctively move to shield her, my heart racing. "Gabriel, please," I beg, but he's already stalking toward me, his face twisted with rage.

I gently nudge Elysse out of the way, out of Gabriel's path to me.

"You're useless, you know that?" he snarls, towering over me. "Can't even manage to have a simple dinner ready on time. What good are you?"

I flinch, my fingers trembling as I try to hold my ground. "I'm sorry, I was—"

"Save it," he cuts me off, his voice dripping with contempt. "I'm sick of your excuses. You're nothing but a burden, Piper. A pathetic, worthless, ugly wife."

I cower under Gabriel's angry tirade. Elysse is against the wall, her eyes squeezed shut as she tries to make herself small. That breaks me more than Gabriel's words.

"At least tell me you managed to unpack my den," he barks.

I swallow hard, forcing myself to meet his gaze. "Y–Yes, It's finished."

His eyes narrow, lips curling in a sneer. "Bring me dinner there, then clean this mess up." He turns away, muttering under his breath. "And don't bother me again tonight."

With that, he strides from the room, snatching up a bottle of whiskey on his way out. I flinch as the den door slams behind him, the sound echoing through the silent house.

Elysse looks up at me, her dark eyes shimmering with unshed tears.

My heart clenches as I gather her into my arms, holding her close. "Shh, it's okay, sweetie," I murmur, pressing a kiss to the top of her head. "Everything's going to be just fine." God. How can she ever believe me?

I thought moving back to Chicago would be a fresh start, a chance to build a better life for Elysse. Gabriel was under so much pressure in England. His transfer here came with a big raise, but also better hours. All things that should make him happy.

With Elio's reappearance and Gabriel's growing volatility, I'm starting to wonder if life is just going to continue to spiral downward. And with it, I'll be taking Elysse, an innocent child.

Carefully, I disentangle myself from Elysse's embrace. I make a plate for Gabriel.

"Wait here, okay?" I say to Elysse. I know I need to get Gabriel's dinner to him, but the thought of facing him again makes my stomach churn. Still, I force myself to carry his dinner to the den, steeling myself as I knock on the door.

"What?" comes the gruff response.

"I have your dinner," I call out, hating the way my voice trembles.

There's a moment of silence, then the door swings open. Gabriel stands there, glass of whiskey in hand, his expression unreadable. "Leave it on the desk." He steps aside to let me in.

I do as he says, setting the plate down and backing away quickly.

"Piper."

I pause, my heart pounding. "Yes?"

"Don't bother me again tonight," he says, his voice low and dangerous. "Understand?"

I nod quickly, not trusting myself to speak. As I leave, I'm relieved he plans to spend the evening in his study. He'll likely be watching porn. Hopefully, he'll take care of his needs himself and not come looking for my help. Sex with Gabriel had never been great. He never seemed to care much about my experience of it. Not like Elio.

God. I can't think about him in front of Gabriel. I hurry out of the room, closing the door behind me with a shaky sigh. Back in the kitchen, I find that Elysse is trying to clean up the mess.

"I'll do that, baby. Let me get you dinner. How was art today?" God should strike me dead for acting like everything is normal. I make her plate and set it on the kitchen table.

"We did flowers."

I study the picture on the table. "Oh, it's lovely. Can I keep it?"

She nods, her movements slow as she picks up her fork to eat. A part of me says to take her now and leave. But where would I go?

Elio.

As a member of the Mafia, he could protect us, right? But no. I can't go to him.

"Why is he always so angry?" Elysse's voice interrupts my thoughts.

My heart breaks at her words. "I guess things were stressful at work. It has nothing to do with you. It's not your fault."

Elysse looks up at me, her dark eyes shimmering with tears. "But he's so mean."

"I'm sorry." I pull her close, pressing a kiss to the top of her head.

She resumes eating and I finish cleaning up the mess. I glance at Elysse, watching the way her small hands tremble as she tries to eat. This isn't the life I wanted for her, this constant fear and uncertainty.

I think back to my previous attempt to escape Gabriel's grasp, the violent consequences I suffered for daring to defy him. The bruises have long since faded, but the memory of his rage, the way he had towered over me as I cowered in a ball on the floor, snarling that he would kill Elysse if we ever tried to leave again, still haunts me.

I shudder, the fear coiling tight in my chest. I can't risk that, can't risk Elysse's life. As much as I hate it, as much as it tears me apart, I know I have to stay. For her sake, I have to endure.

But the hopelessness of our situation weighs heavily on me. I feel trapped, suffocated by the walls closing in around us. Gabriel's control over me is absolute and he knows it. I have no money. No job. No one. I'm powerless to break free.

4

ELIO

I take a deep breath as I walk into the dining room, Lana and Matteo already seated at the table. Ava Rinella, my fiancée, and her father sit across from them. Her piercing green eyes watch me. Is she happy with the match? Is she afraid? I can be a brutal, callous man, but not usually toward women. I offer her a smile that I hope will put her at ease.

I take my seat at the head of the table, with Ava to my left. The opulent room is filled with an undercurrent of tension that sets my nerves on edge, which is unusual for me. This arrangement has been a part of my life for years. I've been dealing with Vincenzo Rinella for years as well. I understand him and how he works. So why am I agitated? The only answer is Piper. My mind is still reeling from my encounter with her. In some ways, I wonder if it was real. After all these years, to run into her at the bank.

"I hope you're ready for a full Italian meal. Seven courses," I say with a nod to Gio, one of the servants who'll be serving us tonight.

Ava offers me a polite smile. "I've heard about your famous D'Amato dinners."

"Good to know someone is saying something complimentary about the D'Amato family."

Lana rolls her eyes at my attempt at humor.

As the servants begin to serve the first course, I force myself to focus on the task at hand. I need to be present, to play the part of the dutiful fiancé, even as my heart yearns for the woman I let slip away all those years ago. I thought I'd moved on, but seeing Piper today proves that wrong. I haven't moved on. I'd buried my feelings, and seeing her today unearthed them. They're back in full force. Longing fills my chest. Longing and questions. Why did she leave? The only answer is her parents moved her away. But was the move for her parents or were they trying to get her away from me? The total lack of contact once she left suggests her parents disapproved of me. And why wouldn't they? My world is full of danger.

Vincenzo's voice cuts through the silence, drawing my attention back to the table. "So, Elio, Caruso has been saying good things about you."

I study him, trying to decide whether he's jealous or impressed that The Outfit's Boss has taken notice of me. What many don't know is Chicago organized crime runs a bit differently from New York. Since Al Capone, there has been one major "family" known as The Outfit. We're organized by areas, but all areas feed up to The Outfit, run by a single Boss, Caruso, along with an underboss, and street bosses, which I and Rinella are. Another secret is that like in New York, the Mafia has seen a decline... or has it? In Chicago, we learned a long time ago that we make more money and are less likely to get arrested if we lie low, hide in plain sight, and don't kill so much. Not that we don't kill if necessary. We're just more clever at it than our bloodthirsty gangster ancestors.

I nod, taking a sip of my wine. "It's nice to be noticed." I'm still young, but my father at one time was in line to take over The Outfit, before he and my mother unexpectedly died in a freak car accident. I know if I'm as smart as my father was, I have a future as a leader in The Outfit.

"I'm sure your father would be proud."

I still can't read his meaning. Is he hoping that with this marriage,

I'll pull him with me? Is he annoyed that at a young age, I'm on Caruso's radar?

"Yes, it's been a lot of work, but I'm honored to carry on his legacy." I pause, choosing my next words carefully. "And of course, I'm looking forward to our upcoming nuptials. It's a union that will only strengthen both of us."

Vincenzo nods. "I'm sure it will. Ava will make you a good wife. She's been raised to serve her husband and The Outfit."

Lana hides her disgust behind a sip of wine.

"Surely, there's more to her than that," I say, earning a smile from Lana. "Do you have any interests? Hobbies?"

Ava glances at her father as if she needs permission. It proves his comment that she's been raised to be subservient.

"She cooks," Vincenzo says.

"Of course she does," Lana quips. "We have an excellent cook." She gestures to her plate. We're on the antipasti course of prosciutto and cheese, no cooking involved.

"Do you have interests and hobbies?" Ava asks me.

My mind instantly flashes to Piper. She's my only interest at the moment. I clear my throat, forcing myself to refocus on the conversation. "I'm afraid my work with the business does consume a great deal of my time and energy." I offer her a small smile, hoping it comes across as sincere.

Matteo shifts in his seat, drawing my attention. "Don't sell yourself short, Elio. You've also got quite the talent for fine wine and art."

I nod, grateful for Matteo's intervention. "Yes, those are passions of mine as well."

Ava's brow furrows slightly, and I can't help but wonder what she's thinking. "How... interesting. I must admit, I don't know much about art and wine—"

"You can teach her," Vincenzo interrupts, earning another hidden glare from Lana.

I give her a look. It's not like our father wasn't the same as Vincenzo. She knows how this world works.

As the meal progresses, we continue to exchange conversation, although it often feels forced. I do my best to play the part of the attentive, devoted fiancé, but my mind keeps drifting back to Piper, to the way her eyes had blazed with a mix of anger and something else I couldn't quite place.

I catch Matteo's gaze. His brows are furrowed as if to ask what's up with me. I smile and turn my attention back to my guests.

"So, Ava. Tell us a bit more about yourself. What are your aspirations, your hobbies? I'm sure a woman of your stature has plenty of interests beyond just managing a household."

Both Matteo and I send her a look to tread carefully.

Ava shrugs. "I do enjoy cooking. I don't know art very well, but I enjoy going to museums."

I have no doubt these are talking points given by her father.

"You have an usual necklace on," Matteo says, surprising me. I glance at the necklace wondering why it stands out.

Ava presses her hand over it and smiles. "I made it."

"Really?" He studies it more. I clear my throat thinking it's not a good idea for my second in command to be staring at her chest.

"Yes."

"Of course, there won't be time for all that when you're married." Vincenzo shakes his head at his daughter. "This is a big home. You'll be busy."

"I'm sure we can set up space and time for crafting, can't we, Elio?" Lana says to me.

"Of course."

"We should get this wedding planned," Vincenzo says firmly. He continues on, emphasizing the strategic benefits of solidifying the D'Amato-Rinella alliance through my marriage to Ava. But thinking of marriage to Ava brings up memories of Piper.

Out of the corner of my eye, I see Lana studying me, her brow furrowed with concern. Once again, I try to refocus.

"I say we get it done. With our contacts, there's no reason why we can't have this wedding in... say... two weeks."

I try to hide my surprise. Two weeks! That fast?

I glance at Ava, who is watching me intently. Like her father, I can't read her. Can she tell that my commitment to this arrangement is wobbling? Before today, I was one hundred percent on board with this marriage. But now, with Piper's sudden reappearance in my life, I'm not so sure.

Matteo clears his throat, drawing my attention. "Elio, what are your thoughts on the matter?"

"What are your thoughts, Ava?" I ask.

Ava's lips curve into a small smile. I think she appreciates someone asking for her input. "Well, I've always envisioned a grand, traditional Italian wedding. With all the trimmings, of course."

I return her smile, letting her know that's what I want too. The problem is, I want it with Piper. But planning a big wedding takes time, months, maybe even a year, which can give me time. "We should do that, but it will take more than two weeks."

"Nonsense." Vicenzo waves my comment away. "Like I said, between our contacts, we can arrange something quickly."

"The D'Amatos do know how to throw a party," Lana adds, earning her a glare from me.

"Two weeks it is," Vincenzo announces.

I can push back on this, but decide now isn't the time. We finish dinner, and I'm eager to have Vincenzo and Ava leave. It takes work to shmooze and I'm exhausted.

As we head to the foyer to say our goodbyes, Vincenzo says, "You seem distracted. Is everything alright?"

I know he doesn't give a shit about me. He's concerned about this alliance. He's either worried that I'm fucking up and the marriage won't gain him anything, or that I'm rethinking the marriage.

I pat him on the back. "Everything is fine, Vicenzo. Just tired, is all."

"You know how important this alliance is. We cannot afford any... distractions."

"I understand. I assure you, my focus is where it needs to be."

Vincenzo studies me for a moment, his eyes narrowing slightly. "See that it remains that way, Elio."

I tense, wanting to remind him that he's in my house and precariously close to disrespecting me with his tone.

Matteo shakes his head at me. I bite my lip. For now.

"Have a good evening, Ava." I give her a kiss on the cheek. "Vincenzo." I shake his hand.

When they leave, I go to my office and pour a stiff drink. The future of the family. My future with Ava. It's all resting on my ability to put the past behind me and focus on the task at hand. But how can I when the woman who's haunted my dreams for the last eight years has suddenly reappeared in my life?

I let out a frustrated sigh, my mind racing with a thousand different thoughts and emotions. I need to get a handle on this, to regain control of the situation before it spirals out of my grasp.

Matteo materializes in the doorway, his brow furrowed with concern. "He's right, you know. You seem off."

Lana enters behind him.

I down my drink. "Long day, that's all."

"Doing what?" Matteo asks. He knows my schedule and therefore knows there wasn't anything challenging on it.

"Just life." I can't tell them about Piper. They won't understand.

"We can't afford to mess this up," Lana says.

I shrug. "We don't need them."

She glances at Matteo, her expression asking him to talk sense into me.

Matteo studies me. "Maybe not, but you'd be a fool to think you have the inside track to Caruso. You're still young, mostly unproven. This alliance gives you more power. Besides, if you don't marry her, he'll send her off to Bianchi and she certainly deserves better than that old mother fucker."

I arch a brow. "You care about what happens to Ava Rinella?"

He clears his throat. "Sure. She's a nice kid."

"You're missing the point," Lana interrupts. "We lost our parents, and Lazaro." She refers to our brother, her twin. "This family is dwindling down to nothing, and I bet it's not by accident."

"We don't know that Lazaro is dead," I say, although I'm sure he is. There's no way my impulsive man-child of a brother who is quick to draw but slow to listen wouldn't be causing a stir if he were still alive. But since we've never found his body, Lana insists that he's still alive somewhere. "And Mom and Dad were in a car accident."

She glares at me. "No one suffers that sort of loss—"

"Families like yours do," Matteo interrupts.

"That's my point," she snaps. "Our numbers are dwindling, big brother. We need an alliance to make sure no one comes looking to get rid of you."

It's a possibility, but I'm not worried. Despite what Matteo says, I am proven and Caruso's support protects me.

I need to reassure them both that I'm on board and moving forward with this marriage. I can't bring my mouth to say the words. "I promise you, I'll take care of this family. I won't let you down."

The weight of that promise settles heavily on my shoulders. In two weeks' time, I'll be standing at the altar, exchanging vows with Ava Rinella. It's what my parents wanted, what they had been planning since I was eighteen. At the time, I was pushing the loss of Piper away by jumping one hundred percent into the business. I had been eager to take on the mantle of leadership, to prove myself worthy of the D'Amato name.

Ava is a lovely girl, and I know she will make a dutiful wife. And yet... fuck. Why did Piper have to enter my life again? She's the one I should be married to. Had she not disappeared, we'd be living in wedded bliss. Hell, we might have kids now. And I wouldn't be standing here on the precipice of a marriage I don't want.

"I hope so, Elio. You're the foundation of this family."

I nod, offering her a reassuring smile. "And I'll continue to be that. For you, for Lazaro, and for our parents. I know this alliance with the Rinellas is crucial. I won't let anything mess that up."

The words taste bitter on my tongue, but I force myself to believe them. Piper is a ghost from the past, a distraction I can't afford. And based on her reception of me today, she doesn't want anything to do with me, anyway. I'm a fool to keep thinking about her and what could have been.

My future lies with Ava and securing the D'Amato legacy. I have to keep my focus on that, no matter how much my heart may yearn for something else.

5

PIPER

I wake before the sun, as I do every morning, dreading the day ahead. The house is still, quiet, and I savor these fleeting moments of peace before the storm begins. Carefully, I slip out of bed, trying not to disturb Gabriel's slumbering form beside me.

I make my way to the kitchen, flicking on the lights and squinting as my eyes adjust. The kitchen shows no signs of Gabriel's volatile temper from the night before. I push down the familiar pang of anxiety and set to work preparing breakfast.

As I crack eggs into a bowl, my mind drifts to the unexpected encounter with Elio yesterday. Seeing him again after all these years stirred up a whirlwind of emotions I thought I had long buried. The anger, the hurt, the love—it all comes rushing back. I grip the edge of the counter as grief overwhelms me. Grief at what I could have had if Elio had fulfilled his promise to me.

Why did I have to run into him? My life was challenging enough without the contrast between Elio's romantic, gentle ways and Gabriel's mercurial moods. I remind myself that Elio changed his mind. He'd arranged to send me away. There was nothing romantic about that.

I take a deep breath and force myself to focus. I need to get breakfast ready before Gabriel and Elysse wake up. Displeasing him is not an option. As I whisk the eggs, I feel a familiar ache in my chest. My daughter deserves so much better than this life of walking on eggshells, never knowing when Gabriel's temper will erupt.

But what choice do I have? I'm trapped, both by my own fears and the threats Gabriel has made. The thought of him hurting Elysse makes my stomach twist in knots. I can't risk it, no matter how much I long to break free.

With a heavy heart I live with daily, I continue my morning routine, preparing Gabriel's plate and keeping an ear out for any sign of movement upstairs. The day is just beginning, but I already feel exhausted.

I'm setting the plate on the table when I hear his heavy footsteps descending the stairs. Bracing myself, I turn around to face him.

"Good morning, darling," he says, his voice uncharacteristically soft. He crosses the room and presses a kiss to my cheek, causing me to flinch involuntarily.

"Gabriel," I reply cautiously, searching his face for any sign of the rage that consumed him last night. "Breakfast is ready."

"Wonderful." He sits at the table. "Thank you, Piper."

I stand there, bewildered. It's not that he's never like this. When I met him, he was kind and calm. But four years of marriage have taught me not to trust it. This sudden change in demeanor unsettles me more than his previous outburst.

Elysse pads into the kitchen, her small face etched with trepidation. She glances warily at Gabriel, then looks at me. My heart aches at the fear in her eyes. This is no way for a child to live.

"Good morning, Ely," Gabriel says, flashing Elysse a smile that doesn't reach his eyes. "Come, sit and have your breakfast."

Elysse hesitates, then slowly moves to take her seat, never taking her eyes off him. I watch the exchange, my own unease growing by the second. What game is Gabriel playing at?

"Piper, why don't you join us?" Gabriel gestures to the empty chair beside him. "I'd like us to have a nice family breakfast together."

I swallow hard, my throat suddenly dry. A nice family breakfast.

That's my assignment. I tense, knowing any small thing will cause me to fail in Gabriel's eyes. Only he knows what a "nice family breakfast" means, and I can't read his mind to know which tiny detail I'll miss that will set him off.

I set Elysse's breakfast in front of her. "I'll need to make more. I only made enough for you and Elysse."

Gabriel's expression darkens for the briefest of moments, and I brace myself for the explosion. But then it's gone, replaced by that unsettling veneer of calmness.

"Get your coffee and sit with us," he says, patting the chair.

Reluctantly, I pull out the chair and lower myself into it, my body tense and ready to spring into action at the first sign of trouble.

As Gabriel reaches over to squeeze my hand, I fight the urge to recoil. The unease I feel is palpable. Whatever game Gabriel is playing, I know it can't be good.

I sit stiffly at the table. Elysse picks at her food.

Finally, Gabriel finishes his meal and stands, giving me a patronizing pat on the shoulder. "That was delicious, dear. Thank you." He turns to Elysse, his expression hardening slightly. "Be good today. I'll be back this evening."

With that, he strides out of the kitchen, leaving Elysse and me in an uneasy silence.

As soon as I hear the front door shut, Elysse turns to me. "He was nice today."

I nod, wanting her to feel good about this change in his behavior. But she knows as I do that it won't last.

Her eyes are intent, like she's building up courage. "Sometimes I wish we didn't have to live with him."

Me too, sweetie. "We're a family."

Her expression drops, and I know I've disappointed her. How long before that turns to resentment? I'm failing my daughter.

I pull her into a tight hug, and her arms tighten around me. For now, I can only offer her the comfort of my embrace, hoping against hope that one day, I'll find the strength to truly protect her.

"I bet my real daddy would be nicer."

I close my eyes as Elio flitters back into my mind. I think back to eight years ago. I had been so young, so naive, when I first fell for Elio. His charm, his passion, his unwavering devotion—it had all swept me off my feet. We'd talked of a future together, of defying the odds and building a life despite the stigma of his family's criminal ties.

But then, the unthinkable happened. I discovered I was pregnant, and my world came crashing down. Elio's father, the Don of the D'Amato Mafia, had other plans for his son. He offered my parents a substantial sum of money to take me and leave town, far away from his son's reach. Faced with the threat of losing everything, my parents had no choice but to accept. I'd prayed that Elio would stop his father, that he'd come and find me. But in the end, he hadn't done either because he didn't want to. It was one thing when it was just me he was committing to. A baby, fatherhood, apparently wasn't something he'd wanted.

"Who is he? Why isn't he here?"

This isn't the first time she's asked about her father. I don't want to lie, but neither can I tell her the truth.

"He couldn't be, sweetie." That is true, sort of. He made a choice. We have to live with it.

When I saw Elio yesterday, he didn't ask me about Elysse. Then again, I wasn't with him very long. Not long enough for him to ask about her. Will I run into him again? Will he ask me about her? The idea of his taking an interest in her now fills me with dread. But why would he want her now when he hadn't wanted her before?

It occurs to me that as much as I resent Elio, he gave me the one bright light in my life. For that I'll always be grateful.

Once she finishes her breakfast and gets dressed, we step outside into the cool morning air. Elysse walks beside me, her small hand nestled in mine. I can't help but marvel at how quickly she's grown. It feels like just yesterday she was a tiny baby, completely dependent on me. Now, she's a vibrant, curious child, wise beyond her years.

When we reach her school, I give her a hug and wish her a good day. I watch her skip into the school until she disappears. Then I make my way back home.

I freeze, my heart pounding as I catch sight of the sleek black car parked in our driveway. There's no reason to believe that it's Elio's, yet he's the one who comes to mind. But how would he know where I live? So maybe it's a colleague of Gabriel's.

As I make my way up the walk, the door of the vehicle opens and a man steps out. Elio. My breath catches, partly in panic and partly at the sight of the man I'd loved so deeply.

He smiles when he sees me. There's no stopping the reaction to his devastating good looks. His dark hair is styled impeccably, and his piercing gaze sweeps over me, sending a shiver down my spine.

Elio's presence is commanding, almost overwhelming, as he walks toward me. He moves with a graceful, predatory confidence. He is as gorgeous and captivating as he was back then.

Memories of our passionate, ill-fated romance come rushing back. Despite the years that have passed, his pull on me is as strong as ever. Conflicting emotions swirl within me, bitter resentment and yearning for the love he once promised. I force myself to remember that Elio was the one who shattered my heart, who let his family tear us apart.

"Piper." His lips curve into a devastating smile that draws me in even as I try to fight against it. I'm as powerless now as I'd been when I'd met him.

6

ELIO

I take a deep breath as I step out of my car, my heart pounding in my chest. There she is, Piper. I feel like my world settles like puzzle pieces into a vision of clarity. Her. She's what I want.

Last night, and even as I waited this morning after seeing her walk up the street with a young girl, I vacillated between duty and desire. But seeing Piper now, duty falls away.

I realize that the young girl must be her daughter. Sadness, and yes, jealousy fills me that she built a family without me. A dull ache settles in my chest as I think about the life we could have had, the future we were robbed of. I can picture it so clearly, Piper and me married, raising our children together, building a life filled with love and laughter. It's a future I've dreamed of for years, one I never stopped hoping for, even after Piper disappeared from my life.

When she left, it was like a part of me died. I spiraled into a dark place, lashing out and embracing the ruthless, violent side of myself that I had tried to keep at bay. I became colder, more calculating, diving deeper into the family business and solidifying my reputation as a merciless leader. But the moment I laid eyes on Piper again, everything changed. I still don't know the details of what happened back then. Why her family left. Why she never let me know where she went. But right now, that doesn't matter to me.

She's a mother. Likely married. Yet I go to her, determined to have what was taken from me.

"Piper." I smile, hoping she'll see the man she once loved or at the very least be disarmed by my presence.

"What are you doing here? How'd you find me?" Her tone is sharp, but it's the way she glances around with fear in her eyes that puts me on edge.

I hold up my hands in a placating gesture. "I haven't stopped thinking of you since we ran into each other." Hell, I never stopped thinking of her. "I had to see you."

Piper's lips thin into a tight line. "You shouldn't be here."

The bitterness in her voice cuts me deep, but I'm not one to give up. "Piper, please. Are you okay? I just want—"

She glances around again. "You can't be here."

Is she afraid of my associations? "I assure you that you're not in danger from me."

"You have no idea." She passes me, heading to her door.

I'm concerned now. Something isn't right and it isn't about my work.

"Just go," she says as she unlocks her door.

I refuse to leave, determined to talk and reconnect with Piper. "I can't. I won't. Not until you tell me what is going on."

"It's none of your business, Elio," she says in exasperation.

"You... you are my business."

She glances around me, and I turn to look to see what is spooking her. "Fine. Come in before someone sees you."

When the door shuts behind me, she glares up at me. "Why are you here?"

I stare at her, wondering where all this animosity is coming from. "I told you. I had to see you. You look beautiful."

She blinks at me like I've taken her off guard by calling her beautiful. Taking a chance, I touch her hand, pulling it up to my chest.

"I've never stopped thinking of you." I feel the familiar spark of electricity, and I'm instantly transported back to all those years ago—the stolen kisses, the whispered promises of a future together. That connection between us is still there, undeniable and powerful. Surely, she feels it too.

Piper's eyes widen in surprise at my touch, and for a moment, I see a flicker of the girl I once knew.

"Elio. I'm married."

"So." I'm not a man who goes after married women as a matter of course. But for this woman, I won't let anything get in the way of recovering what is mine. "Are you happy?"

She tugs her hand away, and I get a sense that it's not because I've made her uncomfortable but because she feels the spark too and doesn't want to be lured in by it.

"It doesn't matter. I'm still—"

"It does matter." I lift my hand to her face. She flinches like she expects me to strike her. I gently trace the back of my fingers along her cheek. "You're so beautiful, but you also look tired... wary. You're not happy."

"It doesn't change anything."

I feel like I'm getting somewhere, that her determination to keep me away is waning. "It does because you deserve to be happy. Do you love your husband? How can you when you're so skittish and unhappy looking?"

Piper's eyes widen slightly at my question, and I see the hesitation flicker across her face. It's barely there, but it's enough to keep the spark of hope alive within me.

"You don't know about me... and you have no right to know. You and I were a long time ago."

She's not denying my statement. She's not telling me she loves her husband. In my mind, if she isn't completely and utterly in love with this man she's married to, then he needs to go.

"I can make you happy, Piper. You know I can." She's the other half of my soul. I know it because being next to her again, I feel like she's filling the hole in my heart created when she left.

"It's too late."

"It's never too late." I cup her face in my hands and look at her, willing her to see my earnestness. "You and your child deserve love and affection... the world." I hold her gaze, silently pleading with her to be honest, to let me in. I need to know if the connection we once shared still has the power to overcome the years that have come between us.

Piper opens her mouth, but no words come out. The seconds stretch on, and I can practically see the wheels turning in her mind as she wrestles with her thoughts and emotions. I hold my breath, hoping against hope that her hesitation is a sign that her heart isn't as firmly committed as her outward actions would suggest.

If she isn't overwhelmingly happy with this man she's married to, then maybe, just maybe, I have a chance to win her back, to reclaim the future stolen from us all those years ago.

I watch Piper intently, searching her face for any clue, any indication of what she's feeling. The vulnerability in her expression tugs at my heart, and I long to pull her into my arms, to comfort her and erase the pain I see reflected in her eyes.

But I resist the urge, knowing that I need to tread carefully. One wrong move, one misstep, and I could lose her forever. I've already lost her once, and the thought of it happening again is more than I can bear.

So I wait, my heart pounding in my chest, as Piper gathers her thoughts and prepares to respond. Whatever she says next will determine the course of our future—whether we have a chance to rekindle what we once had or if I'm destined to spend the rest of my life wondering what could have been.

I take a deep breath, steeling myself as I lock eyes with Piper. "Piper," I murmur, injecting my voice with a hint of the old charm that used to melt her. "I don't know what happened before—"

Her eyes flare with heat. "You know—"

"I don't," I insist. "But the past is done, like you said. What we have is here. Now. Don't you feel it? It's as strong as before. We had something special, you and I. Something I've never been able to recapture with anyone else. And you haven't either."

"That's presumptuous and arrogant."

"Tell me I'm wrong." My gaze drops to her lips. Fucking hell, how I want to kiss her, to taste her again. To stop myself from following through, I return my gaze to her eyes.

I watch as a flicker of emotion flashes across her face, and I press on, my tone low and intimate. "Do you remember how we used to talk and laugh?"

She sniffs and I see tears form. Happy tears, I hope.

"Remember our plans for the future? I never stopped wanting that. Even after you disappeared, I held onto the hope that somehow, some way, we'd find our way back to each other. And here you are."

Piper's eyes narrow, and she takes a step back, putting distance between us. "Elio, that was a lifetime ago. We were just kids, caught up in a fantasy that could never have lasted." Her voice is laced with regret and a hint of bitterness. "What we had, it wasn't real. It was nothing more than a youthful infatuation."

Frustration boils inside me. How can she not see, not feel what's going on here? I shake my head vehemently, refusing to accept her words. "No. You can tell yourself that if it makes you feel better, but it's not true. What we had was real. The way we felt about each other, the dreams we shared, they were real." I reach for her hand, my fingers curling around hers. "I loved you, Piper. I still do."

Her eyes widen, and for a moment, I see a flash of the vulnerability I remember from all those years ago. But just as quickly, it's gone, replaced by a steely resolve.

"Stop." She steps back. I see frustration but also confusion. I don't like seeing it, and yet, I know if I persist, I can make her see what we could still have.

"We were young and foolish, blinded by the thrill of first love." She pulls her hand away, shaking her head. "We can't go back to that, no matter how much we might wish we could."

I open my mouth to protest, to remind her of all the promises we made, the plans we had for our future. "At least you could be honest." I don't hide the hurt and irritation at her dismissing our love. "Don't you dare say what I feel for you is foolish. Fucking hell, Piper... was I really the only one who loved in this relationship?"

I step closer, my gaze locked onto hers. "Tell me you felt it too. Tell me you feel it now. The pull between us. Even after all these years, it's there."

Before she can protest further, I cup her face in my hands and press my lips to hers. Yes, it's born of frustration. I expect her to pull away. Perhaps she'll slap me. She tenses for a moment, but then she surrenders, melting into my embrace.

I settle into the kiss, and the world falls away, leaving just us two. It's new, and yet there's a familiarity in her soft, sweet lips. She returns the kiss with a fervor that mirrors my own. Her hands grip the lapels of my jacket, holding me close, and I know in that instant that the connection between us is as strong as ever. She's mine. Nothing else matters. Not Ava. Not her husband. Finally, for the first time since she disappeared, I can breathe again. I have hope again. There's no fucking way I'll lose her again.

7

PIPER

This is wrong. I know it down to my marrow. And yet... as Elio's lips press against mine, warmth and tenderness flood my senses. It's been so long since I've felt this. Safe. Cherished. With Gabriel, intimacy, when it happens, is a chore. He doesn't care about my feelings, my pleasure. For him, intimacy is devoid of any real emotion or passion. Thankfully, he's found other ways to fulfill his sexual needs. Today, Gabriel's touch involves pain, filling me with fear and dread, not the security and love I crave.

Elio's kiss reignites a long-buried spark within me. His strong hands gently cup my face, his thumbs caressing my cheeks as he pulls me closer. I melt into him, all thoughts of right and wrong fading away. In this moment, there is only Elio and the overwhelming need to feel loved and alive again.

He's right about our past. We did love. We laughed. We made promises to build a life together. Back then, our future had seemed so bright, so full of possibility. But then it was all snatched away, leaving me broken and alone. I should push him away and demand to know how he can waltz into my home acting like he didn't abandon me and our baby. But he slants his head, taking the kiss deeper as his arms wrap around me, holding me like I'm the most important treasure in his life. How can I fight against that?

Despite my better judgment, I respond to his touch, my hands gripping the lapels of his coat as I pull him in deeper. I know this is wrong, that I'm betraying the vows I made to Gabriel. But in Elio's arms, I feel alive again, the dull ache in my heart finally soothed.

His hands stroke my back as his lips glide along my neck. "So fucking beautiful," he murmurs.

Tears prick my eyes at feeling seen. Feeling valued. Elio was always like that even when we were younger. It always felt like he lived for my happiness.

"I need you, Piper... I need you so fucking bad."

No. I should tell him no. But what woman can resist a man desperate for her, aching for her? Not me. Not a woman who desperately needs to feel desired and loved.

His hands slide under my shirt, the warmth of them making me sigh. A rush of desire I haven't felt in years ignites a fire.

"Tell me you feel it... you need it too." His hoarse voice reverberates against my neck.

"Yes." I can't believe I'm doing this. I can't believe I'm giving in to Elio. After all these years, after all the pain and heartache, I'm letting him pull me back into his arms.

Elio lifts me off the ground, carrying me upstairs. I feel like I'm in a romance novel. I know it's wrong. I know it can't last. But for once, I want tender kisses and passion.

He stops at a guest room but then continues down the hall until he finds the primary room. A part of me feels like I shouldn't be taking him to my and Gabriel's bed, but when he looks at me with naked desire and something more... love? I simply surrender.

Our hands are desperate as we remove clothing and then fall onto the bed. Our bodies tangle together. My hands roam over his body, noting the slight differences. There are more muscles. He's broader. He's a full-grown man, not the teenage boy I'd once known.

He moves on top of me, his lips trailing down my neck, and I can't help but moan at the sensation.

"I love the noises you make," he says. His comment reminds me that he liked to talk during sex. That for him, the act was more than simple pleasure.

He kisses me, his tongue exploring my mouth with hunger. It's like he's trying to devour me, to consume every last piece of me. I arch toward him as he kisses me deeper.

"Let me rediscover you, Piper." He moves lower, his lips finding the sensitive skin of my throat before moving down. He licks a nipple before sucking it.

"Oh!" I gasp and arch again as a shock of pleasure jolts through me.

He moves to my other breast, taking it into his mouth, his tongue flicking against it. My body trembles with growing desire.

He kisses a trail down my stomach, his fingers tracing the curves of my body, moving lower still until he reaches the apex of my thighs. My pussy clenches in anticipation. He kisses me there, his tongue tracing the folds.

"Oh... God..." My fingers thread through his thick, dark hair, holding him to me as pleasure ratchets up and up.

"Come, Piper," he murmurs against my sensitive flesh. "Let me taste you." His tongue is on me again, licking, sucking, thrusting. It doesn't take long. My body tightens and then shudders as the sweetest orgasm floods through me. He continues to lick and suck until I'm writhing and another orgasm moves through me.

"Elio." I gasp and tug at him, needing a reprieve.

His lips slide back up my body until they capture my mouth in a firm kiss. I can taste myself on his lips.

"Do you feel how much I want you?" His breathing is ragged as his dick presses against my belly.

I open my legs, needing to feel him inside me more than I need my next breath.

His lips cover mine again as he thrusts inside me, deep and powerful. I wrap my legs around his hips, my arms around his shoulders, and hold him to me. The feeling is more than a physical pleasure. It's like I'm being made whole again, and I want to savor it for as long as I can.

He rocks against me. "So tight, baby... so good. Do you feel it?"

I do. Of course I do. He's thick and full, each movement sending delicious sensations through me. He dips his head, sucking my nipple as he moves in and out. Every nerve in my body is firing from the onslaught of his touch, his taste, his body consuming mine. I give myself over to it, moving with him as need coils tighter and tighter.

"Fuck... I'm close... Piper..." His hand slides between us, rubs over my clit.

I cry out, my body trembling as another powerful orgasm slams into me.

"Yes... Fuck..." He groans, his movements becoming more frenzied, harder, faster until he yells out again, his body bucking with his own release, warmth filling me.

He collapses on me, and even then his dick is pulsing, my pussy squeezing, until finally, our bodies, our hearts, our breaths calm.

He rolls off me but tugs me close, his arms around me as he kisses my temple. The gesture is so sweet that tears come to my eyes. This is wrong, but I'm not ready to let it go just yet. So I lie, my body tangled with his, savoring this feeling of being cherished.

But it isn't long before guilt rises. I've betrayed Gabriel. I can't believe it. I'm not the sort of woman who cheats. Not on someone she loves. Okay, so the love I had for Gabriel left years ago. But it doesn't change that I made a vow. A vow he doesn't keep, but that doesn't excuse me.

But it's not just guilt that is threatening to consume me. It's worry. The joy I felt moments ago is replaced by a growing unease. What will Gabriel do if he finds out? Will he leave? Maybe, but not without hurting me both physically and emotionally. He could try and take Ellyse. Or worse. He's threatened worse.

"I missed you." Elio's lips are gentle on my cheek. I close my eyes, trying to deal with the torrent of emotions warring inside me.

"I missed you too," I admit even though I know I shouldn't.

A phone rings and I tense. If it's mine and I don't answer right away, Gabriel will know something is up.

"Fuck." Elio slides out of bed, finds his pants, and pulls out his phone. "Matty." He listens as he watches me. "I'll meet with him. Reason with him."

There's something about his word choice that tells me he followed his father into organized crime. It seems like that's the sort of thing that should have been a deal breaker, but corruption is everywhere. I don't know the details of Gabriel's work, but I'm aware he uses shady practices. Perhaps I'm just making excuses to justify my feelings for Elio. In the scheme of things, my falling for a Mafia member is low on the ladder. The worst is having Elysse grow up in fear.

"I'll be there in thirty. Listen, can you contact Rinella? I'd like to meet again. Tonight." He hangs up and starts to dress.

I don't want him to leave, and yet I'm relieved. I've just made a bigger mess of my life and I don't know how I'll clean it up.

"I'm sorry. I have... business."

I arch a brow. "Family business."

He nods. "You'll be glad to know we have many legitimate establishments now."

I want to tell him it doesn't matter because we can't see each other again. Ever. But I don't want to ruin this moment. I want to be able to remember this day sweetly, even if it's filled with guilt.

When he's dressed, he comes to the bed and leans over me. "You're mine."

I open my mouth to protest, but he kisses me.

"I'm going to make you happy, Piper. I promise." He gives me another kiss and then exits my room.

I flop back wondering what the hell is going to happen. Danger bells clang. Not just danger from Gabriel finding out and punishing me, but danger for my heart from falling for Elio again.

8

ELIO

The last thing I want to do is leave Piper. When I'd arrived this morning, my goal had been to talk to her and reconnect to rebuild what we lost. Somehow, I ended up in her bed, making love to her like no time has passed. The feel of her soft skin, the sound of her breathless moans, it was all so familiar, yet it felt brand new.

As I held her in my arms, a deep sense of contentment washed over me. This is where I'm meant to be, with Piper. For so long, I had tried to move on from her, to convince myself that my feelings for her were just a fleeting teenage infatuation. But the moment I laid eyes on her again, those feelings came rushing back, more powerful than ever.

Any doubts I might have had are gone. She's mine. Yes, there are logistics to deal with. I need to end my engagement and her marriage. What a fucking idiot her husband must be to not cherish the woman he married, to not spend his time making sure she's happy. And she's not happy. The light in her eyes, that spark of challenge, is gone. There's no way she'd have let me touch her if she was happy with her husband. Piper isn't one to betray someone she loves.

The question is, will he leave quietly? For his sake, he'd better. I have no qualms about making him disappear. I won't let anyone stand in the way of Piper and me being together, not the law or my own family's obligations. I've waited eight long years to have her back in my arms, and I'm not about to let her go again.

I wish I could stay with her now, but I have responsibilities waiting for me. Business, for one. And of course, the matter of ending my impending marriage to Ava Rinella. The alliance between our families is crucial, and ending my engagement isn't going to go over well. I need to figure out a way to appease Vincenzo.

Arriving at my office, my mind shifts into the calculated, ruthless mindset required to lead our organization.

"Where you been, Boss?" Matteo asks as he follows me into my office.

"Busy." I'm not ready to explain Piper or my plans to end the engagement to Ava with him at this time. "What's Alderson?" I ask regarding the call I received that morning.

"He's balking at percentages again."

I roll my eyes. It wasn't so long ago that a man like Alderson would be gunned down on the street. Today, we're more subtle, and it's possible Alderson is working with the Feds. His disappearing now could cause more trouble than putting the fear of God, or more accurately, the fear of me, into him.

"I'll go talk to him. Did you contact Rinella?"

"I did. Is it about the wedding? That's the impression he has."

I nod. "It is." I move on to the next piece of business, bark out a few orders to some of my other men, review reports from both my legit and illegit businesses, then head out to pay Alderson a visit.

I'm on my game except in down moments. During the drive to Alderson's store that fronts for illegal betting, my mind drifts back to Piper. The soft curve of her body as she melted into my embrace. The moment when the shadows of her eyes lifted and I saw into her soul as her body came apart from pleasure.

By the time I leave Alderson, he's back under hand. My threats are subtle, said in a calm, professional tone. If anyone is listening, they're not getting anything that can be used against me, but Alderson is clear that things can take a turn if he doesn't get his shit together.

That evening, I head home. I take a deep breath as I walk through the front door, reviewing my speech in my head. The Rinellas will be arriving soon, and I know I need a solid explanation and consolation prize to end this arrangement with him.

I head to my office, wanting to grab a drink before Vincenzo arrives. My sister is waiting, a glass of wine in her hand.

Her sharp, suspicious eyes greet me. "Why the last-minute dinner with Rinella?"

I shrug and pour myself a scotch.

"All of a sudden, you want to be a part of the wedding plans?"

"Where's Matteo?" I ask, not wanting to discuss my reasons for the dinner beforehand. Like Rinella, Lana isn't likely to take the news well. I love my sister, but I'm the head of this family. I don't have to run my decisions by her. I allow her to give her input on business, but she's not an advisor.

"I'm here." Matteo enters and helps himself to a drink at my bar. "I hear Alderson is behaving. How bad of spanking did you give him?"

I smirk. "Bad enough to hurt."

"He'll whine again."

I nod. "He's going to force us to do something more permanent."

"He likes to go out on the lake. Sometimes shit happens out there."

"Let's see if he can hold it together before we start feeding him to the fishes."

Lana crosses her arms. "You should talk to him about Lazaro. He was one of the last to see him."

I suck in a breath. I wish she'd accept that Lazaro is dead. And I'd already leaned hard on Alderson about Lazaro's movements the day he vanished. Alderson might quibble about his payments, but he's not dumb enough to be involved in my brother's murder.

"Right now, I need to prepare for dinner," I say, taking my drink with me as I exit my office. I head up to my room to freshen up. When my servant informs me of Rinella's arrival, I head down to greet him. I'm a little annoyed that he's brought Ava with him, as I don't want to hurt her. But I suppose he thinks this meeting is about wedding plans.

"Thank you for coming, Vincenzo." I shake his hand. "You too, Ava." I give her a kiss on the cheek. "Come. Dinner is ready."

I escort them to the dining room where Lana and Matteo are already waiting. As we sit around the table, my staff serves wine, and we make small talk.

Once dinner is served, I roll the tension from my shoulders and clear my throat. "I have some unexpected news."

All eyes turn on me. As if he suspects something is up, Vincenzo's eyes narrow.

"I will not be able to go through with our wedding in two weeks' time."

"How much time do you need?" Vincenzo's voice is tight with barely contained anger.

"Let me rephrase that. I will not be marrying your daughter at all." I glance at Ava. "You're a lovely woman and this decision is no reflection on you."

Vincenzo's face immediately contorts with fury as he leans forward in his chair. His hand fists around a knife that I'm sure he wants to plunge into my chest. "What is the meaning of this? Your father would never disrespect me this way."

Lana is gaping at me in shock. Matteo's brows lift in surprise.

I hold up a hand to stop Vincenzo's tirade. "Please, understand that this decision has nothing to do with you or your daughter. It's a... personal matter."

Vincenzo's nostrils flare as he lets out a humorless laugh. "Personal? Did your father raise a pussy? This is business, boy."

I suck in a breath to rein in the violent rage brewing in my gut. I know people see me as soft because I'm polite and often compromising if it can benefit me in the long run. But many people have made the mistake that they can walk over me. They learned the hard way, often with their lives, that I'm not one to fuck with.

"You're a guest in my home," I remind him.

"I deserve to know why you've rejected my daughter. Why you disrespect me."

"Like I said, this is no reflection on you or your daughter. It's personal. The details are not your business."

Vicenzo slams his fist on the table, making the utensils jump. "Not my business? When you renege on a binding agreement between our families, it most certainly becomes my business!"

Lana's eyes are wide with shock, and Matteo, the bastard, has a smirk as if he's enjoying the chaos unfolding before us. Ava, like the dutiful Mafia princess she is, sits quietly, her expression carefully neutral.

"I understand your anger," I say, doing my best to maintain a calm façade. "But there are other ways we can forge an alliance without the need for a marriage."

For a moment, I think Vincenzo will lunge across the table and make use of his steak knife. "You insolent little—"

"Please, let's not lose our tempers here. I understand your frustration. This decision wasn't made lightly. I do respect you and our potential partnership."

Vincenzo's eyes flash with fury. "Not lightly? You make a mockery of our agreement, and you expect me to simply accept it?" He leans forward, his voice dropping to a dangerous growl. "Do you have any idea the position this puts me in, the humiliation I will face?"

I can feel the weight of his glare, the intensity of his anger palpable in the air. He's right, and I need to do better to assure him that I'll make things right. "I assure you that's not my intent. But I cannot follow through on this marriage. I need you to understand that."

"Understand?" Vincenzo scoffs, his lip curling in disdain. "You expect me to simply understand when you're throwing away a union that would have cemented our families' alliance for generations to come? A union that your father made with me. You disrespect him too."

I have no doubt he's right. My father wouldn't have put up with this. When I'd made the decision to promise myself to Piper, I knew he'd be against it. I didn't give a shit then. I don't give a shit now. He's gone. This is my life. This is my business. I make the rules.

"I'm sorry, but my decision is final. I hope we can find another way to—"

"Final?" He leans back in his chair, his eyes narrowing to slits. "I'm afraid that is not how this works, boy."

I feel the weight of his words, the implication behind them. This is no longer just about a broken engagement—it's about power, control, and the delicate balance that holds our world together.

"Yes. Final." I meet his hate-filled gaze, hoping he can see that I won't be fucked with.

He shakes his head, his expression filled with contempt. "You will go through with this wedding, Elio, or there will be consequences. Consequences that you and your family will not soon forget."

The air in the room grows thick with tension. I'm treading on dangerous ground, but I can't ignore the pull of my heart. Nor am I a pussy. I've gone this far, and giving in now would tell Vincenzo that I'm weak. I have to stand my ground or I'll lose all respect and power in my own organization as well as The Outfit.

"We can discuss other—"

"Fuck you, Elio." He shoots up from his chair, knocking it back. "Let's go, Ava." He storms out, Ava trailing behind him with a concerned expression on her face. The sound of the front door slamming echoes through the grand foyer, reaching the dining room.

"Well... that was fun." Matteo cuts his meat, his eyes brimming with amusement.

"What the hell was that, Elio?" Lana hisses. "Do you have any idea what you've just done?"

I sigh and take a sip of my wine, wishing it were scotch. "I know exactly what I've done, Lana, and I'm not going to apologize for it."

Her eyes widen in disbelief. "Are you out of your mind? You've just jeopardized everything we've worked for—everything Dad worked for!"

"Then you marry her. Or Matteo here can marry her."

Matteo blinks. "Me?"

"Sure. You're part of the D'Amato family. Don't you think she'd be a suitable wife?"

A flush comes to his cheeks. He clears his throat. "Well... yes... she's pretty and—"

"The deal was for you to marry her," Lana snaps.

"The deal is off."

She shakes her head. "What is wrong with you?"

"There's nothing wrong with me. I can't marry her when my heart is with someone else."

Lana scoffs, shaking her head in disgust. "Your heart? Since when do you let your heart dictate the decisions that affect this family?"

I decide it's time to come clean. "Piper is back."

"Oh, my God." Lana gapes. "This isn't about some fleeting teenage romance, Elio. This is about power, influence, and the survival of our legacy. Please tell me you're not still living in some fairy tale la-la land. Surely, you've grown out of that."

I open my mouth to respond, but Lana raises her hand, silencing me. "No, you listen to me. You're the heir to this empire, and you have a responsibility to this family that goes beyond your own selfish desires."

I clench my jaw, not wanting to exert my authority over her. We're family. But just like I can't take disrespect from Vincenzo, I can't from her, either. "I'm the head of this empire, this family, not the *heir*. It's already mine. And up until now, you've had no complaints about how I've run it. Not when through me, your income has more than doubled."

"It's not just about money. You're going to turn others against us."

"It is about money in the end, sweet sister. Vincenzo can try to go against me, but he'll lose. He knows it." To be honest, my ego might be bigger than what I can pull off, but I will not be swayed from what

I want. "As far as Piper, it's not a fleeting romance. I love her. I've always loved her."

"And then she left—"

I interrupt Lana because this isn't her business. "I have given all I have to this family. I think I'm owed one bit of personal happiness."

"You know, you could have both," Matteo says. "Marry Ava, have Piper on the side."

I let out a laugh. "Piper isn't an on-the-side woman. Besides, it isn't about sex with her. I love her."

"I don't care, Elio," Lana says, her tone that of a petulant child. "You're going to marry Ava Rinella, and you're going to do it for the good of this family. Anything less is unacceptable."

"He's right," Matteo says to Lana. "Remember how he was when Piper left?" He turns to me. "I wouldn't wish that on you again. You were fucking miserable to be around."

He remembers the darkness that consumed me after Piper's sudden and unexplained departure. I had spiraled into a violent, reckless haze, lashing out at anyone who dared to cross my path. It served me well as I grew into the leader I needed to be for the business. Over the last few years, I clawed back from the dark abyss, so I wasn't the violent asshole I'd been, but I hadn't seen the light nor felt its warmth until I saw Piper again.

"Who's to say she won't leave again?" Lana says.

I won't let her. I don't know why Piper left, but I'll make sure she wants to stay. "Nothing is going to stand in my way. Not even you, Lana."

"You know what's at stake here. The alliance with the Rinellas, the stability of our family's influence—all of it hangs in the balance. You can't just throw that away because of some... some childhood infatuation."

"Piper is the love of my life, and I won't let her go again. Not this time."

Lana opens her mouth to protest, but I rise from the table. "This is not up for debate or discussion."

I leave the dining room and head to the bar. I need a drink. I know I've made my business life more difficult, but the lightness that fills my chest that I'm now clear to pursue a life with Piper far outweighs that.

I hold my glass of scotch up, saluting myself. "Here's to you, Piper. I'm going to make sure all my promises to you come true."

9

PIPER

I rush around the house, my heart pounding in my chest. I'm in shock over my behavior—sleeping with Elio. I'm terrified of what will happen if Gabriel finds out.

I strip the sheets from the bed and toss them in the laundry. I yank open the windows to let in fresh air, desperate to erase any lingering scent of Elio. Once I'm sure I've disposed of any hint of Elio's visit, I resume the job Gabriel has tasked me with. My hands tremble as I sort through the piles of boxes, unpacking them with frenzied movements. I can't seem to settle my nerves. The guilt and shame are overwhelming, and at the same time, those few moments with Elio, feeling like I was the center of the world... I can't quite regret them.

For a moment, I get lost replaying the passionate encounter with Elio. The way he pulled me into his arms, the tenderness in his touch, the burning desire in his eyes. It's been so long since I felt any of that. Elio was always so kind, so loving. Gabriel, on the other hand, is a volatile, controlling man who makes me live in constant fear.

Gabriel is my husband. I made a vow. I made my proverbial bed, and now I have to lie in it, which means getting the house sorted. I'm in a battle with the clock. If I don't make progress on the house,

Gabriel will wonder what I was up to. So I work quickly, hoping he doesn't notice how all our stuff looks like it was put away in a rush.

Late afternoon, I go to the kitchen and prepare lasagna. Once I get it into the oven, I resume unpacking. Just as I finish the last box of books in the family room, the front door opens.

My nerves shake, but I paste on a warm smile to greet Gabriel and Elysse. I hurry to the foyer.

"Welcome home." I hope I'm cheerful without looking like I'm overdoing it. Gabriel notices the most subtle changes in everything.

Gabriel smiles, giving me a kiss on the cheek. I let out a small breath of relief. He's still in a good mood. I know that can change any minute, so I'm still on my guard.

"I got a smiley face on my spelling, Mommy." Elysse holds up a paper to show me her accomplishment as Gabriel hangs up his coat.

"That's wonderful, sweetie. How was your practice today?"

She shrugs. "Good. What's for dinner?"

"Lasagna."

Gabriel sniffs the air. "Is something burning?"

I freeze, my mind racing. "Oh, no." I rush to the kitchen as I realize in horror that I forgot the lasagna in the oven. The acrid smell of burnt food fills the air. Immediately, I'm chastising myself for forgetting to turn on the timer, for not checking on the lasagna sooner.

Pulling open the oven, I wince at the sight of the blackened, charred mess. "No, no, no." Panic is growing as I use potholders to remove the lasagna from the oven.

"I hope that's not dinner."

I don't have to look at him to know his good mood is a thing of the past. It's evident in his tone.

I don't want to look at him, but he feels disrespected if I don't. I turn to him. "I'm so sorry. I got distracted and lost track of the time."

His expression darkens, the anger building like a storm in his eyes. "Distracted, huh?" he sneers. "Is that what you call it?"

Before I can react, his hand lashes out, striking me hard across the face. The force of the blow sends me reeling, and I stumble back-ward, colliding with the kitchen counter.

"You useless, incompetent woman!" he roars, towering over me. "Can't you do anything right?"

Cowering, I raise my hands to shield myself, but it's no use. His hand lands another blow. Pain explodes in my skull, and I cry out as I fall to the ground.

"Mommy!"

I want to protect Elysse, but Gabriel is standing over me, fury in his eyes. His hands ball into fists. "You don't do shit all day. Why is it too much to expect a home cooked meal when I get home?"

"I was unpacking." My voice trembles. "I lost track of time—"

"You're worthless, you know that?" His foot kicks out, catching me in my side.

"Stop it!" Elysse's terrified scream pierces the air. My heart leaps into my throat as she launches herself at him, her small fists pounding against his leg. "Leave Mommy alone!"

Gabriel whirls on her, his hand raised mid-strike.

"No!" I reach up and grab his arm to prevent him from hurting her. "It's my fault." I glance at Elysse. "Go to your room, sweetie."

Her expression is torn.

"Gabriel." I say his name, wanting to pull his attention back to me. "I'll be better, I promise. Just... don't hurt her. Please, don't hurt my baby."

The desperation in my voice seems to give him pause, and he glares at me, his chest heaving with rage.

"You'd better not mess this up again, Piper," he growls, his fingers flexing as if he's still considering lashing out. "I'm going out." He sucks in a breath and straightens his tie. "Don't think of leaving or your brat will pay. Do you understand?"

I'm still on the floor as I nod. "Yes. I understand."

With that, he turns on his heel and stalks out of the kitchen, slam-ming the front door behind him. I slowly climb up from the floor. Elysse rushes into my arms, her small body shaking with sobs.

"Shh, it's okay, baby," I murmur, holding her tight and pressing a kiss to the top of her head. "He's gone now. You're safe."

I know, though, that the respite is only temporary. Gabriel will be back, and I dread the moment when he returns, knowing that he'll likely be in an even worse mood, especially if he's been drinking. If I'm lucky, he'll find comfort in the arms of another woman and won't return tonight at all.

Tears sting my eyes as I hold Elysse. I hate myself for not having the courage to simply pack us up and run. I would if his threat wasn't always directed at Elysse. He knows the way to control me is through her.

I take a deep, shuddering breath, trying to steady my own emotions. I need to be strong for Elysse's sake. She's looking to me for comfort, for guidance, and I can't let her down. Not again. We can't continue living this way. The fear, the abuse, the constant walking on eggshells—it has to end. Elysse deserves so much more than this. We both do.

My heart pounds in my chest as I consider my options. I know I need to find a way out, for Elysse's sake.

"He hurt you again."

"I'm so sorry, baby," I whisper, my voice thick with emotion. "I'm going to make this right, I promise."

I think of Elio.

I'm going to make you happy, Piper. I promise.

For a moment, I think about calling him and asking for his help. But how can I? Elio's sort of help could lead to murder, and I don't want to be a party to that. I don't know the specifics of how Mafia families and businesses run, but I know there is a great deal of risk. What's that saying about jumping from the frying pan into the fire? That's what asking for his help would involve, moving from one dangerous situation to another.

I hold Elysse close, vowing to find a way to break free, no matter what. It's time for me to be the protector. I can't expect a man or anyone to save me, to save Elysse. That's my job.

"Let me fix us some dinner, okay?"

She sniffs. "Okay."

A few minutes later, I have pasta and cheese on the table. "Tell me about school." I work to make my voice light, but Elysse isn't having any of it. She pokes at her food. It won't be long before she sees me for what I am and resents me. I'm a coward.

After dinner, I clean up the kitchen and air out the burnt smell. Because Elysse has withdrawn and won't talk to me, I turn on a movie and we sit together watching it until her bedtime.

Once she's asleep, I go to the bathroom in my room. I look at the woman in the mirror. The woman I've become. I'm worn down. Weary. A dark bruise mars my cheek. I've come to learn it's one reason Gabriel doesn't want me to leave the house. He doesn't want anyone to see the evidence on me that he's a monster.

What am I teaching my daughter? The idea that someone would do this to Elysse guts me. Yet here I am, the model of succumbing to domestic abuse.

I find my phone and open my web browser. I start to enter a search term to find shelters or services to help me. But I only have two letters entered when I consider that Gabriel often checks my phone. The image of Gabriel, his hand ready to strike Elysse, flashes in my mind. His threat to harm her if I try to leave...

I set my phone down, and my soul cries out at my cowardice.

10

ELIO

I wake up with a renewed sense of purpose, my mind racing with thoughts of Piper. The connection we shared all those years ago still burns hot, wild, perfect. I'm determined to rekindle that flame.

As I get ready, I can't stop thinking about how I'll approach this. I know I need to be cautious, to tread carefully. I can't assume that all is well between us simply because we had sex. I remember her wariness, which I'm not sure is specifically about me or life in general. I smile as I think back to having to breach her defenses with charm and patience in high school. I can do it again. I will do it again.

Needing to see her, I drive to her home, planning to arrive about the time she returns from taking her daughter to school the day before. A daughter. I can't deny how envious I am of the man who made a child with her. A child who should have been mine.

But I still hold to the fact that Piper isn't happy. I know I can fix that for her. I haven't met her child, but I'm fully prepared to embrace her.

As I drive to Piper's house, I map out the conversation in my head. I suppose the first thing is to find out why she left, and if I was at fault, to find a way to make amends. I'll tell her that I never stopped thinking about her, that she's the only one who's ever made me feel truly alive. And I'll ask her, straight out, if there's any chance we can start over. Maybe I should make my case a bit more before I ask that. I don't want to give her any reason to doubt me.

My heart races as I pull up to her house. I feel like I'm on the edge of finally having everything I ever wanted. I'm excited, yet nervous. What if she says no? I shake that from my head. I know she and I are meant to be together. She might try to push me away, but not even she can deny our connection.

I trot up to the front door ready for the next phase of life. I knock, one last time replaying what I want to say.

The door opens only a crack. I can barely see Piper, and what I do see is a woman wearing large, dark sunglasses. I lean in because I think I see the hint of a bruise on her cheek. Alarm bells start ringing in my head.

"Piper, what's wrong?" I push the door open, ignoring her attempt to keep me out.

"Nothing. You can't be here, Elio."

"Something is wrong." I shut the door. I reach for her glasses.

She jerks away. "Just... leave me alone."

I stare at her, feeling a sense of helplessness. "I can't." I reach for the sunglasses again, gently removing them. She's caked on makeup, but there's no doubt that she has a black eye. "Fucking hell. Did your husband do this?" He's a dead man. The deed is as good as done.

"No. I drank a little too much wine last night out of guilt for cheating on my husband."

She's lying. "I don't believe you."

She scoffs. "You always did think the world revolved around you."

"No. I always thought it revolved around you."

For a moment, I see something in her eyes that gives me hope. But as quickly as it's there, it's gone.

"What happened?" I ask, reaching out to brush the bruise on her cheek.

She flinches at my touch, and my stomach twists with dread. Something is very wrong here.

"Did he do this?" I ask. The haunted look in her eyes is all the confirmation I need. "Did he find out about us?"

"There is no us, Elio. Why are you here? You need to leave."

"Is he here?" I'll kill him with my bare hands.

"No. He's not. But he's my husband. What we did was wrong—"

"No!" I point my index finger at her. She recoils like she thinks I might hit her. "Fuck. Piper. I would never hurt you. And if he's—"

"He's not." she insists, but not very convincingly. "I've been unpacking and a book fell off a shelf and hit my cheek. That's all."

Lies. It's all a lie, but why? "I can help you. Let me take you away—"

"I don't need a knight in shining armor. Especially one like you."

What the fuck does that mean? "What the hell, Piper? You're not a woman to put up with this bullshit."

"And yet you're still here."

I'm the bullshit? "I'd never hurt you—"

"That's a lie. You did hurt me."

"I never... your husband struck you. Fucking hell, you have a daughter."

Her eyes flash with heat. "Don't you judge me. Gabriel is a good provider."

I scoff, wondering if I fell through Alice's looking glass. "So the fuck what? That gives him a right to hit you? Why are you defending him?"

"I told you, it was an accident unpacking. Why are you even here? You got what you wanted yesterday."

"No, I didn't." The perfect life I'd imagined for us is slipping away. I reach for her, desperate to make her understand. "What I want is you, in my life, like we planned. You and your daughter."

She shoves me away, her expression hardening. "Save it, Elio. You've already proven that you don't really care, so why should I believe you now?"

Her words cut me deep. I'm shocked, but also angry. How can she accuse me of all this? I made promises to her. She's the one who left.

"At the very least, let me help you—"

"I don't need your help, Elio. I can take care of myself."

I stare at Piper, my dream dying again.

"What we had is dead."

How can she say that? "No. You can tell me to take a hike, but you can't dismiss what is between us."

"I'm married. I have a daughter. My life is here, with Gabriel."

Murderous jealousy fills me. "I can give you everything you want, and you still want a man who hurts you—"

"You're no better."

If she drove a stake through my heart, it wouldn't hurt as much as those words. "Piper, don't do this."

She shakes her head, her voice barely above a whisper. "It's too late, Elio. I made my choice a long time ago. You need to go and stay away from me."

I want to argue, to tell her that it's never too late to change her life, but the haunted look in her eyes stops me. I want to pull her into my arms and make her feel the truth of feelings. Something is fucked up here, and I might walk away now, but I'm sure as hell going to do whatever needs to be done to keep her and her child safe.

"Please," I ask one more time. "Let me help you. I can't just leave you here, not like this."

She stares at me in an attempt to be strong, but underneath I see anguish. "You have to. I... I made a mistake letting you back into my life. I never should have given in to you."

Her words feel like a punch to the gut, and I have to fight to keep my composure. "Don't say that."

"I don't want you in my life. I need you to leave, now."

Her tone is final, and I know there's no arguing with her. Defeated, I nod. "Okay. If that's what you want, I'll go."

I turn to leave, my heart shattering. But I can't bring myself to walk away, not without one last plea. "Promise me you'll be safe. Call me if you need anything—"

"I won't." She averts her gaze. "I'll be fine. Just go, and don't come back."

I linger for a moment, desperate to change her mind, but she opens the door to let me out.

I turn and make my way to the porch, pausing only to glance back at her one last time. "I love you, Piper. Always."

Her breath hitches, but she doesn't respond. Instead, she shuts the door.

I stand on the porch, my mind racing as I try to make sense of what just happened. Piper is in trouble. That much is clear. And she's pushing me away, denying what's between us. Okay, so maybe I have to accept that she doesn't want me. But she's also refusing to let me help her. She has to know that I can protect her. Maybe I should have been clear that I could save her without expecting anything in return.

The sound of the deadbolt sliding into place tells me I won't have the opportunity to say any more today. But this isn't over. I may be leaving her house, but I'm not giving up. I'll find a way to protect her, to get her and her daughter to safety.

11

PIPER

I watch Elio leave, my emotions a tumultuous mix of grief, confusion, anger. As soon as he's out of sight, I break down in tears. The pain I feel is overwhelming. Even after all these years, Elio still has the power to shake me to my core. Each time he begged me to let him help me, saying he'd treat me well, saying he loved me, all I wanted to do was let him. But I couldn't. Elio isn't my answer. His world isn't any safer. And I can't trust him.

As I work through all the emotions, anger rises to the top. I'm furious with him for showing up here thinking he can waltz back in and pick up where we left off. As if it's that simple? He'd abandoned me and Elysse once before. I'd be an idiot to give him the opportunity to do it again.

And yet, a part of me still yearns for him. The way he looks at me, like I'm the center of his world, almost makes me forget what he did. Oh, hell, I did forget yesterday and let myself succumb to his charm. I hate myself for giving in to that temptation, for betraying the vows I made to Gabriel.

I hope Elio got the message and will stay away. Even as I tell myself that, the thought of never seeing him again, of his walking out of my life for good, fills me with sadness. Why couldn't Elio have fought for me and Elysse eight years ago?

The memory of Elio's promise to me and the aftermath floods back. I was so young, so naive, believing that our love could conquer anything. Little did I know that it would all come crashing down a day later.

I remember sneaking back into the house. I made it only to the hallway bath before I felt sick and had to make use of the bathroom. The retching must have been loud enough to wake my parents because the next thing I knew, they were standing in the doorway, faces etched with concern and suspicion.

"Piper, what on earth is going on?" my mother asked in concern.

I tried to come up with some excuse for sneaking in, but what could I say?

"Have you been drinking?" my father demanded. "Is that why you're sick?"

I shook my head. "No... it just must be something I ate."

"Were you out with that boy again?" My father's voice was laced with disapproval.

Ultimately, I had to confess that I was Elio. At first, they hadn't been too concerned by my dating him, but over the last few months, after articles about potential crimes committed by his family and our growing infatuation, my parents wanted me to stay away from him.

My parents' expressions shifted from concern to outrage, and I braced myself for the inevitable lecture that was sure to come. But nothing could have prepared me for what happened next. They sent me to bed, and I thought all was well until the next morning when my mother handed me a pregnancy test she'd run out and bought first thing that morning. I told her she was being ridiculous, but I couldn't get out of taking the test.

My hands trembled as I stared at the little pink plus sign, the confirmation my parents suspected. I was pregnant.

My parents were disappointed but immediately took action. Hours later, Elio's parents showed up at our home to discuss the situation.

"Where's Elio?" I asked. I'd always been a strong young woman, but at that moment, I felt outnumbered. I needed him.

"Elio doesn't want to be a part of this," his father said, his expression and tone not hiding his disdain for me.

His words shook me to my core. Elio didn't want me. After all the promises he made, he turned his back on me, on us, on our child.

While I was present during their discussion, I wasn't included in the decisions. What I wanted didn't matter. By the time Elio's parents left, my father was holding a small fortune with which to move somewhere else and live in financial comfort. My parents chose England. I felt like I'd been sucked into a tornado, spinning, spinning, the world gone mad. Two days later, I was in a suburb of London.

My bitterness at Elio's abandonment isn't the only resentment I carry. I still haven't forgiven my parents. Sure, they made sure I was taken care of during my pregnancy. They helped me finish school and get a degree. They are loving grandparents to Elysse. But they forced me to leave Elio and my friends, the life I knew. They pushed me to marry Gabriel so that Elysse could have a father. When I told them about his anger issues and how I wanted to stay in England while he took a job in Chicago, they encouraged the move back to the United States with him, saying the move would reduce his stress and how we were a family. They were wrong.

I wonder what they'd think about Elio showing up and wanting to be a part of my life again. It's so odd that Elio acts like nothing happened. He looks at me like he's genuinely confused about my resistance toward him. I'm convinced that he was in on the plan, that he had agreed to let me go because he didn't want to be a father. Now, I wonder if I was wrong all along. Could it be possible that he had no idea that our parents arranged for my family to leave town?

No. I shake my head. There's no reason for him not to be at the meeting with my family since it involved him as well. The only reason he didn't come was as his father said. He didn't want to. Elio didn't fight for me, didn't come after me. And that's all that matters.

I realize I'm still standing at the door. I make my way to the kitchen for a glass of water, but the memories continue to torment me. It occurs to me that it was the moment I first started losing myself, when my life stopped being my own. My parents decided my fate without consulting me. Today, Gabriel does the same. The way Elio tries to bend me to his will suggests he's not much different.

I pour myself water and drink the glass, wishing the water could wash away all the pain, all the fear. That's the problem, I realize, wanting something, someone else to fix all that is wrong in my life. But there is no magic pill, no knight in shining armor. I have to save myself and Elysse. Despite the danger we're in, I'm determined to find another way forward. I won't let Gabriel's abuse and my past with Elio dictate my future any longer. It's time I take control of my own life, for Elysse's sake if not my own.

Filled with a renewed sense of strength, I consider my options. I can try to leave Gabriel again, but the memory of his violent reaction last time still haunts me. The bruise I carry today is a reminder of what he's capable of, and I can't bear the thought of Elysse being caught in the crossfire.

Perhaps I could reach out to the authorities, but I've heard horror stories about the limitations of law enforcement. A protective order isn't a guarantee that Gabriel won't come after me and Elysse.

And how would I support us? I haven't worked since I married Gabriel. While four years isn't that long, I imagine it's long enough that I'd have a difficult time finding a job that would pay enough for me to afford a new place to live.

Frustration eats at me that I can't find the solution. I'm left where I always am, doing my best to keep the peace through subservience. This time is no different as I head out of the kitchen to finish unpacking the house. But I let my mind ruminate over ideas to stop this madness.

That evening, Gabriel and Elysse arrive home. Everything is the same. Gabriel isn't jovial but he's not angry, either. Elysse shares her day at school and after school programming, her eyes wary as they track Gabriel for any potential outburst.

For me, there is a change. Deep down, I'm starting to feel my agency return. I don't have answers. I'm still stuck. But I'm building the confidence to know that a solution will come. I will save Elysse and myself.

"I'm going to Vegas this weekend," Gabriel informs me over dinner.

"Okay." I don't bother asking questions. I learned a long time ago that questions bother him when he's planning to gamble, drink, and sleep with other women. Besides, I'm glad he's going. A few days of respite are what Elysse and I need.

Gabriel glances at me, his eyes narrow with suspicion. I sit quietly, waiting for him to ask his question or demand something of me.

He pokes at his salad. "I'll leave you some money if you want to do something fun." It's his attempt to placate me.

I'll take it. "Thank you."

"But the house needs to be done by the time I get back. It's ridiculous how long it has taken you to unpack."

"It will be done." It's nearly done. He's just looking for reasons to remind me of what a loser I am.

When dinner is finished, he leaves again, heading to the bar. Elysse and I watch TV and then I tuck her into bed.

"How about you and I go out for a fancy dinner this weekend?" I say as I pull the blankets over her.

"Fancy?"

"Remember how we used to go for proper tea back in England? We can do something like that but for dinner. We'll dress up nice and go to an expensive restaurant. Maybe we'll have dessert for dinner."

Her eyes light up. I don't see that as often as I should.

"Can we go roller skating?"

I laugh. "Okay."

She's smiling as her eyes close, and she snuggles into bed. I watch her for a moment. She's my strength. My purpose. For her, I'll find a way to get away from Gabriel.

12

ELIO

I'm not sure what to do about Piper, but I do know that I'm not going to stand around and let her be abused. I'm going to find out who that bastard is and give him a taste of his own medicine.

When I arrive at my office, I do a public records search on the house Piper lives in and discover it's owned by a Gabriel Collins. Sounds pompous. It takes a bit more research to learn he's from a rich family in New York but attended advanced studies in economics in England. See... pompous. He works for an international financial firm and was recently relocated to Chicago.

A knock on my door interrupts my research.

"Boss?" Matteo's voice calls out.

"Yeah. Come in."

"We got a problem," he says as he enters my office followed by several of my highest ranking men. That gets my attention. This problem isn't some little hassle.

"What's happened?" I push my focus on Piper and her asshole husband aside as Matteo and my men provide reports of retaliation from Vincenzo over my ending the engagement to his daughter.

I rise from my desk and pace the length of my office as I listen to the reports from my trusted lieutenants. The tension between the D'Amato and Rinella families has reached a boiling point, and it feels like the very territory we've fought so hard to control is now up in flames. The tentative agreements we'd already had with the Rinellas are now broken.

I don't make any decisions yet. My first step is to talk to Vincenzo. Once I dismiss my men, I call him.

"If I didn't know any better, Vincenzo, I'd think you were glad I broke off the engagement so you had an excuse to come after me."

"You brought this on yourself, boy."

My teeth grind as his use of the word *boy*. He thinks my younger age and fewer years of experience make me weak. I'll show him differently. However, because I don't want to fuck with our business or have issues with Don Caruso, I'll use diplomacy first.

"I told you I'd find a way to make things right. Did you forget, old man?" There. I swipe at his old age.

"What I want is for my daughter to be married to a D'Amato."

Fucking hell. "That's not going to happen. But I can arrange—"

"No. Your father and I put this agreement together eight years ago. He'd be rolling in his grave if he knew you'd do me dirty like this."

"He'd also think you're an idiot for attacking me on my turf. It works both ways, you know."

"All I did was tell my boys to cut you off from the waterfront. If you had any other issues... well, that wasn't me."

"My father always said you were a liar. A bad one at that." I'm talking a big talk, but I'm off my game some at this turn of events. I rake my fingers through my hair. For a moment, I reconsider my situation. Piper doesn't want me. Am I about to start a war with another family for no reason? I can't be sure Caruso will be on my side if things fall apart between me and Rinella. He likes me more, I'm sure. I'm innovative and smart. But I did break an agreement.

When I think of a life with Ava, I feel dead inside. It has nothing to do with her. She's lovely. But Piper... she's the one I want. Since the day I met her, she's been mine. I won't let anything stop me from having what's mine. I don't know how I'll convince her to give us another chance, but I'll keep trying until I take my last breath. Which might be sooner than later if things with Vincenzo escalate too much.

"Fuck you, D'Amato." The line goes dead.

I let out a breath and call Matteo to have him come back to my office. He's not really a strategist, but I need to bounce ideas off him. I might have talked to Lana about this, but she'll bust my balls about breaking the engagement.

He walks in with his usual easygoing swagger. "Rinella concede?"

"No."

He laughs. "The guy has a hard on for you to marry his daughter."

I nod. "Do you think he plans to use her to worm his way into my business?"

"Wouldn't put it past him. She gives you a male heir, you have an untimely death, and all of a sudden, he's looking after the D'Amato business."

"Fuck."

"Works both ways. In fact, you're at a better advantage. She's your in to take over his business."

"He has a son."

Matteo laughs. "That moron?" He has a point. Vinny Junior is about as dumb as they come. He spends all his time drinking and gambling away his father's profits. "Be glad he's not proposing that Lana marry him."

I let out a bark of a laugh at the idea of that. "Lana would eat him alive."

"I bet he'd enjoy every moment of it until she slit his throat."

"I need to figure this out." I sit behind my desk and will my brain to find the answer.

"You could marry Ava."

I glare at him.

He holds his hands up in surrender. "Okay, so not that. I hope this woman is worth all this. It's not just you who's affected, you know?"

"You're not being asked to marry a woman you don't love."

He looks down. "She seems nice."

"Then you marry her." I have a sense of déjà vu. Didn't we have this same exchange the other night? "Let's get back to the issue at hand."

"We need to respond swiftly. Show them we won't be pushed around," Matteo says.

I nod, my mind racing as I consider my options. "I'd rather appease him with a new arrangement than retaliate for encroaching on my territory and blocking us from the waterfront."

He stares at me. "That's not what your old man would do. You know as well as I do that you'll look weak."

He's right. I can't afford that. "Okay. So we retaliate. But where does it end? I need something he'll want as much as a marriage between our families."

"I can't imagine what that is unless you walk away and let him have it all."

"That's not happening." I sit back in my chair. "What about Kiplinger?"

"Vice?"

I nod. "We could hand over some information." I have what Rinella doesn't have, friends in high places, including law enforcement and local government. They keep me from being arrested and I keep them financially secure.

"I've heard a few rumors."

"Anything definitive? Catch him in the act?"

"Maybe. Let me check with Robbie. He's the one closest to Rinella's area."

"Good. Keep me posted." I suck in a breath. "We need to keep an eye on all our businesses... legit and otherwise. I think I'll go to the restaurant tonight."

"You think he'll try to hit you there?"

"I think he knows that hurting the name I've worked to build as a legitimate businessman will bother me more than fucking with our other business. I have a good reputation even if there are whispers of the old family business."

"I'll have guys at the clubs. What about the construction sites?"

"Maybe put a few more men."

"You know, Elio," Matteo muses, "Lazaro would have known exactly how to handle this situation with the Rinellas. He was like a rabid dog. He could have married Ava or scared Rinella enough to make him back down."

"True." My brother Lazaro had always been on the edge of crazy. It made him unpredictable, which made our enemies and our associates nervous. The memory of him is bittersweet. I miss him. God, I'd lost so much in the span of a few years. First, Piper. Then Lazaro. Next, my parents.

I scrub a hand over my face, trying to push back the tide of grief and regret. Lazaro's absence left a void emotionally, but also professionally, that no one else can fill. Many times, I've wondered how things would be different if he were here. No doubt, Rinella would be second-guessing ever crossing us. I'm left with him thinking I'm weak, and it doesn't sit well.

"I miss him too, you know," Matteo says, his gaze filled with empathy. "He was a crazy motherfucker, but God, was he good for a laugh."

I smile. "He was." I can't get Lazaro back. I don't know what happened to him, but I have no doubt he's dead. In the past, he'd have been gunned down and we'd have a body to bury. Today's Mafia isn't so in-the-face with its killings. I imagine Lazaro is at the bottom of Lake Michigan or under a crop of corn somewhere in a rural part of the state.

I can't get my parents back, either. I suppose it's a comfort to know they died in a car accident together instead of a hit. They could be brutal SOBs, but they were my parents.

Piper, however... She's alive and well. I've lost a lot, but she's one person I can get back. At the very least, I need to make sure she's safe.

I write down Gabriel's name on a piece of paper and hand it to Matteo. "I want you to see what you can find out about this man."

Matteo takes the paper, reads it, and frowns. "Is he new in Rinella's business?"

I roll my shoulders knowing Matteo isn't going to like this assignment with Rinella trying to burn my business down. "No. He's Piper's husband."

Matteo's eyes widened. "She's married?"

I nod.

"Fucking hell, Elio. You blew this deal over a married woman."

"He abuses her." I state it like it should answer all Matteo's questions and concerns.

"So... what? You're going to kill him and then take her for your own?"

My jaw is tight. "She's mine. That's all you need to know."

He blows out a breath. "Lana is going to—"

"I'm the boss here!" Have I been too lenient? Weak? Is that why Rinella and now Matteo and Lana think they can disrespect me? Well, that's going to change.

He holds his hands up in surrender. "Okay, okay. Do you want eyes on him?"

"I want you to find out everything you can about him." If I'm lucky, I'll find the skeletons in his closet and will use them to make him leave of his own accord.

"Sure thing." He tilts his head to the side. "Can't she just leave him and go with you?"

"It's complicated." But it won't be for long. Piper and her child will be mine. I just need to figure out how.

13

PIPER

The silence that settles over the house as Gabriel's car pulls out of the driveway is both eerie and peaceful. I let out a breath, my shoulders sagging with relief. Elysse looks up at me with her big blue eyes, a tentative smile on her face.

"He's gone?"

I nod, brushing a strand of hair from her face. "Yes, sweetie."

Elysse's smile widens. "So it's just us?"

"That's right. We get to have a fun girls' weekend, just the two of us." I force a note of cheer into my voice, even as my mind is already racing ahead. Gabriel's absence is a brief respite, a chance to breathe without the suffocating weight of his presence. But more than that, it's an opportunity. An opportunity to think, to plan, to figure out how Elysse and I can finally escape this unbearable situation.

A part of me wishes Gabriel would tire of me and leave us. I know he's in Vegas drinking, gambling, and sleeping with other women. When I first learned of his extracurricular activities, it broke my heart. Now, his activities and infidelities are a relief. If only he'd decide to not come home. He clearly doesn't love or respect me. Why he insists on staying with me is baffling. I imagine many would ask the same of me. Why stay when he's so heinous? I would leave in a moment if I knew I could keep Elysse safe from the threats he's made on her.

But this has to end. What I need is a plan, a way out for Elysse and me. I curse myself for not being better prepared, for not having an escape route already mapped out. If I did, we could leave now, while Gabriel is gone. But I know I need to be strategic about this. Rushing into things could put us in even more danger.

So for now, I'll focus on giving Elysse a lovely weekend. We'll spend the day enjoying Chicago, have a fancy dinner, and roller skate. That I have planned. Later, when she's asleep, I'll begin to map out our escape. I'll make a plan to get us out of this nightmare once and for all.

"We're going to explore the city today, just you and me. I want to show you all my favorite places from when I was growing up."

Elysse's eyes light up, her smile wide and eager. "Really? Like where?"

"Well, I was thinking of the pier. There is a huge Ferris wheel and other rides. Then maybe we can have tea at the American Girl Doll store."

She bounces up and down, clapping her hands. "Yay. Can we still go skating?"

"Yes. I thought we'd do that later. After I take you to a nice dinner at my favorite Italian restaurant. We'll have a full day of it."

She throws her arms around me, and I hug her close. She deserves so much more than I've been giving her. I can't wallow in my difficulties anymore. I've been so consumed by fear that I've lost myself, my strength. I need to find it and do better by Elysse.

We get dressed and head out, hand in hand, ready to take on the city. Our first stop is the pier, where we ride the Ferris wheel and carousel. Elysse's cheeks are flushed, her eyes sparkling with joy, and my heart feels lighter than it has in years.

We see the children's museum, so we go in, where we enjoy a dinosaur expedition and then join the circus. Inwardly, I wonder if there are any real circuses that Elysse and I could run away with. She and I could feed the elephants.

We take a ride share the few blocks to the American Girl store where we have a tea lunch. I share with her stories of my childhood, of the adventures I had with my friends growing up in Chicago.

"Mommy, did you always want to be a mommy when you grew up?" Elysse asks, her head tilted to the side.

I pause, considering. "I always knew I wanted to have a little girl, someone to love and take care of. But I also wanted to travel the world, to have adventures of my own." I don't want to lie to her about the circumstances of her birth and how it changed the trajectory of my life. But neither do I want her to feel like she's negatively impacted my life. She's the only bright star in it.

"Can we still do that someday? Have adventures together?" she asks, licking whipped cream off her fingers from a pastry.

"That would be fun. Where would you like to go?"

Her little face scrunches up in thought. "Can we go to the fairy places?"

"You mean back in the U.K.?" I have no idea if there are fairy places in the United States.

She nods.

"I don't see why not." But even as I say it, I wonder if I'm giving her false hope. I'm committed to finding a way out from under Gabriel's abuse, but deep down, I don't know if I can. I push my doubt away and silently renew my promise to myself and to Elysse. I will get us out of this nightmare. I will give us the life we deserve. No matter what it takes.

After lunch, we head to the park to play mini golf and enjoy the playground. For a time, we sit on the grass, relaxing, and I wonder if I've packed in too much activity for one day. We still haven't roller skated.

But as dinnertime approaches, we both get a second wind. I order us a rideshare to take us to the restaurant.

"This was my absolute favorite place to eat when I was your age," I say as we exit the car in front of the Italian restaurant. It looks slightly different from what I remember. A bit more upscale than when I was younger. "My parents would bring me here for special occasions." I'd planned to come when I graduated from high school, but that didn't turn out. I shake that thought away.

"What do they have?" Elysse holds my hand as we enter. A wave of emotion overwhelms me. It's not from the memories of my family. It's from Elio. This was the place Elio took me on our first date. I can still picture it perfectly—the nervous flutter in my chest as I walked through the door on Elio's arm. The way he looked at me across the table like I was the center of the universe for him. I'd already been smitten with him, but that night, I fell head over heels for him.

I shake the memory away. "Spaghetti and meatballs, your favorite."

"Yay." Elysse bounces on her toes, her excitement palpable.

The hostess greets us with a warm smile, leading us to a cozy booth in the back. As I slide in across from Elysse, I'm hit with a fresh wave of memories. The night he gave me the promise ring, he'd arranged our meal from this restaurant to be delivered to the rooftop. Maybe bringing her here wasn't a good idea.

Refocusing on the present, I read the menu. It hasn't changed except for a few new items. "They have mozzarella sticks."

"Can we get them?"

"Of course."

As Elysse pores over the options, chattering excitedly about mozzarella sticks and spaghetti and meatballs, I feel the knot in my stomach start to loosen. Yes, this place is inextricably tied to Elio in my mind. But it doesn't have to stay that way. I can reclaim it, make it a special place for Elysse and me.

A flutter of activity near the door has me looking up. My heart leaps into my throat as Elio strides through the restaurant, looking every inch the charismatic, powerful man he's become. He's wearing a perfectly tailored suit, his dark hair artfully tousled, his eyes scanning the room with a cool, assessing gaze.

For a moment, I'm frozen, torn between two equally powerful urges. Part of me wants to run to him, to throw myself into his arms and beg him to save me from this nightmare of a life. He said he wanted to help me, protect me.

But the other part of me, the wiser, warier part, knows better. Elio abandoned me when I needed him most, left me to face the consequences of our actions alone. I can't put my faith in him again. I have to be my own hero now.

I duck my head, hiding behind my menu. Moments tick by, and I can't help myself. I peek over the top of my menu. Elio's eyes land on me, followed by a slow, devastating smile. He starts making his way toward our booth, his stride confident and purposeful.

Panic rises in my throat, and I feel the sudden urge to flee. I plaster on a smile, for Elysse, not him. I don't want her catching on to Elio's past with me.

"Piper," he says warmly as he reaches our table, his voice sending shivers down my spine. "What a pleasant surprise."

I keep smiling, but it's possible I'm grimacing. "Elio. What are you doing here?"

His eyes flick to Elysse, then back to me, a question in their depths. But he doesn't ask, just slides into the booth next to Elysse, ignoring the tension crackling between us.

"And who is this lovely young lady?" he asks, turning his megawatt charm on my daughter.

A new sort of panic fills me. For the first time ever, Elysse is sitting next to her father. Will he figure it out? He knew I was pregnant. Did he forget?

Elysse, always eager to make a new friend, introduces herself. "I'm Elysse and I'm seven years old." She holds up seven fingers.

Elio grins and holds out his hand to shake hers. "Hello, Elysse. I'm Elio D'Amato and I'm twenty-six years old."

My heart constricts as Elysse beams back at him and shakes his hand, clearly charmed. I watch, both worried and at the same time strangely moved. I study Elio's face, trying to reconcile the man in front of me with the boy I loved so fiercely, so recklessly.

As if sensing my gaze, Elio looks up, his eyes locking with mine. And in that moment, I see a flicker of something—concern, perhaps, or regret. His gaze lingers on my cheek, on the spot where I know the faint shadow of Gabriel's bruise still lingers beneath my makeup.

I look away, shame and anger burning in my chest. I don't want his pity, don't want him to see how far I've fallen. I just want him to leave, to let me get through this dinner with my daughter in peace.

"That's my mom."

"We've met."

Elysse's brow furrows. "Really?"

"I met your mom when I was in high school." His eyes are on mine, shining with a mixture of amusement and mischievousness.

"Really?" Her eyes widen like saucers.

"It was a long time ago." A lifetime ago. I'm only twenty-five, but I feel ancient, all of a sudden. That woman I'd been eight years ago, young, vibrant, bold... she's long gone, and it fills me with sadness.

"It feels like yesterday?" His gaze stays on me.

"Was he your boyfriend?" Elysse makes a face. She doesn't think much of boys right now. I'm not thinking very much of the one sitting with us.

"I was head over heels for your mom," Elio says. "I brought her here, you know. It's her favorite."

"Like I said, that was a long time ago." I shift, discomfort growing. How can I sit here and watch my daughter fall under the spell of the man who broke my heart? The man whose family sent me away all those years ago?

But even more than that, I'm terrified of what Elio's presence in Elysse's life could mean. He's not just my ex-boyfriend. He's the head of a powerful Mafia family. A family with enemies and secrets and a violent way of doing business.

Is it safe for Elysse to even be around him? What if his enemies find out about her, try to use her as leverage against him? The thought makes my blood run cold.

And even if the danger isn't physical, there's the emotional toll to consider. Elysse has already been through so much with Gabriel's abuse and volatility. The last thing she needs is to get attached to someone else who might disappear from her life without warning.

Because that's what Elio does, isn't it? He makes grand promises, sweeps you off your feet, and then vanishes when things get tough, leaving devastation in his wake.

I can't let that happen to Elysse. I won't. She deserves stability, security, a father figure she can depend on. And much as it pains me to admit it, I know that can't be Elio.

But as I watch them together, heads bent conspiratorially as Elio entertains her with some wild story about losing a meatball, I feel a flicker of doubt. Is it really fair of me to keep Elysse from her father, to deny her a chance to know the man who helped give her life?

I push the thought away. It's not about fairness. It's about protecting my child. And right now, the best way to do that is to keep Elio at a distance.

"Elysse and I are having a private dinner." I hope he gets the hint and leaves us.

He flashes me that infuriatingly charming grin. "Let me buy."

I shake my head. "I can ask the manager to show you the way out."

He flinches, and I don't blame him. My words are caustic, but I'm feeling desperate to get my bearings again.

"She wouldn't dare." He leans over the table toward me. "I own this place."

My jaw drops. "You... you own it?"

He nods, looking far too pleased with himself. "Bought it a few years back." There's something in his tone, in his expression that suggests it was more than a business deal, but I don't want to examine it too closely.

"Well, then," I say coolly, "as the owner, surely, you have more important things to do than sit with us."

To my utter frustration, Elio just laughs. "Sweetheart, there is nowhere else I'd rather be. Let me buy you and Elysse dinner. I promise I'll be on my best behavior. Deal?"

Before I can tell him exactly where he can shove his deal, Elysse pipes up from beside him. "Can Mr. Elio stay, Mommy? He's funny!"

I close my eyes briefly, feeling a headache building behind my temples. How can I say no now without disappointing Elysse or making a scene?

Slowly, reluctantly, I nod. "Fine. You can stay. But don't think for a second that this changes anything."

Elio's smile is blinding as he signals the waiter. "Of course."

We order our meals, and Elio arranges for an expensive wine for us. He makes sure there are three cherries in Elysse's Shirley Temple.

As our food comes, Elio and Elysse talk and laugh with an easy camaraderie. Watching them together is like a knife twisting in my gut. The way she lights up at his jokes, the easy rapport between them—it's everything I would want for my daughter. Everything all of us should have had... in another life.

But this isn't another life. This is now, the life I've built in the aftermath of his betrayal. He made his choice eight years ago. I'll be damned if I'll give him the opportunity to abandon and break the heart of my daughter.

14

ELIO

Fate is on my side. That's the only explanation for Piper being here. Okay, so it is her favorite restaurant, and she didn't know I now owned it, but still. For her to be here on the one night I decide to come in has to be fate.

I can't take my eyes off Piper, except to talk to her daughter, Elysse. What a charming, precocious child. She reminds me of Piper when I first met her, brilliant and bold. I find myself enchanted by this little girl, wanting to make her laugh, to get to know her hopes and dreams. To make them come true.

She must take after her father. She doesn't have the blonde hair and blue eyes of her mother. And yet, I can still see Piper in the shape of her face.

I glance at Piper. God, she's still so beautiful it nearly takes my breath away. But there's a wariness in her eyes now, a hardness that wasn't there before. She's built walls around herself that I long to break through. I want to be there for her, to support her, no matter what she's going through.

As we eat and chat, I feel the warmth and closeness between Piper and Elysse. They have their little jokes, their knowing looks. Despite whatever hardships they've faced, their love for each other shines through. Motherhood is a new side of Piper I haven't seen, nurturing, patient, playful. It gnaws at the deep longing inside me.

I have to fight the overwhelming urge to pull them both into my arms, to protect them from whatever demons they're battling. I want to be a part of this little family, as crazy and impossible as that seems. I know I have no right. They belong to someone else. Someone else who mistreats them. I could be what they need. I want to be what they need, but it's clear that Piper doesn't want me around. What I can't figure out is why? She seems bitter and resentful toward me, like I did something wrong. Is it guilt from cheating on her husband with me? No, because she was like that from the moment I saw her at the bank. I want to ask her what's going on but know I can't in front of Elysse.

I focus on keeping things light, on making Elysse giggle with silly stories, on coaxing reluctant smiles from Piper. For now, I'll take what I can get. But one way or another, I'll tear down the fortress Piper has erected. I'll prove to her that she can trust me, that I'll move heaven and earth to keep her and Elysse safe. Or I'll die trying.

As dinner comes to an end, I'm desperate to find an excuse to stay by their sides. "Can I walk you to your car?" I ask.

"We don't have a car," Elysse says. "Mommy isn't allowed."

Piper's expression is stricken. "It's not that, sweetie."

"They drive on the wrong side here," Elysse says.

I try to keep things light as I say, "That depends on who you ask." But I glance at Piper, wondering why she's not allowed to have a car. A flare of anger flickers at the thought of her husband exerting that kind of petty control over Piper and Elysse. The Piper I used to know was vibrant and independent. She never would have tolerated this.

"We just haven't made arrangements for another car. Besides, we can get an Uber whenever we need, right?"

"Please let me drive you home," I say.

"We're going skating now, aren't we, Mommy?"

"Yes, we are."

"You can come with us." Elysse's little hands rest on my forearm, her eyes pleading. I've fallen in love for the second time in my life. I have to make them mine.

Piper looks adorably flustered as she glances at my tailored suit. "Sweetie, I don't think Elio is dressed for roller skating—"

"I just need skates," I say.

She gives me an exasperated look. "I'm sure you have more important—"

"I don't." *There's nothing more important than you two.*

Piper hesitates, biting her lip in that way she does when she's uncertain.

But Elysse is already bouncing on her toes in excitement. "Please, Mommy."

"I'm going with or without you," I state. "Since I'm going, I could give you a ride." I wait a moment, then shrug and make like I'm leaving. I nod toward one of my men, extra security for tonight. "Can you get my car? I'm going roller skating."

His brow furrows at the unusual request, but he does as I ask.

"So, are you riding with me or no?"

Elysse presses the palms of her hands together in front of her heart. "*Pleeease*, Mommy."

"Oh, alright. I suppose it would be faster than waiting for a ride."

"Yay!" Elysse cheers. She takes my hand, and my heart nearly beats out of my chest. I glance up at Piper, wanting her to see that her daughter thinks I'm one of the good guys. What I see is worry in Piper's eyes. Why?

I'm glad I drove the SUV instead of the Porsche. It will be safer for Elysse. I wonder if she needs a car seat? But then I realize that if it were the case, Piper would have one.

I help them into the vehicle. As I move to the driver side, I text my men to let them know where I'm going. I have extra security, as do most of my businesses with Vincenzo on his retaliation tour. I'm not worried he'd kill me or anyone in my family, but better safe than sorry.

"Do you know how to roller skate?" Elysse asks from the back seat.

"Depends on who you ask. The last time I had skates on my feet was over eight years ago with your mother." I look over at Piper, wondering if she remembers our time together fondly.

Her lips twitch upward, but she quickly schools them back into neutral. "If you ask me, no. He has terrible balance."

"My talents always lie elsewhere." I wink at her, then think twice about the innuendo of that statement.

As we arrive at the roller rink, a wave of nostalgia washes over me. Memories of high school outings with Piper flood back. She's right. I sucked at skating, but I endured it because it always made her laugh. Then we'd have pizza and I'd steal kisses.

We get our skates and move to a bench to put them on. Inwardly, I laugh as I lace up the skates, wondering what I'm getting myself into. But I'm happy. Excited. Hopeful. I haven't felt like this for a long, long time.

From the first step, my awkwardness on wheels is immediately apparent as I wobble out onto the rink. Piper and Elysse glide over to me, their faces lit with amusement.

"Try not to fall," Elysse says helpfully.

"I'll try. I'm a bit rusty."

Elysse giggles and grabs my hand. "Don't worry, we'll help you!"

With Piper on one side and Elysse on the other, I find my balance. We make a few tentative laps, their encouragement helping me build my confidence. I don't have much control, and when I drift toward Piper, her hand brushes mine, sending a jolt of awareness through me. I'm playing with fire. I have no right to insert myself into their lives. But for tonight, I let myself believe that anything is possible. That maybe, just maybe, I can win back the only woman I've ever loved.

As we pick up speed, I grow bolder, but my skate catches and I tumble down, my arms flailing, grabbing for something to keep me upright. I end up accidentally pulling Piper down with me. We land in a tangle of limbs, Piper sprawled on top of me. For a breathless moment, we stare at each other, our faces inches apart. The rest of the world falls away and it's just us. My heart stutters in my chest.

The urge to kiss her is almost more than I can resist. I want to taste her, to pour out all my longing so she can feel the sincerity of my heart.

Elysse's laughter stops me. It wouldn't be right to kiss Piper in front of the child. Not when she has a father, the ungrateful fuck wad that he is.

"Mommy, Elio, are you okay?"

Piper quickly scrambles off me, her cheeks flushed. "We're fine, sweetie. Just a little tumble."

She helps me to my feet, and we brush ourselves off, carefully avoiding eye contact. The charged moment has passed, but it still crackles through my blood.

"I think I'm getting the hang of this," I say lightly, trying to defuse the tension.

Elysse claps her hands. "You're doing great! Let's race!"

"I need to visit the ladies' room. Elysse, come with me."

"Do I have to? Me and Elio can skate." She takes my hand.

She glances at me. "I guess it would be okay."

I fight feeling offended at Piper's distrust of me. I remind myself that I'm a stranger to Elysse. Not that she's worried about me. Elysse is pulling on me to keep skating.

"Looks like it's just you and me for a bit, kiddo. Think you can teach me some of your fancy moves?"

Elysse's face lights up. "Sure! Watch this!" She turns around and begins to skate slowly, but surely, backward. I applaud her efforts.

She turns to the front again and takes my hand, and we skate on.

"So, your dad's not big on family outings, huh?" It's wrong for me to probe, but I have to know what I'm up against.

Elysse's smile falters, but it's not sadness I see. "He's away a lot. For work and stuff. But it's okay. I like when it's just me and Mom."

"Must be tough, him being gone so much."

"I don't mind, really," Elysse says. "He's not my real dad, anyway."

I nearly stumble over my skates at her casual revelation. Not her real father? My mind reels with the implications.

"Oh? What do you mean?" I hope my voice sounds neutral.

"Mom says my real dad is somewhere else."

"Like where?"

She shrugs. "Maybe in heaven." Elysse's voice is matter-of-fact, but I can hear the wistful note behind it.

My heart clenches. She thinks her father is dead? Why doesn't Piper tell her? Is Elysse too young to know the truth? And who is this guy? I do some mental calculations, deciding she must have gotten pregnant soon after she moved away. Unless... no. Piper would have said something if I were the father. Wouldn't she?

I swallow hard, my mind spinning with unanswered questions.

Elysse looks up at me, her eyes wide and innocent. "I wish my real dad could have been someone nice like you."

Her simple, heartfelt statement rocks me to my core. Emotion rolls through in a large, powerful wave, humbled and awed by this little girl's trust in me. It's combined with a yearning to be the man, the father, she deserves.

"That's very sweet of you to say," I manage. "I'm sure your real dad, wherever he is, loves you very much."

"Do you have kids?"

I shake my head. "I don't."

"Do you want some?"

"I do."

She beams up at me, her smile brighter than the neon-colored lights overhead. And for a fleeting moment, everything feels right in the world. But then I catch sight of Piper emerging from the restroom, her face pale and drawn. Reality comes crashing back, reminding me of the obstacles that still stand in our way. Obstacles that I'm determined to overcome.

15

PIPER

I can't believe how well the night has gone, despite my initial trepidation over Elio spending time with Elysse. Watching them together, laughing and joking as they skate around the rink, fills me with a bittersweet mixture of joy and anxiety. Joy because it's been so long since I've seen Elysse this happy, her eyes sparkling with delight as Elio helps her perfect her skating technique. And anxiety because with every passing moment, I worry that Elio might start to notice the little things about Elysse that remind me so much of him.

But even with that underlying fear, I can't deny that this has been one of the best nights I've had in a long time. Elio is a natural with Elysse, patient and kind, making her feel at ease in a way that Gabriel never has. It's clear that he genuinely enjoys spending time with her, and the feeling seems to be mutual.

As I watch them together, I feel a sense of contentment wash over me, a feeling I haven't experienced in years. For just a moment, I allow myself to imagine what life could be like if things had been different. If Elio kept his promises. But I quickly push those thoughts aside, knowing that dwelling on what-ifs is a waste of time.

For now, I'll cherish this moment, this brief respite from the harsh realities of my life. Tonight, I'll let myself enjoy the company of the man I once loved and the daughter we created together.

As the evening draws to a close, Elio insists on driving Elysse and me home, not wanting us to order a car this late at night. My heart races at the prospect of spending more time with him, even as my mind screams that it's a terrible idea. But with Elysse's eager agreement and Elio's charming insistence, I find myself agreeing.

The drive home is filled with laughter and easy conversation, Elysse regaling Elio with stories of her favorite books and movies while he listens attentively, asking questions and sharing his own experiences. I try to focus on the passing streetlights, but my gaze keeps drifting to Elio's profile, his strong jawline and the way his lips curve into a smile as he chats with my daughter.

Too soon, we arrive at our house, and Elio walks us to the door like a true gentleman. As I fumble with my keys, Elysse pipes up, her voice filled with hope. "Elio, do you want to come inside for a bit? Maybe we could play a game."

I freeze, my heart leaping into my throat. "Oh, sweetie, I'm sure Elio has other plans. It's getting late, and we shouldn't keep him."

But Elio just smiles, his eyes locking with mine. "I'd love to."

I hesitate, torn between the desire to spend more time with him and the knowledge that it's a dangerous path to tread.

"Please, Mommy."

Elysse's pleading eyes and Elio's earnest expression are difficult to refuse. "Okay, sure. Come on in."

As Elio steps inside, I can't shake the feeling that I'm inviting more than just a man into my home. I'm inviting danger. Danger if Gabriel finds out. Danger from Elio's profession.

As I go get some wine, Elio and Elysse play a game of Chutes and Ladders. When she wins, I send her up to get ready for bed.

"Will you tuck me in?" she asks Elio.

His expression is sweet, nearly awed, and it makes my heart swell. He recognizes the beautiful nature of my daughter.

"I'd be honored."

She rushes up to her room, leaving me and Elio alone.

I hand him one of the glasses of wine and settle on the couch. I'm sitting several feet away from him, but the air around us feels charged, a mix of familiarity and uncertainty. I take a sip, the rich, red liquid warming my throat as I gather my thoughts.

"Elysse seems to have taken a real liking to you," I say, breaking the silence. "She's not usually this open with new people."

Elio smiles, his eyes crinkling at the corners. "She's a great kid, Piper. You've done an amazing job raising her."

I feel a flush of pride at his words, mixed with a twinge of guilt. If only he knew the truth about Elysse's parentage. "Thank you. It hasn't been easy, but she's worth every sacrifice."

"I'm ready," Elysse calls from the hall.

"We're coming." I rise, and Elio follows me to Elysse's room.

"What do you think of my room, Elio?" Elysse asks as she jumps into bed.

He takes in Elysse's version of a fairy garden, with pastel floral flowers in greenery, a sheer canopy over her bed, and fairy lights everywhere.

"It's wonderful."

"It's fairies."

"Aren't fairies naughty?" he asks.

She laughs. "Some are. Not me."

"You're a fairy? Where are your wings?"

She giggles, and while it's wonderful to watch, it fills me with guilt that she's not happy like this all the time.

Elysse gives Elio a hug and a kiss on the cheek. There's no missing how moved he is by her affection.

"Goodnight, sweetie," I say to her as I tuck her in.

"Goodnight, Mommy. Thank you for the fun day."

"It was fun, wasn't it?" I feel like I can see the light dimming in her eyes as we return to reality. "We'll do it again soon." I hope I'm not giving her a false promise.

"Can Elio come?"

"We'll see. You go to sleep now. You must be exhausted." I give her a kiss and exit her room where Elio is waiting.

We stare at each other, and my heart stops as I wonder if he's figured it out yet. How can he not realize this is the child he'd been adamant that he didn't want to know about all those years ago?

We head downstairs, and I think I should ask him to leave, but I don't. Instead, we return to our wine. We chat for a while, catching up on the years we've missed. The details aren't deep or detailed. It's like small talk, each of us not wanting to share too much.

The way Elio looks at me holds more weight than the words we're saying. His gaze is intense and searching. For a moment, I wonder if he's piecing together the timeline, realizing that Elysse's age lines up with our past together. But he doesn't say anything, and I push the thought aside, not wanting to shatter the calm, sweet moment.

"Tonight didn't go as I initially planned. But it's been the best night I've had in years," he says.

I tilt my head, curious. "What do you mean? How did you plan for it to go?"

"To be honest, I showed up at the restaurant for business. But when I saw you and Elysse there, I couldn't help myself. I had to come over, to talk to you."

"I can't believe you own the restaurant."

Elio's eyes lock with mine, his gaze intense and sincere. "I bought it because of you. Because I knew it was your favorite. I never forgot about you, not for a single day."

My ego needs his attention, and it's getting harder to push my yearning for him away. To remember that he hadn't wanted me or Elysse. To remember I'm married to someone else.

I shake my head, a wry smile tugging at my lips as I meet Elio's gaze. "I can't believe you still haven't improved your skating skills after all these years. It's like high school all over again."

Elio laughs, his eyes sparkling with mirth. "I didn't have my roller skating partner. Besides, I had to grow up. Join the business."

"Fair enough," I concede, my heart fluttering at the sound of his laughter. "But I have to admit, it was kind of nice seeing you look a little vulnerable out there. The great Elio D'Amato, stumbling around like a newborn colt."

He grins, a hint of mischief in his expression. "Well, I'm glad my lack of skating prowess could provide you with some entertainment." He looks down for a moment. "Being with you is like skating."

I narrow my eyes. "Off balance?"

He reaches out, his hand gently cupping my cheek. "Exhilarating, challenging, and capable of sweeping me off my feet in an instant. After all this time, the feeling is as strong as ever."

I lean into his touch, my eyes fluttering closed for a brief moment. When I open them again, Elio's face is mere inches from mine, his breath warm against my skin.

"Elio, we shouldn't—"

"Just tell me you feel it too, Piper."

I should deny it. "I do, but—"

His thumb brushes across my cheekbone. "I've missed this. Talking with you, spending time together. It feels like no time has passed at all."

I swallow hard, my heart racing at his touch. "I've missed it too," I admit, my voice barely above a whisper. "But things are different now. We're different people."

Elio nods, his expression thoughtful. "Maybe so, but some things never change. The way I feel about you, Piper... that's never changed."

A lump forms in my throat, tears pricking at the corners of my eyes. I want to believe him, to let myself fall into his arms and forget about the past. But I know I can't, not without risking everything I've built for Elysse and myself.

"Elio, I—" I begin, but he cuts me off, his finger pressing gently against my lips.

"I know things are complicated. But for tonight, can we just enjoy each other's company? No expectations, no promises. Just two old friends catching up."

I hesitate for a moment, then nod.

He leans in. His lips press against mine, soft yet insistent. My mind screams that this is a mistake, that I shouldn't be kissing him back, but my body betrays me. I melt into his embrace, my fingers tangling in his hair as I pull him closer. The kiss deepens, and I can taste the wine on his tongue, the flavor mingling with the intoxicating essence that is purely Elio.

His hands roam my body, leaving trails of fire in their wake. I should stop this. I'm playing with fire, but I can't seem to find the strength to pull away.

Elio's lips trail down my neck, his teeth grazing my sensitive skin. I arch into his touch, a breathy moan escaping my lips. It's been so long since I've felt this way, so alive and desired. With Gabriel, intimacy is a chore, a duty to be fulfilled. But with Elio, it's electric, a connection that transcends the physical.

His hands slip beneath my shirt, covering my breast. The friction against my nipple sends waves of need through my body. I moan, and it's like it opens the floodgates. All of a sudden, our hands are a flurry of activity as we try to get to each other's skin.

"Fuck." Elio tugs at his sleeve, unable to pull it off his arm because of the cuff link.

I glance at it and then him. "I bought you those." They were nowhere nice enough for a rich businessman like him, but at the time, I'd spent all my allowance and side job earnings to buy them for him.

His smile is sweet. "I know." He laughs. "How many times do I have to tell you that you've always been with me?"

If that is true, then why didn't he stop his parents from sending my family away? I can't ask the question, though, because his lips wrap around my nipple and all other thoughts fly away.

I gasp, holding him to me, needing to get closer... closer. Except we're half naked on the couch in the living room where Elysse could find us if she got up for some reason. God, if she saw us and then told Gabriel... I don't even want to think about what would happen.

I pull away, straightening my shirt as I prepare to tell him he needs to go.

"Piper." Elio's voice sounds desperate. "I want you, more than I've ever wanted anything in my life."

I stare into eyes that show so much. They look at me, and I feel seen. "Not here."

It takes him a moment, but then he nods. He rises and scoops me up like he did before and carries me to the bedroom. I'll feel guilty about it later, but right now, I'm powerless to resist him. He's a romance hero come to life, treating me like I'm his most precious treasure.

His eyes are on me, intense, reverent as he undresses me. He lays me on the bed, rising over me, his hands caressing me gently, coaxingly, slowly building the burn.

"So many times I've dreamed of this," he says as his lips trail along my neck. "You've haunted my dreams."

"Haunt?" The word comes out on a gasp as his tongue flicks over my nipple.

"I tried to forget, but you're always a dream away."

I imagine that Gabriel isn't giving me another thought on his trip. And here Elio is, telling me that I still appear in his dreams after all this time. I can't make sense of it. Why didn't he come find me? But the questions disappear as his fingers slide over my clit and his lips tug on my nipple, working me up and up until I come apart.

"You're so beautiful when you come." He brings his fingers to his lips, sucking my essence off them. "Mmm... I want more."

Elio had been a generous lover back when we were younger, but we were both new to sex. He's had more experience, I can tell. So, while I might have haunted his dreams, he wasn't celibate. I'm envious of those women he's honed these skills on.

He moves down my body, lips and hands brushing over my skin, making me come alive again. "Open for me, Piper."

I do as he asks, and he settles between my thighs.

"Such a wet pussy," he murmurs. He kisses my inner thigh, and I writhe with need and anticipation.

"Don't tease me."

"I wouldn't think of it." His mouth consumes me until my pussy is on fire.

"Elio!" A second orgasm blasts through me, more powerful than the one before. He doesn't stop, though, and soon, another one steals my breath.

My pussy is quivering as he moves up my body. He sits back on his heels, gripping my hips and tugging me to him, driving into me.

"Oh, God." My fingers clutch at the sheets as he moves in and out, forcefully, deeply.

"Yes... oh, fuck... so good... so good."

I watch him, his jaw gritted, his head tilted back as he reaches for the apex. It's so sexy that immediately, I'm on the edge again.

"Elio... oh..." My body tenses and then floods with pleasure again.

"Yes!" He lets out a feral growl, followed by his release. Our bodies move together in a synchronicity I haven't felt since... well, since he and I were together before.

He collapses on me, rolling to his side, tugging me close. I push away the guilt and regret that try to infringe. I nestle next to him.

"Buying that restaurant was the best thing I've done," he says, kissing my temple. "I suppose deep down, I always hoped you'd return to it, and tonight, you did."

My heart fills with emotion at how romantic he is. So, what happened eight years ago?

"This has been the best night I've had in a long time. Seeing you, spending time with your daughter. She's a delight, Piper."

"I think so."

"She told me your husband isn't her father."

I tense.

"She thinks her real father is dead."

I swallow, wondering what he's asking. What he might have figured out.

"Is there something you want to say about that?"

He's figured it out and now he's judging me, disapproving of my choices. And he just fucked me to what... soften me up so I'd fall for his charm and confess everything? What is he playing at?

He has some nerve. Maybe I should have told her that her father was a Mafia criminal who didn't care about me or her. Perhaps I should tell him that, see if he really wants Elysse to know the sort of man he truly is.

I scramble out of bed and grab an old T-shirt, jerking it over me as I shake in a mixture of anger and self-loathing that I'd fallen for his charm again. "You have no right to judge me."

16

ELIO

"You have no right to judge me for my choices," Piper seethes.

I sit up, startled by the sudden shift in her demeanor. "I'm not judging—"

"Aren't you? I have every right to protect my daughter from the man who decided he didn't want her." She laughs bitterly, tears welling in her eyes. "You have no idea what it's like, Elio. No idea how hard it was to find out I was pregnant, to have my entire life uprooted because the father of my child decided he wanted nothing to do with us."

My heart clenches at the pain in her voice, and I reach for her, but she jerks away from my touch. "I'm sorry, I didn't realize—"

"Don't patronize me. How could you possibly think I'd tell her about her father who didn't want her?"

Her words hit me like a punch in the gut, and I stare at her in stunned silence. I can't imagine any man walking away from Piper, from the chance to be a father to a child as amazing as Elysse.

Piper's tears flow freely now, and she covers her face with her hands, her shoulders shaking with silent sobs. "You have no idea what it was like," she chokes out. "To be so young and scared and alone, to have the person I loved most in the world abandon me when I needed him most."

My heart aches for her, and at the same time, I wonder about the man she loved most in the world. I thought that had been me.

I exit the bed and slip on my boxer briefs. "I'm sorry that happened."

She laughs humorlessly, wiping at her tears. "Yeah, right."

I shake my head, frustration building in my chest. Why the hell is she so mad at me? I didn't abandon her.

"You just walked away like a coward, leaving me to deal with the fallout on my own."

What the fuck? "Piper, I don't know what the hell you're talking about. "

Piper shoves my chest, her eyes blazing with fury. "You have some nerve, coming back into my life like nothing happened, like you didn't abandon me when I needed you most."

I grip her wrists, holding her in place as I search her face for answers. "I swear to God, I have no idea what you're talking about. I never abandoned you. You're the one who left me, remember? You disappeared without a word, without even saying goodbye."

She wrenches her hands from my grasp, her lips curling into a sneer. "Yeah, you tell yourself that if it helps you sleep at night."

Anger surges through me at her accusations. "Damn it, Piper, I'm telling you the truth. I have no idea what you're so pissed off about."

"Well, it's too late now. I want you to leave. I want you to stay the hell away from me and *my* daughter."

My temper flares. "What the fuck, Piper? One minute you're hot, falling into bed with me, and the next you're cold, telling me to leave and stay away. What the hell do you want from me?"

"I want you to leave me and Elysse alone!" Piper shouts, her face flushed with anger as she jabs a finger at my chest.

I stare at her completely confused. "Is this about your husband—"

"No. He's just proof that I make terrible choices in men. First you, and then him."

"Me? All I did was love you." I feel like I'm in an alternate universe. Nothing she's saying is making sense.

"Until it was inconvenient. Then you sent your parents to do your dirty work, to pay off my parents and send me away so you wouldn't have to deal with the consequences of your actions."

My heart stops at her words, and I feel like I can't breathe. "My parents? They... they paid you to leave town?"

Piper nods, her eyes brimming with tears. "They showed up at my door the morning I learned I was pregnant. Offered my parents a fortune to take me away."

I run a hand through my hair, my mind spinning with this new information. I can't make sense of it. "They wouldn't do that." *Would they?*

She scoffs, crossing her arms over her chest. "If you really want to know the truth, why don't you go ask them yourself? I'm sure they'll be more than happy to fill you in on all the sordid details."

I shake my head, a humorless laugh escaping my lips. "I can't. They're dead."

She flinches.

The pain of the last few years, of all I've lost, pierces my chest. "Should I ask Lazaro? Oh, wait, he's dead too. Do you think Lana knows? She's all I have left."

Her eyes widen in surprise, and for a moment, I see a flicker of sympathy in her gaze. But it's quickly replaced by anger once more. "Well, then I guess you'll never know the truth since you don't want to believe me."

All the information is swirling in my head. I'm fighting to make it coherent. I think back to eight years ago. I'd made a promise to Piper, and the next day she was gone.

They showed up at my door the morning I learned I was pregnant. Offered my parents a fortune to take me away.

Piper's words hit me like a punch to the gut, and I stagger back, my mind reeling with the implications. My parents paid her to leave town, to hide her pregnancy from me.

I look up at her. "I'm Elysse's father?" I feel like the world is tilting on its axis, like everything I thought I knew has been turned upside down. I have a daughter. A beautiful, amazing little girl whom I've already fallen in love with. And I've missed seven years of her life because of my family's brutally cruel act.

"Don't act like you didn't know."

Betrayal cuts through me, and I can't breathe. They took everything from me. The woman I loved, the chance to be a father to my child. And for what?

I close my eyes as I remember right after Piper disappeared, I was told that I'd be marrying Ava Rinella when she came of age. Did my parents really pay Piper's family off to secure some bullshit alliance with the Rinellas?

I look at Piper, really look at her, and I see the pain and anger in her eyes that I'm only now beginning to understand. If this is what she believes, then of course she'd be angry.

Except... I would never do what she's accusing me of. How could she believe I would? The pain of that is beyond anything I've ever felt, worse than when she disappeared.

I shake my head as a toxic brew of anger and hurt swirl. "I loved you. How could you think I would abandon you, abandon our child? Fucking hell, Piper. I promised you everything. I gave you all of me."

She watches me, blinks as if she wasn't expecting that response.

"No... this isn't on me. What you and your parents and my parents did... that's on you. I bet that was it, wasn't it? All that time, you and your family struggled. You saw a way out. My father was an asshole, but he knew people. He took one look at you and your family and knew money was all you wanted."

She looks at me with desperation. "What? No. They made me leave."

"You could have called me. Emailed—"

"They wouldn't let me—"

"How convenient. So you won't believe me that I knew nothing about this deal you and my parents struck up, but somehow, I'm supposed to believe you couldn't contact me?"

"It's the truth. They told me you didn't want to be there."

"And you believed them? Just like that?" I'm seething now with so much anger and pain. "The night before, I vowed to love you forever, but instead, you believed my father whom you'd never met."

Piper's eyes fill with tears, and she wraps her arms around herself. "What was I supposed to think, Elio? We were eighteen. Your family had all the power, all the money. I was just some girl from the wrong side of the tracks who got knocked up by the heir to a Mafia empire."

I run a hand through my hair, frustration and hurt warring in my chest. "You knew me. You knew how much I loved you. How could you think I would ever agree to something like that?"

She's looking at me like the proverbial deer caught in the headlights. "They... they never told you?"

"No. They never mentioned a word. One night, I was high on love, and the next day, you were MIA. I showed up at school on Monday and was told you'd moved. That was it."

"Your parents made it seem like—"

"Every time you say that, it guts me, Piper, because it proves you didn't trust me... didn't believe in me."

She closes the distance between us, her hand coming up to cup my cheek, but this time, I'm the one who backs away.

"Elio, I'm so sorry. I... should have known better." A sob escapes her lips. "I... God..." She sinks onto the edge of bed. "Everything happened so fast. I..." She presses her hand to her temple. "I was scared and confused... and then all of a sudden, I'm on a plane to England."

I guess that explains how she met Gabriel. The idea that she gave herself and our daughter to that fucker over me cuts deep.

"You think I'm a fucking monster, so you married a man who abuses you?"

Her eyes jerk to me, and the pain and confusion I see there makes me feel like shit for being an asshole.

"I did love you, Elio. I was so scared, so alone. And when your parents showed up with that money, telling me you wanted nothing to do with me... I didn't know what to think."

I turn away, not wanting to be swayed by her words. At the same time, I have to concede that she was in a difficult position. My father was a powerful, feared man even to those not in our world. She was eighteen. Her parents didn't like me because of my Mafia connection. Neither she nor her parents could take on my parents and win. She was in an impossible situation.

I let out a sigh and sit on the bed next to her. "I'm sorry. I should have been there for you, should have fought harder to find you when you disappeared."

"I didn't know what else to do."

I brush my thumb across her cheek, wiping away her tears. "I understand. But I need you to know that I never would have abandoned you or our child. Not for anything in the world."

She nods, her eyes searching mine. "I'm sorry."

I take a deep breath, my mind still reeling from the revelation that I have a daughter. "Elysse is really mine?"

Piper's lips curve into a soft smile, and she nods. "Yes. She's yours. Ours."

Joy explodes in my chest, overcoming the pain and anger. "I can't believe it. I'm a father."

Piper leans into my touch. "I used to dream of a moment like this, of telling you and your being happy about it."

I brush my lips against hers in a soft, tender kiss. Everything is changing. Piper is mine. So is Elysse. There's nothing Gabriel can do about that. And if he thinks he's going to get his hands on either of them again, he's got another coming.

"I'm sorry," Piper says again as she pushes me back. "I'm so sorry, Elio... so sorry..."

"It's the past, baby. We're here now, together."

"I did love you. I Never stopped."

I arch a brow considering what she thought of me.

"I was angry and hurt, but... I never could stop loving the boy I knew in high school."

"What about now?"

She smiles, moving to straddle my thighs. "I feel like I have a lot to make up for."

My dick perks up at that, but I need to be sure she believes me. "Tell me you believe me."

"I believe you." She kisses me, hard, fervently, and so full of promise. There is a lot we need to discuss, decisions to be made. But right now, having her touch me is enough. I need her to soothe away the pain of what my parents did, of her failure to believe in me.

She moves off my thighs and onto the floor on her knees. She tugs my boxers off and my dick springs out, hard and proud.

"What are you doing?" I ask. It's not that I don't know what she's doing, but I want to hear from her lips what she plans to do to me.

"It's not obvious?" She strokes my dick, and delicious sensations race out.

"Tell me." I thread my fingers through her hair.

"I'm going to suck your dick." She arches a brow. "Are you okay with that?"

I feign thinking about it. "Yeah, I guess so."

"Maybe you should be sure."

My dick is aching. "Suck my cock, Piper."

She wraps her lips around my shaft, and the feeling is so fucking good. I feel it in every cell of my body. Her mouth is wet and hot, and I'm in heaven as she slides up and down, sucking, licking. Power gathers like a storm at the base, and it won't be long before I come.

"Baby..." I tug at her to stop. "Come up here." I lift her, setting her over my thighs. "Fuck me."

She wraps her arms around my neck and kisses me, and I swear I can feel it down to my toes. She rises up over my dick and then takes me in. Our groans of pleasure echo off the walls. I hold her to me, savoring this moment. For the first time in eight years, she's mine again. Finally.

She rocks, and I let go, let her take me to the place that only she's ever been able to take me. Sure, over the years, I fucked other women. But it was always like scratching an itch. With Piper, there's so much more. She rides me, harder, faster, until I hit the edge. My orgasm slams into me like a freight train. My dick pulses, pumping, pumping into her.

She cries out, her pussy squeezing, and stars blast behind my eyes as pleasure peaks again. We ride out the pleasure until I fall back on the bed, taking her with me. She kisses me, and at that moment, my world is perfection. I vow it will stay that way. I won't let anyone or anything take what's mine again.

17

PIPER

The truth hits me like a freight train, shattering everything I thought I knew. Elio never abandoned us. He wasn't part of the plan to pay me off to disappear and raise our child alone. The pain and anger that have fueled me for the past eight years evaporate, replaced by a whirlwind of confusion and regret.

Even lying in his arms after making love, guilt twists in my gut as I remember the venom I spewed at him. I was so quick to believe the worst of him. But looking into his eyes now, I see the same shock and heartbreak that I feel. We were both victims, manipulated by forces beyond our control.

"I'm sorry. I should have trusted you. I should have known you would never abandon us."

Elio holds me tighter, kissing my temple. "We're here now."

I melt against him, finally letting myself feel the love and connection that've always been there. We cling to each other, both of us reeling from the weight of this revelation. There's so much to process, so much lost time to mourn. But for now, all that matters is that we're together.

"How much time do you need to pack up your and Elysse's things?"

I tilt my head up to look at him. "What?"

"You'll move in with me tomorrow."

I pull back, a flicker of irritation sparking within me. At first, I'm not sure why. But then it hits me. He's telling me what's going to happen. Not asking. Not conferring. Elio is a powerful man. A man who lives in the shadows. All of a sudden, I wonder if he's all that different from Gabriel. Not that Elio would hurt me physically. But I can see him as a man who sets the rules and expects everyone to follow.

"You just decided that?"

His brow furrows in confusion.

"You can't just make decisions for me like that."

He continues to stare at me like I'm crazy. "What do you mean? You're not seriously considering staying with your husband, are you?"

His words hit a nerve, and I feel my defenses rising. "That's not the point," I snap, moving out of his embrace. "I've been bossed around and told what to do since the moment our parents made me leave all those years ago. I had no say in the matter then, and I can't let anyone else make my choices for me now."

Elio's frustration is evident in the set of his jaw. "I'm not telling you what to do. I just assumed that you'd want to be with me over that fucker you married. Am I wrong? What is this, Piper? If you think this is a little affair, you're wrong." He cocks his head. "You really want to stay here? To have your daughter exposed—"

"No. But I can't be a doormat anymore. I need to make my own choices, to regain control of my life. I'm not a damsel to be saved, Elio. At least, I don't want to be. I want to save myself."

He runs a hand through his hair, clearly struggling to understand. "If that's the case, why are you still here? Why have you stayed with a man who hurts you, who terrorizes our daughter? If you could leave, surely, you would have already."

He's not wrong. But I realize now that Gabriel's power over me came on slowly, like that story about the frog in warm water that slowly heats to a boil. The change is subtle, so it's not noticed until it's too late.

When I don't have a response, Elio's frustration mounts. He gets out of bed, pacing the room like a caged animal. "What's your plan, Piper? What decisions have you made to leave your husband, eh?" His tone more than his words cut me deeply, striking at the heart of my helplessness and fear.

I've been trapped in this nightmare for so long, I've almost forgotten what it feels like to have control over my own life. But I refuse to let him see how much his question unsettles me.

"You think I haven't tried?" I think about the threats Gabriel made against Elysse when I told him I was leaving. The sheer terror I felt as his dark, deadly eyes bore down on me while he outlined what would happen. The memory makes me wonder why I'm arguing with Elio about this. Elio solves all my problems. A place to stay. Protection. But would I be going from one domineering man to another? By letting Elio save me, am I once again giving up my personal power?

"I can protect you, Piper."

I nod. "From Gabriel, yes, but your own world isn't so safe. You have enemies. The constant threat of incarceration. The Mafia, the violence, the constant risk... Is that really any better for Elysse?"

His eyes flash with indignation, and I can see his temper rising. "I would never let anything happen to either of you," he growls, his fists clenching at his sides. "I'd protect you both with my life."

I believe him. It's another part of him that is different from Gabriel. Gabriel will protect what's his, but not out of love or devotion, and surely, not with his life.

"Why did he give you that bruise?" Elio demands.

I press my hand to my cheek. "What? Why?"

"Why?" he barks out.

"It was an accident. I burned dinner."

"Jesus fuck, Piper. That's not an accident. That's abuse. You really want to stay here?"

"No. But I need to find myself again. I need to make my own decisions."

"Back to that. Fine. What choices do you have? Call the cops and get a restraining order? How long will that take? And will a piece of paper really protect you?"

He's being patronizing, even if he's speaking the truth. A court order wouldn't deter Gabriel. Not forever.

"Do you have money? A job? I know you don't have a car. Who pays your phone bill? Your husband, I bet, will use it to find you or cut it off."

Helplessness overwhelms me. I sink to the edge of the bed.

"There are shelters, I suppose. So, Piper, what choice are you going to make?" He stands in front of me, his eyes blazing with frustration and maybe hurt. "I'm not going to stand by and watch you and Elysse suffer. If you won't leave him, then I'll do whatever it takes to get you both out of there. I won't let my daughter live in a home where she's in danger."

His threat rips through me. The thought of losing Elysse, of having her taken away from me, is more terrifying than any abuse Gabriel could inflict. But I know Elio is right. I can't keep putting my daughter at risk, no matter how scared I am of the alternative. Even if it means handing over control to Elio.

Tears fall. "I feel so powerless, like I'm just a pawn in everyone else's game."

Elio's expression softens, and he takes a step closer, reaching out to cup my face in his hands. "You're not powerless. You have choices. You can go to a shelter or call the cops. But you could also choose to come with me. Why aren't I a choice you can make?"

His words send a shiver down my spine, and I feel a flicker of hope ignite within me.

"I'm more invested than anyone in keeping you and Elysse safe and happy. I can protect you. I can give you the life you deserve, the life we were meant to have together. There was a time when you wanted that."

I search his eyes, looking for any hint of deception or ulterior motive. But all I see is sincerity, a fierce determination to make things right. And in that moment, I realize that this is what I've been waiting for all along. A chance to take control of my own life, to choose the path that leads to happiness and love.

I nod. "Okay."

"Okay what?"

"I choose you."

He sits on the bed next to me. "Are you giving in? Giving up?"

I shake my head, even though a part of me feels like I am. Yes, I'm choosing Elio, but it's the choice that offers the best outcome for Elysse.

He puts an arm around me. "I don't want to take away your power. Quite the opposite, actually. It guts me to see the strong, assertive woman I love beaten down, literally and figuratively. I'd like to return the favor to your husband."

My gaze jerks to his. "You can't kill him, Elio."

He arches a brow. "I didn't say I would. I'd rather him live in fear like he's made you live in fear."

I can't deny there's a petty part of me that would enjoy that. "I just want to be free of him."

"Then you will be. And if you're not ready for us... my house is large. You and Elysse can have your own suite of rooms."

I can hear in his voice that it's not what he wants. But I appreciate the offer. He's giving me choices.

"Thank you."

He leans in and kisses me. "So... when would you like to move?"

I smile at how he's rephrased the statement to include my input. "Tomorrow. Elysse and I can be packed with our bare necessities by lunchtime."

"Thank fuck." His smile is wide, like he'd just won the lottery. Then he pushes me back on the bed. "Speaking of fuck..." He rises over me, sinks into me, and I give myself over to him, to my decision to be with him.

18

ELIO

I gaze at Piper's sleeping form beside me, her face still etched with worry even in slumber. Seeing her like this, so helpless and afraid, ignites a fierce protectiveness within me. I vow that I will save her and Elysse from Gabriel's clutches, no matter the cost. Of course, that's the thinking she's fighting me against. She wants to have a sense of control in her life.

My mind wanders to the vibrant, strong-willed girl Piper used to be when we first fell in love. The acts by our parents and then years of abuse and fear have dimmed her light. I'm determined to help her reclaim her strength. She deserves to live freely and without fear, to make her own choices and chase her dreams. And our daughter deserves a childhood filled with love and safety, not violence and instability.

As I pull Piper closer, she stirs slightly, nestling into my embrace. In this moment, holding the woman I love and the mother of my child, I feel a sense of completeness I haven't known in years. This is my family. For a time, I'd been sure any family I created would be arranged, an alliance to boost business. Now I have a real family, and I'll fight for them with every fiber of my being.

Exhaustion finally takes hold and my eyes grow heavy. I press a tender kiss to Piper's forehead before allowing sleep to claim me.

A shrill ring pierces the quiet, jolting me from a deep slumber. I groan, reaching for my phone on the nightstand. It's not there. Then I remember I'm at Piper's. I slip from bed and find my phone still in my coat pocket.

The caller ID reads *Matteo*. This can't be good.

"What is it?" I grumble, my voice thick with sleep.

"We've got a situation, Elio. Several of our guys were arrested last night."

I'm suddenly wide awake. "What happened?" I glance at my watch, noting that it's nearly six in the morning.

"Not sure yet. But our usual contacts at the precinct aren't playing ball. We're on our own here."

I curse under my breath, glancing over at Piper's sleeping form. She looks so peaceful. I want to keep it that way.

"Call Tony and meet me at home. I'll be there in twenty."

There's a pause, and I'm sure he's wondering where I am in the middle of the night.

"On it, Boss." The line goes dead.

I quickly dress and then take a moment to take Piper in. My heart clenches at the thought of leaving Piper and Elysse unprotected. But I have no choice. If I don't handle this now, it could come back to bite us all later.

I sit on the edge of the bed, my hand sliding down Piper's delectable form. "I'm sorry, baby. Something's come up with work and I have to go."

"Is everything okay?" Her voice is heavy with sleep.

"It will be. Just some business I need to take care of." I hesitate, not wanting to leave her alone. "When is your husband expected back?"

Piper's face falls slightly. "Later tonight."

I nod, my jaw clenching at the thought of that bastard laying a hand on her again. My first instinct is to tell her to pack a bag now, to come home with me where I can keep her and Elysse safe. But I stop myself, remembering her words from last night. She needs to make her own choices, to regain the agency that was stolen from her all those years ago.

I sit on the edge of the bed, taking her hand in mine. "I'm not sure how long business will take, but then I want to come back and help you and Elysse pack. Is that alright?"

Her smile is sweet, like I've given her a gift. "Yes."

I have the realization that Elysse doesn't know the truth yet. What will she think when she finds out? Will she be happy?

Piper and I need to talk to her, but now isn't the time. First, I need to get them safe.

"Put my number in your phone, okay?" I pick up her phone and hand it to her. "Call me if anything comes up."

She keys in her code and hands me the phone. I put in my number and hand it back to her. Then I lean in, capturing her lips in a tender kiss. It takes every ounce of willpower I possess to pull away, to leave the warmth of her embrace.

"Take care of my girls." I rise from the bed to leave. I stop at the door, taking one last lingering look before heading out.

Twenty minutes later, I enter the foyer of my home, the one I inherited from my parents. It's twenty-five thousand square feet of opulence and luxury one would expect from an aristocrat or a Mafia Don. It's more than I need, except now I'm imagining filling it with more children. And if Piper wants to change up the décor, she can.

"Where the hell have you been?" Lana demands, her eyes flashing with annoyance. "We've been trying to reach you for hours."

Huh? I look at my phone and only then notice the missed texts and calls. "I had personal matters to attend to." I make my way to my office where Matteo is waiting. "What's the situation?"

Matteo steps forward, his brow furrowed. "Our men got a call about a disturbance, and when they went to check it out, they were taken in."

I arch a brow. "How convenient."

He nods. "Sounds like a setup, but our contacts at the precinct aren't being helpful."

I curse under my breath, the gravity of the situation sinking in. "Have they been charged or just detained?"

"I'm not aware of charges. Tony is on his way."

I nod. Tony is a good lawyer. I have faith that he'll sort this out. And yet, something feels off. I pay an obscene amount of money to cops to avoid situations like this. "I should go down there."

Lana scoffs, crossing her arms over her chest. "Oh, now you're going to do your job? Where was this dedication earlier when we needed you?"

I bristle at her accusatory tone. "Watch it, Lana. I'm still the head of this family."

She steps closer, her eyes narrowing. "Then start acting like it. You've been distracted lately, letting things slip through the cracks. We can't afford any weaknesses, not with Vincenzo breathing down our necks."

My temper flares, the stress of the past few days boiling over. "You think I don't know that? I'm doing everything I can to protect what's ours."

Lana laughs humorlessly. "Really? Because from where I'm standing, it looks like you're too busy chasing after some ghost from your past to focus on the present."

I clench my fists, my voice dropping to a dangerous growl. "Careful. You're treading on thin ice."

She meets my gaze unflinchingly, her eyes filled with a defiant fire I know all too well. "I'm not trying to undermine you, Elio. But we need to face facts. Piper's return has thrown you off balance, and we can't afford any distractions right now."

I open my mouth to argue, but Matteo interjects, his tone placating. "Lana's right, Elio. We need to focus on the task at hand. We still haven't done anything to placate Vincenzo. I wouldn't put it past him to have organized the issue we have now. We know he's trying to worm his way closer to Caruso, and you and I know he'll use that to undermine you."

I take a deep breath, trying to calm the storm raging inside me. As much as I hate to admit it, they have a point. My personal life has been occupying too much headspace at a time when I need to be focused.

"What is it about her, anyway?" Lana demands. "She was just a high school—"

"Don't." I whirl on Lana, shoving my index finger in her face. "Don't you dismiss her importance to me."

Her brows rise as she looks at my finger.

I take a breath. "While we're on the subject, there's something else you both need to know. Piper and her daughter, Elysse, will be moving in with us. As soon as I deal with this issue, I'll be going to pick them up."

Lana rolls her eyes. "Really, Elio? You've torched an alliance with Vincenzo to get your rocks off with your high school sweetheart? What are you thinking?"

I meet her gaze head-on, my resolve unwavering. "You tell me I need to be more of a leader, so here it is, Lana. You will speak to me with more respect. You'll treat Piper and Elysse with respect as well. This is not your home, and I'll have no qualms about forcing you out if you insist on being such a bitch."

Her eyes flare with heat, but then she sniffs. "For once, you've found your balls."

"Does her husband know she's moving in with you?" Matteo asks.

"Oh, my God, she's married?" Lana's momentary retreat reverses.

I scrape my hand over my face. "I don't have time to explain everything, but the short version is that yes, she's married to an asshole who beats her but has felt powerless to leave because of the child."

It occurs to me I haven't given all the important details. "The other thing you need to know is that the child, Elysse, is my daughter."

The silence that follows is deafening. Lana's eyes widen in shock, her mouth falling open. Matteo looks equally stunned.

"What?" Lana finally manages, her voice barely above a whisper. "How is that possible?"

I sink into the chair behind my desk, suddenly feeling drained. "Piper found out she was pregnant, and our parents paid her parents a shit-ton of money to leave town, to keep me from finding out. I only just learned the truth last night."

Lana shakes her head, a rare display of empathy crossing her features. "Elio... God. I knew Mom and Dad were assholes, but... wow. I'm so sorry."

"So this is more than just saving her from that fucker she married," Matteo says.

I'm reminded that I asked him to investigate her husband. "What have you learned?"

"Same stuff you found out... he's the son of a rich family from New York. Got advanced degrees in business and economics in England. He now works for an international finance firm that transferred him here a few weeks ago. He married four years ago."

"Anything I don't know?"

"He's a serial cheater. He was arrested five years ago for shoving his girlfriend, not Piper, down the stairs, but the charges were dropped. It appears the woman was paid a lot of money. She now lives in a villa in Italy. Right now, he's in Las Vegas. Bet you can't guess what he's up to."

I don't have to guess. What does anyone do in Vegas? Drink. Gamble. Fuck. What did Piper see in this man? Why didn't her parents help her escape him?

"The question is, will he be a problem for us?" Matteo gives me a pointed look, letting me know my plate is full of issues to deal with already. "Men like that don't give up control easily."

"What do you mean?" Lana asks.

"Will he come after them?"

"He can try," I growl. But he has a point. I can't assume Piper's husband will go away without a fight. "Let's increase security here at the house." Already, I'm dreading the discussion with Piper in which I have to tell her that she'll need to lie low until we can be sure her husband won't do anything to retaliate. She'll see it as my taking away her power, her independence.

"Look, I don't mean to be a bitch. I'll do my part to welcome them into our home, but right now, we need to deal with our guys sitting in a jail cell," Lana interrupts.

"What do you suggest?" Matteo's question is patronizing, but Lana ignores that aspect.

"We need to hit Vincenzo where it hurts."

"We're not even sure he's behind this," I point out. "I don't want to further aggravate him if I don't have to."

She purses her lips at me. "Who else could it be?"

"Well, considering our inside men aren't doing shit, perhaps they're part of it."

That shuts her up, which annoys me further. Her lack of faith in me, her belief that I'm a pussy, pisses me off.

"I'm not inept, Lana. Maybe I don't live up to your Michael Corleone idea of a Mafia leader, but I know what I'm doing."

Lana scoffs, shaking her head. "Sometimes, you have to get your hands dirty to protect what's yours."

I stand and fix her with a hard stare, my voice low and dangerous. "You don't think my hands are dirty?" I laugh, and it must be menacing because she flinches. "I guess you were too young to remember how I earned my access to Caruso. Access Dad didn't have. He'd be fucking jealous of me. Don't mistake my attempts to do business strategically as a sign of cowardice or weakness. I can be merciless when I need to be, and that includes with you, little sister."

For the first time, I see fear in her expression. A part of me is glad to wipe her smirk off her face, but at the same time, I don't want her thinking I'm going to kill her in her sleep.

"If you want to stay a part of this family, live in this house, have input on business, and live in the luxury you've grown accustomed to, you will talk to me with the respect I deserve... that I've earned."

"Fine." She bites off the word.

"So, what's next?" Matteo asks, likely trying to break up the tension between me and my sister.

"I shower and change, and then we go to the police station." As I pass Lana, I stop. "You can come if you want."

She sucks in an indignant breath. Like how dare I suggest that I have a say in whether she can go or not. But she's the one who is pushing me to be an aggressive leader. I wait a moment to see if she'll say anything. She presses her lips together, clearly fighting a retort. She knows I can and will make her stay home if she disrespects me again.

With a nod, I exit my office heading up to my room. In the shower, I wash away the tension. I learned a long time ago, calm and cool goes a lot further in getting what I want over asshole behavior, Lana notwithstanding. The idea that others might see me as weak doesn't bother me so much. It's easier to fuck up someone who underestimates me. And right now, someone has severely underestimated me. I'm going to find out who and deal with them.

19

PIPER

I lie in bed now alone, staring at the ceiling, feeling hopeful. For the first time in a long time, I have a chance to make a change. A change for Elysse. The sun is peeking through the curtains, and it's a metaphor, I decide. A new day is dawning. Light is finally going to chase away the darkness.

Even so, the idea of leaving Gabriel fills me with uncertainty and dread. I've tried to leave him before, when we were in England, but he found me. It wasn't hard. I'd gone to my parents' house. I suppose I was naïve in thinking he'd take a hint and let me go. Why would he come after me when he so obviously thought I was worthless?

Of course, he was apologetic and made promises, begging me to come home. I didn't want to. I knew by then who he was. But my parents insisted I needed to return to him, to give him a chance. The more I tried to tell them the truth, the more they said I was selfish. Elysse needed a stable home. I was lucky that Gabriel was willing to be her father.

I can remember like it was yesterday, their saying I have no way to support myself if I leave him. I told them they could give me Mr. D'Amato's money. After all, I was the one he wanted to get rid of. I was the one carrying his son's child. My parents didn't see it that way, but the truth was, the money was gone.

I had no job. No place to go. And so I returned to Gabriel.

The memory of his rage, the bruises he left on my body, the scars I still carry, sends a shiver down my spine. But worse than that, I remember his threat—if I ever tried to leave again, he'd hurt Elysse. He knew that was the one thing that would make me behave. And it is, because the thought of him laying a hand on my daughter makes my blood run cold.

I have one chance to escape and I have to take it. I've agreed to accept Elio's help, but a part of me questions the wisdom of being with him. It's been so long. Do I really know him anymore? He's been kind and sweet, but so had Gabriel when I first met him.

And then there's Elio's work, the danger that comes with being involved with the Mafia. Is it fair to bring Elysse into that world?

Despite my fears, I know Elio is right. I can't stay with Gabriel. Every day I spend with him is another day I'm risking not just my life, but Elysse's as well. She deserves better than this. We both do. I have to trust that Elio is the man I remember. He is, after all, Elysse's father.

I get out of bed to prepare for the day. I shower and dress, then strip the bed to wash the sheets. I realize that if I'm leaving today, I don't need to cover my tracks. But I still need to consider how I'm going to leave. There's no doubt that I can't talk to him alone and expect him to let me leave. If he catches wind of my plan, he'll stop at nothing to keep us here, hurting Elysse to insure my compliance.

I should just pack up Elysse and slip away without a word. However, that feels cowardly. My heart clenches at the thought of not confronting him, of not looking him in the eye and telling him that we're done, that he no longer has power over us. But how can I do that? The risk is too great. He's too volatile, too dangerous.

Once Elio gets here, we can wait for Gabriel, and I can tell him I'm leaving, tell him he can't hurt me or Elysse ever again. I shake my head. Gabriel will get angry, and I can see Elio doing something drastic, like killing Gabriel. I don't want Elio to get in trouble.

I pull out a bag and start packing just the essentials. My hands tremble slightly as I fold clothes and gather toiletries. It's partly fear, but partly excitement at being free.

I hear Elysse stirring in her room and go to her. She's rubbing sleep from her eyes, her hair a tousled mess. My heart swells with love for her. I'm doing the right thing, letting Elio take us away. I now wonder why I ever questioned it. It doesn't matter whether I have a choice in this. The most important thing is her.

"Hey, baby," I say softly, sitting on the edge of her bed. "We're going to go on a little trip, okay? I need you to pack some of your favorite clothes and toys."

She looks at me, confusion in large, dark eyes, eyes like Elio's. "Where are we going?"

I brush a strand of hair from her face. "Somewhere safe, sweetie. Somewhere we can be happy." I don't want to burden her with too many details, to scare her unnecessarily. She's been through enough already.

She watches me for a moment, and I can see a glimmer of hope in her expression. Even without the details, she senses a change.

She nods and gets out of bed. I help her pack, guiding her to choose her most cherished possessions.

Paranoia has me hiding the bags in the hall closet as we go downstairs for breakfast.

"When are we going, Mommy?" Elysse's voice holds concern, like she worries Gabriel will return and keep us prisoner. I can't deny that I'm feeling anxious as well. But he's not due back until later tonight. We're fine.

"Soon. Probably around lunchtime. Elio has—"

"Elio is going with us?" Her smile is wide and bright, and it fills me with joy that he makes her feel happy and safe.

"Yes, baby. We're going with him." For a little while? Forever? That I don't know. I don't need that answer right now.

"Will he be my new daddy?"

The question catches me off guard. Elio and I haven't talked about how or when to tell her the truth. Now isn't the time, though. He should be here.

"Would you like that?"

She nods so vehemently she looks like a bobblehead. "Yes. He's nice to us. And he's funny. He roller skated with us. Gabriel never did that."

It occurs to me that while Elysse would refer to Gabriel as her daddy, she never actually called him that. She never called him anything.

After we eat breakfast, Elysse and I play a game. Despite trying to keep things light, the tension builds the longer we sit and wait for Elio to pick us up. I keep glancing at the clock, my anxiety mounting with each passing hour. Where is Elio? Is he okay? Has something happened to him?

I fight the urge to call him, to hear his reassuring voice. He's a busy man with a lot of responsibilities. Something, clearly important came up this morning that he needed to deal with. I have to trust that he'll be here when he can, that he won't let us down.

I've sent Elysse to wash her hands as I go to prepare lunch when the front door opens. Relief floods through me as I make my way from the kitchen to Elio.

Except it's not Elio.

Gabriel enters the house looking like he just stepped out of a smoky strip club.

"Gabriel. I didn't expect you home so early." Terror fills me. I'm looking around to make sure there is no sign of our plan to leave.

He drops his bag by the door, his gaze raking over my body in a way that makes my skin crawl. "Did you miss me?" He grabs me and pulls me into an embrace. "I bet you missed this." He grinds himself against me. The feel of his erection makes my stomach churn.

I stiffen, fighting the urge to push him away. "You must be tired." Why did he take an earlier flight?

"I want to fuck my wife."

"Mommy?"

I close my eyes as Elysse's quavering voice reaches me. I gently push Gabriel away.

"It's okay, sweetie. I'll go make lunch. Are you hungry, Gabriel?" I hope I sound normal.

He tugs me back. "I told you, I want to—"

"Elysse is here."

He turns and glares at Elysse. "Go upstairs. Now. Don't come down until I say so."

I nod to her, willing her to comply.

"Elio doesn't talk to us like that."

My heart stalls in my chest.

"What?"

I move us, pulling his attention back to me. The tension rises. The air crackles. I have to defuse this, fast.

"Elysse, sweetie, go play in your room. Your dad and I need to talk."

She hesitates, looking between me and Gabriel. "Okay." I watch until she disappears down the hall.

"Finally." He pushes me onto the couch, his body looming over mine. "It's been a long time, Piper."

"You seem to prefer other women." I wince at the wisdom of provoking him.

"I do. But I've decided it's time I have a son. You're going to give me one."

Oh, God. Where is Elio?

Gabriel tugs at my clothes, and I close my eyes, knowing I'll have to endure this. But then he stops. "What the fuck is this?"

I freeze as Gabriel holds up a cufflink, his eyes blazing with fury. My heart pounds in my chest, my mouth going dry.

He moves off me but stands over me. "Who was here, Piper?"

I swallow hard, my mind racing for an explanation. "It's... it's nothing. Just an old piece of jewelry."

He leans over, his face in mine. "You think I'm stupid? You think I don't know this is a man's cufflink? A cheap one at that. Who are you spreading your legs for?"

I try to stand up to move away, but he pushes me back. "Gabriel, please. It's not what you think."

He grabs my arm, his fingers digging into my flesh. "Then what is it, huh? Door to door salesman?" He sneers. "I'm not an idiot. Who are you seeing behind my back?"

Tears sting my eyes as I shake my head frantically. "No one. Just an old friend from high school stopped by to say hi. That's it."

His grip tightens, his face inches from mine. "I don't believe you."

"Gabriel, stop," I plead. "You're hurting me."

But he's beyond reason, consumed by jealous rage. He shoves me back, his hand wrapping around my throat. "Who is he, Piper? Who have you been fucking behind my back?"

I gasp for air, clawing at his hand. "No one. I swear, there's no one else."

Out of the corner of my eye, Elysse appears standing in the hallway, her eyes wide with terror. Oh, God, not in front of her. Please, not in front of my baby.

I try to catch her eye, to silently plead with her to run, to hide. But she's frozen in fear.

Gabriel follows my gaze, his grip loosening slightly as he sees Elysse. "Get out of here," he barks at her. "Go to your room."

I take the moment to catch my breath.

"Mommy," Elysse whimpers.

Gabriel takes a step toward her. "You'd better listen to me if you know what's good for you."

I fly up from the couch. "No. Don't touch her." I lunge at Gabriel, grabbing him, knowing this could be the last thing I ever do.

He grabs and pushes me hard. I stumble back, falling over the coffee table. "You fucking bitch. You think you can tell me what to do?"

"Go to your room, Elysse," I call out as Gabriel lifts me from the floor like I'm a rag doll.

Elysse's eyes dart around, and I know she's looking for a way to help. No, baby. Just hide. Her gaze settles on my phone next to my purse. Her little fingers snatch it up, clutching it close as she backs away.

My baby is so brave. Braver than I've ever been.

Gabriel's hand cracks across my face, sending me sprawling to the floor. I taste blood, my vision blurring.

"This is all your fault." He spits, grabbing my hair and yanking me to my feet.

I whimper, tears streaming down my face. "Please, don't do this."

But he's beyond reason, beyond mercy. He pushes me against the wall, his hands wrapping around my throat once more.

I struggle for air. Darkness closes in. I think of Elio. Will he get here in time to save Elysse? I hope so. I have a moment of gratitude that he knows the truth. He'll take care of Elysse.

As if Gabriel knows I'm thinking of Elio, his grip tightens around my neck. My lungs burn. My vision fades. Everything goes black.

20

ELIO

I t's just after eight in the morning when I stride into the police station, my annoyance simmering beneath the surface. What a waste of my goddamn time. I've got a million other things I need to be doing right now, namely, getting Piper and my daughter the hell away from that abusive dick she married. But instead, I'm here, cleaning up yet another mess.

Lana and Matteo flank me. Their expressions mirror my own impatience and irritation. Neither of them wants to be here, either. Lana's arms are crossed over her chest, her dark eyes flashing with barely restrained temper. Matteo just looks bored, but I catch him scanning the station, always on alert for potential threats.

I spot the cops on my payroll huddled together in the corner, talking among themselves. They straighten up when they see me coming. I have to play this cool. I'm in the middle of a police station, so it won't be smart to give away that I own these men. At the same time, I need to know what's going on.

"Officers."

The cops exchange uneasy glances. They know they need to play it cool too so as not to give away that they work for me.

"Someone want to tell me what the fuck is going on? Why are my men being detained?" I keep my voice calm.

"Finster got a tip about a burglary down by the docks," Officer Jones reports.

"Who the fuck is Finster?"

"Detective. He's been working on a string of burglaries in the area." Jones looks at his buddy, Colliers, who nods.

"We called Matteo—"

"What I care about is that they're here at all." I lean in closer and speak low. "I pay you a shit-ton of money to prevent just this sort of thing."

Collier crosses his arms over his chest and narrows his eyes at me. "We can't be everywhere all at once. Why were they there, anyway? We didn't get any heads up that they were going into Rinella territory."

He's right. I look at Matteo. "Do we know why they were there?"

He shakes his head. Fuck. That means my men fucked up.

I turn back to the officers. "Why aren't you getting them out?"

"Your lawyer is here, and it would look sus if we poked our noses in," Jones says.

I shake my head, wondering if I'm wasting my money with these two. "Where are they now?"

"Interrogation. The lawyer is there. We can call you when they're done—"

"I want it done now. Who can I talk to that will make it happen?"

Matteo leans in next to me. "Maybe we let this play out. The head of the D'Amato family throwing his weight around might cause undue attention."

He's not wrong. "Where can I wait?"

The officers guide me to a room. "No one should bother you here."

"Well this was a waste of time," Lana says, scrunching her nose at the drab room.

"This has Rinella written all over it," Matteo says, pulling out a chair and sitting down.

"I agree. But why were our guys there? That doesn't make sense. I didn't send them. Did you?"

"No. I guess we'll have to wait and see."

"Must we wait here?" Lana asks. "We're not helping and it will look suspicious. Plus, Rinella's men are probably reporting to him that he's won."

"I'm not leaving until I know what happened. And I don't give a fuck about what Rinella is told. He's an idiot if he thinks this little adolescent stunt means he won."

"Yeah, he's just fucking with you," Matteo agrees.

"And you're letting him," Lana quips.

I sigh. "If you don't want to be a part of this, you can go."

She makes a face but sits down next to Matteo.

Time moves slowly when waiting for something. In this case, it was over an hour before Tony, the family lawyer, strides through the door.

"Elio." He holds out his hand, and I shake it.

"What the fuck, Tony?"

He shakes his head. "It's all bullshit. They got nothing on our guys. No evidence, no probable cause, nothing. They're just jerking us around."

I clench my jaw, my anger rising. "So why the fuck are they still in there?"

Tony holds up a placating hand. "Relax. They're processing the paperwork now. Should be out within the hour."

I pace back and forth, my impatience growing. I can't wait around here. Not when I need to be helping Piper and Elysse pack and move in with me.

"Why so long?"

"You know how it is. It's like trying to buy a cell phone or a car. The process is slow."

"This is unacceptable," I growl. "I want to know who ordered this. And I want them out now."

"They've got a protocol—"

"I don't give a fuck about protocol. These are my men, and I want them released. Now."

"I'll go see what I can do." Matteo exits the room.

I turn back to Tony, my frustration boiling over. "How did this even happen?"

"They got a text about taking a looksee at the docks. So they went down and were then picked up by a detective... Finster, I think."

"Text? From who?"

"They thought it was from Caro."

I frown. Joey Caro is one of my street men.

"In hindsight, they see now that it wasn't."

"Contact Caro," I say to Lana.

"When do you want to see him?"

"As soon as I get home." I turn back to Tony. "What else did they say?"

"That's about it. They were walking along, checking things out, when Finster showed up and took them in on suspicion of burglary."

"Is this Finster with Rinella?" I ask.

"Doubt it. He seems straight. Apparently, he got a tip, though."

I nod as I see the situation clearer. "Rinella forged a text to my men to lure them down to the docks and then tipped off Finster."

"Looks like it. There's been a lot of burglaries in the area, so it would make sense that he'd follow up on the tip."

I'm ready to be done with all this. At this point, I can have Matteo deal with my men.

"I'm heading home. Bring the men there. And get Caro there." I stride out of the room and see Matteo, giving him the same order.

On the ride home, I consider stopping by Piper's to pick them up, but Lana is with me and I don't need her harping on me about being distracted. Piper said her husband wasn't due back until tonight, so they should be safe.

Back in my home office, Lana doesn't waste time reminding me how this will look. "He might be just fucking with you, Elio, but it makes you look vulnerable."

"Fucking hell."

She doesn't back down, meeting my glare with one of her own. "You heard me, Elio. This whole thing makes you look weak. Like you can't control your own men."

I clench my fists at my sides, struggling to keep my anger in check. "Watch yourself, Lana."

"Threaten me if you want, but you know I'm right. You're so busy chasing after your high school sweetheart that you can't see what's happening right under your nose. Vincenzo is playing you like a fiddle, and you're too distracted by lust to even notice."

That's it. I snap, slamming my hand down on my desk. "Enough!"

She flinches but then purses her lips at me like I'm a petulant child.

"You want to talk about distractions? How about the fact that you're too busy sticking your nose into my business to actually contribute anything useful to this family?"

Lana's eyes widen, but she still doesn't back down. "I'm looking out for our best interests. Someone has to, since you clearly can't be bothered."

I let out a harsh laugh, shaking my head in disbelief. "You know what, Lana? I've had just about enough of your shit. I wasn't joking about cutting you off... not just from the house but your allowance as well. It's easy for you to sit back and judge me when you have no real skin in the game."

Lana's jaw drops, her eyes flashing with anger. "Maybe if you'd give me a real job to do, I'd have skin in the game. I can help you, Elio. Or you can be a petty jerk."

I take a deep breath, trying to rein in my temper. As much as I hate to admit it, Lana has a point. We need to focus on the bigger picture here—namely, how we're going to handle this bullshit with the Rinellas.

Matteo enters with my men and Caro. They all look a little nervous. Good. Someone fucked up somewhere, and I need to know who and how.

"I didn't text them," Caro says right away. He holds out his phone. "You can check, Boss."

"How would Rinella have made it seem like a text was from you?"

"Spoofing?" Matteo suggests.

"We were just looking around," one of the men says.

"For what?" I ask.

They shrug. "Anything that you might want to know about. That's what the text said."

"So you were spying?"

They nod. They verify my suspicions. I feel like I need to reprimand them, but for what? Being gullible? Clearly, I need to put in more protocol about orders given via text.

"You can go. Lie low." I dismiss them.

The men and Caro leave my office, relief on their faces.

"We can't let Rinella get away with this," Lana says, perched on the edge of my desk.

"No, we can't." I sit down behind my desk.

"What do you have in mind? she asks.

I lean back in my chair, steepling my fingers together. "Nothing."

Matteo frowns, looking at me like I've lost my mind. "Nothing?"

I shrug, a slow smile spreading across my face. "Exactly what I said. We do nothing. Vincenzo wants a reaction out of us, wants to provoke us into doing something stupid. But we're not going to give him the satisfaction."

Lana gapes at me. "So what, we just let him get away with this little stunt? Let him think he can mess with us whenever he feels like it?"

"Oh, he's not getting away with anything, Sis. Trust me on that. But we're not going to stoop to his level. We're going to hit him where it really hurts."

Matteo leans forward, his eyes narrowing. "And how, exactly, are we going to do that?"

I pause for a moment, savoring the anticipation. "I'm going to marry Piper."

Lana's jaw drops, her eyes widening in shock. "You're going to what?"

Matteo looks equally stunned, his brows shooting up to his hairline. "Marry her?"

I nod, my grin turning smug. "Vincenzo thought he could strong-arm me into marrying his daughter. Or he just wanted to fuck with me in this petty prank. So I'll be petty back. Not only have I rejected his daughter, but I'm going to marry someone else. He'll see that as a bigger slap in the face." I like this idea a lot, but not as retaliation. No. I want to make sure Piper is mine. "Plus, I get back what was stolen from me, the woman I love and my child. It's a win-win."

"What about the fact that she's married?" Matteo asks.

"That can be undone."

Matteo runs a hand through his hair, looking skeptical. "And you think that's going to be enough to get back at Vincenzo? Marrying some girl from your past?"

I level him with a hard stare. "She's not just some girl. She's the love of my fucking life. And yeah, I think it'll be more than enough. Because it hits at his pride. Plus, his only real asset for building an alliance with us has been through his daughter. But now? It's useless. And he knows it."

My phone rings, and I pull it out of my pocket, glancing at the screen. Piper's number flashes up at me, and I feel a sudden rush of excitement. Maybe she's calling to tell me she's ready, that she's packed and waiting for me to come get her and Elysse. Perhaps I'll have time to stop by a jeweler and pick up a ring to make my intentions official.

I poke the answer button. "Are you ready?"

A sob comes through the phone, putting me on alert. "Piper?"

"*Elio?*" It's Elysse. "*He's hurting Mommy.*"

Oh, fuck. I feel a cold dread wash over me, my heart clenching in my chest.

"*I'm scared.*"

For a moment, I can't breathe. Can't think. All I can see is Piper's face, bruised and battered, her eyes wide with fear. And Elysse, my little girl, watching it all happen, powerless to stop it.

I pull my shit together, jumping up from my desk and heading out the door. "Where are you?"

"Mommy told me to go to my room, but I'm hiding. I don't want him to hurt me."

"Good. That's good. You stay hidden. I'm coming right now."

"What's going on?" Lana says as she and Matteo follow me out.

"I've got to get to Piper's."

"I'll get the car." Matteo rushes ahead of me. I'm grateful that even without details, he knows this is serious.

"Hurry," Elysse's terrified voice comes over the phone.

"I'm on my way," I manage to choke out. "I need you to be brave, okay? Stay hidden until I get there. Can you do that for me?"

"Okay... hurry. I'm so scared."

"I know, baby girl. I know. I'm coming as fast as I can. Just hold on, okay? I'm going to make everything alright. I promise." God, I hope I can keep that promise.

"What can I do?" Lana asks.

I'm heading out the door when I call back, "Hold down the fort."

I drive like a maniac, Matteo white knuckling it in the passenger seat. I screech to a halt and send up a prayer to a God who has probably written me off that Piper is okay. That I'm not too late.

I screech to a stop and am out of the SUV's door like a flash. I burst through the front door of Piper's house, my heart pounding in my chest. I see Gabriel's hands around Piper's neck. She's not moving, not fighting back. Then my heart stops. I'm too late. Too fucking late.

Rage consumes me, a red haze descending over my vision. I cross the room in three strides, grabbing Gabriel by the back of his shirt and hauling him off Piper. He stumbles back, caught off guard by my sudden appearance.

"Get the fuck off her!" I roar, shoving him hard.

He hits the ground but scrambles back to his feet, his face twisted with fury. "She's my wife. I'll do whatever the hell I want with her."

I grab him and manhandle him over to Matteo. "Hold this piece of shit. I need to check on Piper."

Matteo doesn't hesitate, grabbing Gabriel by the arms and wrenching them behind his back.

I turn back to Piper, my heart in my throat. She's slumped on the floor, her eyes closed, her breathing shallow.

I drop to my knees beside her, cupping her face in my hands. "Piper? Baby, can you hear me?" My heart is cracking open. Have I failed her again? "Please, open your eyes. Look at me, sweetheart."

"Are you the one who's been fucking my wife behind my back?" Gabriel snarls at me.

I don't look at him. "Matty, kill him if you have to." Matteo pulls his gun out, holding it to Gabriel's head. His eyes widen, and I think he's finally understanding that he's messed with the wrong woman.

I turn my attention back to Piper. I'm terrified that I'm too late, that Piper's gone. But then her eyelids flutter and she lets out a soft groan. Relief floods through me, so intense it would bring me to my knees if I weren't already on them.

"That's it, baby." I brush her hair back from her face, holding back the rage that's growing at the sight of new bruises. "You're okay. I'm here now. I've got you."

I pick her up, carrying her to the couch. She sinks down onto the cushions, her breathing still ragged.

I kneel in front of her, taking her hands in mine. "What do you need? I can call a doctor—"

"I just need a minute." Her voice is hoarse.

I nod. "Rest. I'm going to deal with this scumbag."

Piper nods weakly, her eyes drifting closed again. I press a soft kiss to her forehead before standing and turning to face Gabriel.

I stalk toward him. "You think you're a big man, hitting a woman? You're pathetic."

Gabriel's eyes flash with fury, but he's smart enough not to say anything. Matteo steps back slightly to give me room.

"You're a pussy-ass man. Real men don't have to terrorize women and children to feel important." I lunge at him, my fist connecting with his jaw with a satisfying crack. He reels back, spitting blood, but

I don't give him a chance to recover. I grab him by the front of his shirt, slamming him back against the wall.

Gabriel tries to look defiant but fails. I can smell the fear radiating off him.

"She's my wife. I can do whatever I want with her."

I slam my fist into his stomach, doubling him over. "Wrong answer. You crossed a line, you piece of shit." I grab him by the hair and wrench his head back. "You put your hands on the woman I love, the mother of my child. There's no coming back from that." I lean in close so all he can see is my face. "You're going to pay with your life."

Gabriel's eyes widen, his mouth falling open in shock. His eyes slide to the right toward Matteo as if he might help him.

"Now you know what it feels like, don't you? The fear? The pain?" I let loose, raining blows on him, channeling all of my rage and fear into each punch.

If he's saying anything now, I don't hear it. The roaring in my ears is rage and retribution.

21

PIPER

I step out of the house, my arm wrapped protectively around Elysse who's gripping my leg. Elio walks on my other side, his arm banded around me. I feel safe in his presence and yet, unsettled as well. I'd always known Elio to be affable, easygoing. Tonight, I saw murder in his eyes.

As we approach Elio's sleek black SUV, Elysse trembles against me. Her small fingers dig into my leg, and I can sense her fear. I worry about what's going through her young mind. Is it the adrenaline from the terrifying situation we just escaped? Or is she scared of Elio and the imposing man standing next to his car? He clearly works for Elio as he'd done Elio's bidding while in the house.

The stranger crouches down to Elysse's level and offers a gentle smile, but Elysse buries her face in my side, refusing to look at him.

"This is my cousin, Matteo," Elio explains, his voice soft and reassuring.

Matteo rises, stepping aside, giving us space. Elio moves forward, opening the back door of the SUV. He extends his hand to help me in, and I hesitate for a moment before accepting it. His touch sends a jolt through me, a mix of familiarity and uncertainty.

"Come on, sweetheart," I murmur to Elysse, guiding her into the vehicle. She clambers in, still clinging to me as if her life depends on it. I slide in after her, pulling her close as Elio shuts the door behind us.

The car ride is a blur, my mind still reeling from the events that just unfolded. Elio's voice cuts through the haze as he instructs Matteo to call the doctor. I glance over at Elysse, who has curled up against me, her eyes closed but her body still tense. I stroke her hair, trying to offer what little comfort I can.

As we pull up to Elio's home, a sense of unease settles in my stomach. I've never met his family before, only his parents when they caused my family to leave town all those years ago. The memory stings, but I push it aside, focusing on the present.

We step out of the car, and Elio guides us toward the entrance. The door swings open, revealing a striking woman with dark hair and piercing eyes.

Elio tenses for a moment, as if he's anticipating negativity from the woman. "This is my sister, Lana. Lana, Piper and Elysse."

She regards me with a mix of curiosity and skepticism, her gaze lingering on Elysse. "Welcome."

"Thank you for having—"

"This is your home now." Elio's voice leaves no room for discussion. What I don't know is whether he's convincing me or his sister. I don't want to be bossed around anymore, but right now, I don't have the energy to confront him.

Elio leads us upstairs, his hand resting gently on the small of my back. He shows Elysse to a room.

"This is your room. Anything you want or need, you tell me, okay? We'll redecorate it however you want. It can be a princess castle. A jungle. Whatever you wish," Elio tells her.

Elysse hesitates, looking back at me with uncertainty.

I give her a reassuring nod. "It's big, isn't it?"

"Is it too big?" Elio almost sounds like he's desperate to make sure Elysse likes the room. Likes him.

"It's fine," I say.

Elio then turns to me. "There is a room next door or... mine is across the hall there." He points down the hall.

I'm not quite ready to face the intimacy of sharing his space, nor am I ready to leave Elysse alone.

"I'm just going to stay with her for now."

He nods. "What can I get you?" His eyes are filled with concern.

"I just want to rest."

"Okay. I'll be downstairs if you need anything."

"Thank you, Elio." I don't want him to feel that I'm ungrateful. I'm just sore and tired and worried about Elysse.

I guide Elysse to the bed. "Let's lie down for a bit, okay?"

She climbs onto the large bed, curling in a little ball against me. I hold her, kissing her head.

Just as we settle in, there's a knock at the door. Elio pops his head in. "Doctor Albert is here."

I don't want to be examined, but considering what I've just been through, perhaps I should be.

Elio excuses himself again, giving me and Elysse privacy with the doctor.

"Sounds like you had quite the ordeal," Dr. Albert says as he approaches me.

I nod. He glances at Elysse. "She wasn't hurt physically, but she witnessed more than she should have."

"Let's make sure you're okay," he says. As the doctor examines us, I feel a sense of relief wash over me. It's sinking in that Elysse and I are safe, away from Gabriel's abuse.

The doctor checks and cleans my wounds. I wince as he tends to the bruises and cuts. This is the worst they've ever been. My sense of calm vanishes for a moment as I realize that Gabriel would have killed me.

"You're shaking." Dr. Albert takes my hand and looks me in the eyes.

"I'm just thinking of how close I came to..." I don't finish the sentence, not wanting to vocalize my near demise in front of Elysse.

"You don't appear to be in shock."

I shake my head. He continues to examine me, determining that he doesn't believe anything is broken and I'm not showing signs of an altered state.

"How about I check the little one?" he asks.

I sit on the bed, holding Elysse close as the doctor examines her. My heart clenches as I watch my daughter, so small and fragile, enduring this ordeal. The doctor asks her gentle questions, trying to assess her physical state. Elysse responds in soft whispers, her voice trembling. I restate that Gabriel hadn't touched her.

"Some injuries are mental, though, are they not?"

Tears fill my eyes along with the guilt that I'd put her through all this. Maybe I need to get her counseling. Maybe I need counseling.

Once the doctor leaves, Elysse and I lie down on the bed together. She curls up against me, her small body fitting perfectly into the curve of mine. I wrap my arms around her, holding her close, trying to provide the comfort and security she so desperately needs.

"I'm sorry, sweetie. I'm sorry you had to experience all that."

"Elio looked mean... like—"

"He was protecting us. You called him and he came to save us. You were so brave to call. I'm so proud of you."

"Will we be Elio's now?"

I wonder if she believes women and children are owned by men. I can't blame her for thinking that considering she hasn't known anything different.

"Elio will keep us safe, sweetie."

Elysse nods, burying her face in my chest. I stroke her hair, murmuring soothing words of reassurance. Gradually, her breathing slows, and I feel her body relax against mine.

As I lie there holding my daughter, exhaustion washes over me. The events of the day, the terror and the relief, have taken their toll. My eyelids grow heavy, and I succumb to sleep.

I wake disoriented. Looking around, I remember I'm at Elio's. I reach out for Elysse, but she's not here. Worry surges through me as I frantically scan the unfamiliar room.

"Elysse?" I get out of bed, checking the bathroom. She's not there. I exit the room, calling her name as I go down the hallway. Eventually, I end up downstairs, following a trail of voices and laughter.

I reach a kitchen that has a large bay window with a breakfast table. Elysse holds a sandwich in one hand and game cards in the other.

Across from her, Elio and Matteo lean in, their faces scrunched in concentration. A deck of cards lies between them.

"Got any threes?" Elysse chirps, her voice lighter than I'd expect.

Matteo groans dramatically, handing over a card. "You're cleaning us out, kid."

Relief washes over me as I watch my daughter giggle, clearly at ease with these two men who, just a few hours ago, made her wary.

Elio glances up, catching my eye. He sets down his cards and approaches me, concern etched on his face. "How are you? There's coffee and food if you're hungry."

I nod, still processing the scene before me. "Elysse... how long has she been up?"

"I went to check on you about an hour ago. I found her awake and coaxed her down here to let you rest. I think before, she was afraid of us, but now we're afraid of her."

I smile. "Not many people beat her at cards. Or board games."

"I should take her to Vegas."

I arch a brow at him. He laughs. "I'm kidding."

"Go fish," Matteo tells Elysse.

She picks up a card from the pile. "Fish, fish, I got my wish!" she exclaims triumphantly.

Matteo dramatically slaps his forehead. "Good thing we're not playing for money."

"Can I get you something to eat?" Elio asks.

Actually, what I want is to clean up. I feel like I have Gabriel on me. "What I really want is a shower."

"Let me show you to your bath." Elio puts his arm around me. "Will you two be okay while I take Piper to clean up?"

"Do you know how to play Crazy 8s?" Elysse asks Matteo.

"I don't, but you can teach me." Matteo nods toward Elio in what I determine means he's happy to hold down the fort.

"I can ask Elysse to come."

Elio rubs his hands up and down my arms. "She's fine. Give yourself a moment."

"I'm going to clean up, okay?" I say to Elysse.

"'K," she responds absently as she picks up her cards.

I follow Elio upstairs, eager to wash away the trauma of the day. Elio guides me into the room he mentioned earlier was his.

"I have the nicest shower and tub," he says sheepishly, as if he doesn't want me to think he's trying to push me into sharing his room. I do have some unease about all this. Am I moving too fast, jumping from one man's arms to another's?

Elio seems to sense my hesitation. He pauses outside the bathroom door, turning to face me. "If you're not comfortable, I can show you another bathroom. I won't deny that I'm ready to have the life we always said we would, but I understand you may need time."

I meet his gaze, seeing the sincerity in his eyes. He's giving me a chance to set the pace. Knowing that shifts something inside me. He's not telling me how it is. He's not pushing me. He's giving me a choice.

Resistance falls away, and I give in to my heart. "This is fine."

Elio's hand rests gently on the small of my back as he guides me into the bathroom. It's spacious and luxurious, with a large walk-in shower and fluffy towels hanging on the rack.

"Take as much time as you need." He hands me a fresh towel.

I reach out for the towel, wincing from the ache at the movement.

"Piper." His eyes fill with emotion. I see the murderous rage he has for Gabriel, but also caring for me. "Let me help you." He hangs the towel outside the shower, then reaches in to turn on the water.

I begin to strip off my clothes, trying to hide the pain as the fabric grates against my bruises, as my muscles cry out from injury.

"Fuck." Elio's voice is a low rumble as his gaze takes me in.

I check the mirror, seeing the damage Gabriel inflicted on my body. I turn away, stepping into the shower, letting the hot water cascade over my body. The heat soothes my aching muscles, and I close my eyes, letting the water wash away the pain and fear.

Once again, doubt about staying with Elio creeps in. Is this really the right thing to do? Falling into Elio's arms so soon after leaving Gabriel? What kind of example am I setting for Elysse?

But where else could we go and be certain that Gabriel wouldn't try to find us? Elio was right. I don't have my own money. I don't have a job or a means to get a place for me and Elysse.

I remind myself that Elio isn't Gabriel. He's kind and gentle, and he's offering me a safe haven. Right now, that's what Elysse and I need more than anything.

All of a sudden, Elio is with me in the shower. He doesn't say anything as he takes the soap and lathers it in his large, strong hands. Hands that earlier today wanted to kill Gabriel. Now, those hands are gentle as his fingers gently slide over my skin with tenderness.

His eyes roam over my body, taking in the bruises and marks that mar my skin. Concern etches his handsome features as he gently traces the outline of a particularly nasty bruise on my ribs.

"Piper." His voice is thick with emotion. "Did Dr. Albert see this? You could have a broken rib."

I give him a reassuring smile despite the dull ache that throbs beneath his fingertips. "The doctor checked them. Nothing's broken, just bruised."

Elio's jaw clenches, a flash of anger darkening his eyes. I know he's thinking about Gabriel, about the harm he inflicted upon me.

"How often did he do this to you?" he asks, his voice tight with restrained anger.

I shrug. "I don't know." I'd lost count.

"Why didn't you leave?" His question feels like an accusation, making me feel exposed and vulnerable. I look away, shame and embarrassment washing over me.

Elio swears under his breath, his fingers tracing an old scar from a years ago attack by Gabriel on the back of my shoulder. "If I ever get the chance, I'll kill him for what he's done to you." Elio's voice is low and dangerous.

His words send a chill down my spine, and I turn back to face him. "Elio, no. The violence has to stop. Elysse and I... we can't handle any more violence."

Elio's eyes fill with torment. He wants to protect me, to make Gabriel pay for the pain he's inflicted, but I hope he understands that I can't endure it anymore.

As quickly as the anger appears, it's replaced by a softness that steals my breath. Elio's the only man who's ever looked at me like that. With raw emotion. Like I'm the center of his world.

His lips find my skin, trailing gentle kisses over my bruises and scars. Each touch is a silent promise to comfort and protect me. His tenderness brings tears to my eyes, and I lean into him, allowing myself to be vulnerable in his arms.

"I want to erase every scar, physical and emotional," he murmurs against my skin. "To make it all go away." Elio's hands are gentle as they explore my body, his touch a soothing balm to my battered soul. It feels like he's trying to heal me. I lean into him, allowing myself to be vulnerable in a way I haven't been in years.

As the water cascades over us, I lose myself in the sensation of Elio's touch. His fingers caress my curves, igniting a fire. I arch into him, craving more of his touch, more of the connection that pulses between us.

Elio's lips find mine, his kiss tender yet passionate. In this moment, the rest of the world falls away. The pain, the fear, the uncertainty—all of it fades into the background. I wrap my arms around him, kissing him with a desperate fervor.

He laughs softly. "I'm sorry, I didn't mean to make you aroused."

"Touch me." I need him more than the shower to wash away all of Gabriel.

"Baby, you're injured—"

"Touch me." My voice is more demanding.

He stares at me like he's looking for something in my eyes. I hope he finds what he's looking for because I need him to soothe the pain and fill the hole that's been living inside me for too, too long.

22

ELIO

I t doesn't seem right to have sex right now. But as I look into her eyes, I see that something deeper is going on. Perhaps she needs hands that love her, not ones that brutalize her. That I can give her.

I trail gentle kisses over Piper's bruises and scars, wishing I could erase every mark that bastard left on her. My blood boils thinking about what she's endured, but I force myself to stay calm. She needs tenderness now, not more violence.

"I'm sorry," I murmur against her skin. "I'm sorry I wasn't there to protect you all these years."

Piper trembles slightly under my touch. "You're here now."

I plan to be here forever. But I'm not sure she's ready to hear that. She needs to feel in control. It's taking more effort than I thought I had to hold back and not state that she's mine.

I cup her face gently in my hands, careful to avoid the bruise on her cheek. "I'm not going anywhere. You and Elysse are safe with me." I lean in and kiss her again, giving her what she asks for. My lips and fingers glide along her body, revering her. I never want her to be afraid of my hands.

I knead her tits, gently sucking on her nipples. She lets out a sweet mewling sound that makes my dick harder than steel, but I tell it to calm down. This isn't about me.

I kiss her again as my hand slides over her abdomen. I think about Elysse growing there. A sharp pain pierces my heart at how much I missed. The pregnancy. The birth. Elysse's first steps. Did she call Gabriel "Daddy"? I shake my head of these thoughts because they're starting to piss me off and that's not what Piper needs right now.

I brush my finger on her clit. She gasps against my lips. I lift her leg, hooking it over my hip, giving my fingers greater access to her warm, soft pussy. I slide one, then two fingers inside her.

She moans. Her hips rock. "Elio..."

"I'm here, Baby." I glide my lips down her neck, over her tits, stopping to suck her nipples again. Then I continue down, dropping to my knees. I lift her leg again, hooking it over my shoulder. I hold her hips steady with her back against the tiles. I swirl my tongue around her clit.

"Yes. Oh... mmm." Her fingers grip my head almost painfully. But I stay with her, using my mouth and tongue to drive away the demons and fill her with pleasure. I slide my tongue inside, lapping at her pussy walls. Her body trembles. Her hips rock. She cries out, and her juices flow over my tongue and down my chin.

I guide her down and then stand, gathering her into my arms. "You're safe." *You're mine. Forever.*

Her hand wraps around my cock, but I take her wrist and move it away.

"What about you?" she asks.

I reach around Piper to turn off the shower. "My dick is fine." He doesn't think so at the moment, but he'll be fine. I grab a fluffy towel and wrap it around her, then get one for myself.

"Let me help you." I gently pat her dry.

She winces slightly as the towel brushes over some of her bruises. "I'm sorry."

"I'm okay," she insists, but I can see the pain in her eyes.

I retrieve a soft robe from a hook on the wall and help her into it.

It's mine and so too big for her, making her look small and vulnerable. "You don't have to be strong all the time. Let me take care of you."

Piper leans into me, and it feels like a gift that she's surrendering at least in this moment. I press a kiss to her forehead, savoring this moment of intimacy and trust between us.

I help Piper into my room, sitting her on the side of my bed... our bed. My heart swells with love for her, but there's also an ache of longing for the daughter I've just discovered. A daughter Gabriel raised as a father. The rage tries to ignite, but I clamp it down. Still, I don't want to be left out any longer.

"We should tell Elysse about my being her father."

Piper's eyes widen, and I can see the conflict in them. Perhaps I misworded that. It was a statement, not a question. But this isn't a choice Piper needs to make. I'm Elysse's father.

"I... I don't know, Elio. It's a lot for her to take in, especially after everything that's happened."

Her hesitation stings, but I nod, trying to understand. "I know it's complicated, but I've missed so much already." The guilt and anger about that builds and I can't hide it in my tone. "I've lost seven years of her life, Piper. Seven years! I can't get that time back. I'll be damned if I'm going to lose any more."

Piper's eyes flash with equal irritation. "It's not my fault that you—"

"Fuck!" I turn away as I rein in my anger. Then I look at her again. "I'm not blaming you. But fucking hell, Pipe, I'm her father. Are you really going to keep me from that any longer?"

Piper's expression softens. She reaches out and takes my hand. "I'm sorry I got defensive. I'm upset too at what happened all those years ago. Right now, I'm just thinking of her. I want to protect her."

"Protect her from me?" What the hell? Five minutes ago, Piper was begging me to touch her and now I'm a danger?

"No." She shakes her head vehemently. "Protect her emotionally. A lot happened today."

I'm trying to understand, but it's not easy. "It's because she was afraid of me, isn't it?"

"No—"

"But if she knew I was her father, she wouldn't look at me as another stepdad, one who could be an asshole."

"Elio—"

"Don't keep this from me, Piper."

Piper is quiet for a moment, then nods slowly. "You're right. She deserves to know the truth. And you deserve the chance to be her father."

Relief and joy flood through me, along with fear that Elysse won't be equally as happy to learn I'm her father.

We dress and then go downstairs. The sounds of laughter and music greet us as we enter the living room. Elysse is standing in front of the TV, her little body swaying to the upbeat tune of a children's movie. It's a relief to see Elysse acting like a carefree child, especially after the trauma she's witnessed. I don't imagine the emotional scars are gone, but this scene gives me hope that she'll be okay.

Matteo sits on the couch, watching her with an amused grin on his face.

Elysse giggles and beckons for him to join her. "Come on, Matteo. I'll teach you the steps!"

Matteo shakes his head. "I don't know, kiddo. I'm not much of a dancer."

She grabs his hands and tugs him off the couch. "It's easy. Just follow me."

To my surprise, Matteo relents. He stands up and lets Elysse guide him through the silly dance moves. They hop and spin, their laughter filling the room.

I laugh at the sight of my tough-as-nails cousin, my second in command, being led in a dance by a seven-year-old girl. It's a side of Matteo I've never seen before.

Piper leans into me, a soft smile on her face as she watches our daughter. "She looks relaxed and happy."

"She does. I'm glad she feels safe and comfortable here." I hope that means Piper feels more at ease telling Elysse the truth.

Elysse spots us standing in the doorway and waves excitedly. "Mommy, Elio, come dance with us!"

I grin and lead Piper into the room. "How can we resist an invitation like that?"

We join Elysse and Matteo, letting the music and laughter wash over us. Turns out I'm worse than Matteo when it comes to dancing. But that's okay because in this moment, all the horrors earlier in the day are gone. Right now, we're just a family enjoying a silly moment together.

As I twirl Elysse around, her little hand in mine, I catch Piper's eye. She's smiling at me, her eyes shining with love and gratitude. I know we still have a lot to figure out, but I know everything is going to be okay. Finally, after all this time, I have what I wanted from the moment I first laid eyes on Piper in high school.

As the movie credits roll, we catch our breaths.

"I'm done in," Matteo says, ready to leave us.

"Where's Lana?" I ask him.

Matteo shrugs, a mischievous glint in his eye. "She's working. Probably plotting her takeover of the family business."

I chuckle, shaking my head. I consider that I'm open to the idea of her taking on more responsibility. It would free me up to spend time with Piper and Elysse.

"Or maybe she's trying to get out of babysitting."

"You seem to have a knack for it," I say.

He shrugs. "I like kids."

As much as I'm enjoying this lighthearted moment, there's a serious matter I need to discuss with Matteo, so I walk with him toward the hall.

Once we're out of earshot, I lower my voice. "I need you to do something for me. Find someone to keep an eye on Gabriel. I don't trust him."

"Okay. For how long?"

"Few days, at least... oh, and when he's served divorce papers. I've called Tony about pulling those together."

"Consider it done."

With that weight off my shoulders, I return to the living room, ready to enjoy more precious moments with Piper and Elysse. For the first time in years, I feel like I'm exactly where I'm meant to be. I just hope Elysse feels the same.

Nervousness twists in my gut as Piper and I sit down with Elysse. I've faced down dangerous men without flinching, but the thought of my daughter rejecting me fills me with a fear I've never known.

Piper takes Elysse's hand, her voice gentle as she begins. "Sweetie, there's something important we need to tell you. It's about your dad."

She covers her ears and shakes her head. "I don't want to know about him. He's mean and scary—"

"No, sweetie, not Gabriel." Piper pulls Elysse closer, holding her. I'm afraid she might change her mind. "About your real dad."

Elysse's brow furrows, confusion in her large, dark eyes. I remember thinking that Elysse must take after her dad. And now I see it. She has my eyes.

"You said he was gone."

Piper takes a deep breath. "I know, but I was wrong."

Elysse's gaze darts between us, her little mind working to make sense of this revelation. "Who is he?"

I lean forward, my heart pounding. "It's me."

Her eyes widen, and for a moment, she's silent. Then, in a small voice, she asks, "Like my new daddy?"

I shake my head. "Like your *real* dad."

She looks at Piper, who nods. When she turns back to me, her expression fills me with dread. "Didn't you want me?"

Her words are like a knife to my heart.

"Sweetie, he didn't know about you," Piper explains.

"If I did, I would have been there," I add. "And now that I do know, I'm here because I want you more than anything."

Elysse is quiet for a moment, processing this information. "Really?"

"Really. Even before I knew the truth, when I met you at the restaurant, I wanted to be there for you. I'm so sorry that we missed so much time. I hope you'll forgive that and let me be your dad."

It takes a moment, but then a smile spreads across her face. She launches herself into my arms, hugging me tightly. "I wished you were my dad instead of Gabriel."

I've never been moved to tears before, but the overwhelming love and acceptance from this little girl—my little girl—has tears stinging my eyes.

"I'm here now and forever," I promise. That includes Piper too, whether she realizes it or not. I glance at Piper, who wipes a tear from her cheek.

"Can we watch the movie again?" Elysse asks. I have whiplash at how quickly she's moved on to the next thing. But then I realize that she doesn't need more time to process this. She's accepted that I'm her father and is ready to move on.

"Sure thing."

Elysse grabs the remote like a pro and turns the movie on again. She grins as she starts dancing, her little feet tapping out the rhythm. I do my best to follow along, feeling a bit silly but loving every moment.

Piper watches us from the couch, a soft smile on her face. She looks relaxed and comfortable too, and more than ever, I feel like my dream has finally come true.

As the movie ends, I scoop Elysse up and spin her around. She giggles and wraps her arms around my neck. "That was fun, Daddy!"

My heart swells at hearing her call me 'Daddy'. "Daddy needs a break. I think it's time for some dinner. What do you say, little dancer?"

Elysse nods enthusiastically. "I'm hungry."

We enter the dining room to find Lana and Matteo already seated at the table. They both smile warmly at Elysse.

Elysse stops and hides behind my leg when she sees Lana.

"I know how you feel," I joke, "but she's more bark than bite. In fact, she's your aunt."

Lana arches a brow at me but then smiles again at Elysse. "Come with me, kid, and I'll tell you all the dirt on your dad here."

Elysse looks up at me.

"She won't don't do that. I have more dirt on her." I lead Elysse to a spot at the table near me. It's where I used to sit when my parents were alive. In that moment, I finally have a feeling of being head of the family.

"I never had an aunt before. Or a cousin."

I'm beginning to sense how small Piper and Elysse's worlds were, especially with Gabriel.

"Well, get used to it. We're going to spoil you rotten," Lana says playfully. I smile at her, hoping she sees how appreciative I am at her accepting Piper and Elysse, even as doing so fucks up things with Vincenzo Rinella.

Matteo grins. "Just wait until Christmas, kid. Your aunt and I are going to make sure you have the biggest pile of presents ever!"

For once, dinner isn't filled with me and Lana griping or all of us discussing dinner. Instead, we learn about Elysse and her love of dancing. I make a mental note to find out about dance classes for her. Elysse also shares different words she used when in England, like biscuit for cookie.

"I don't hear an English accent," Matteo says.

Piper laughs. "She has an American mom and grandparents." It makes me ridiculously happy that she doesn't mention Gabriel's influence, that she's already culled him from Elysse's past.

"Are your parents still there?" Lana asks, innocently enough. But I see the glimmer of light in Piper's eyes dim.

"Yes." She looks down.

Lana glances over at me, a brow arched in question.

"I believe they were in league with Mom and Dad." No sense in keeping the truth a secret. What I don't understand is why they were so eager to get her away from danger they perceived from me but didn't help her leave Gabriel.

"What's in league?" Elysse asks as she pokes a cooked carrot.

"In cahoots," Matteo says.

"What's cahoots?"

"It means they worked together," Piper finally says.

Elysse looks up at Piper. "To do what?"

Piper turns to me. I'm not sure if I'm supposed to shut up or answer or do anything at all. But I have my fatherhood to defend.

I put my hand on Elysse's. "Remember when we told you that I didn't know about you?"

She nods.

"That's because my parents and your mom's parents didn't want me to know. They worked together to make sure I didn't."

Elysse's eyes widen. "That's mean. Why?"

I shrug. "I don't know." Of course, I can guess. My father wanted to build an alliance with Rinella. Piper's parents didn't like me. Plus, I'm sure my father offered more money than they could earn in a lifetime.

"Grandma and Grandpa did that?"

Piper sighs but nods.

"They didn't help you with... you know who?"

She shakes her head, her expression telling me not to talk about it in front of Elysse.

"Well, thank God Matty and I are here," Lana exclaims. "We're the best family ever. You'll see."

After dinner, Piper and I play with Elysse until her bedtime. For the first time, I put my daughter to bed, reading her a story from a stack of books Lana found somewhere that had been hers as a kid.

Tucked in bed, Elysse smiles sleepily up at us, her eyes heavy with exhaustion from the eventful day. After everything she went through, seeing her smile and feeling safe is an accomplishment.

I sit on the edge of the bed, smoothing Elysse's hair back from her forehead. "Goodnight, Elysse. Sweet dreams."

Piper leans down and presses a kiss to Elysse's cheek. "Love you. Sleep tight."

Elysse yawns, her little voice soft with drowsiness. "Love you too, Mommy. Love you, Daddy."

My heart swells to the point I can't believe it hasn't come out of my chest.

Piper and I each give Elysse one more kiss before quietly leaving the room, leaving the door slightly ajar.

As we step into the hallway, I pull Piper into my arms, holding her close. "Thank you for giving me this chance to be a father, to be a family with you both." I add the last bit to test the waters, to find out if Piper is seeing this thing between us as a done deal. Her and me forever. Just like we planned at eighteen years old.

Piper looks up at me, her eyes shining with what I hope are love and happiness. "I never thought we'd have this. After everything that's happened, I didn't dare to hope."

I cup her face gently, my thumb brushing over her cheekbone. "And yet, here we are. Didn't I tell you we were meant to be?"

She laughs. "You always were so sure of everything."

"Not everything. Just you. Us." I give her a soft kiss. "I promise you, as I did then, that I will always love you. And I will do everything in my power to keep you and Elysse safe and happy."

"It's about time."

I snort out a laugh. It's been a long time since I've heard that irreverent banter of hers. Unable to resist any longer, I capture her lips in a passionate kiss.

"It's time for bed." I scoop her up and carry her to my room.

"You have a thing about carrying a woman to a bed for sex."

"I do?" I think about the last times I've been with her, and indeed, I've carried her. "Well, it's what dashing knights in shining armor do."

Her eyes narrow. "I'm no damsel in distress—"

"No, you're a damsel about to be thoroughly ravished." I set her down in my room, only then remembering why I didn't fuck her in the shower. "Although not tonight."

"Why not?" She almost looks as if she's pouting.

"You're injured."

She purses her lips and shakes her head. "I'm not broken. But..." Her fingers walk down my chest and lower, lower. "I imagine you have blue balls."

My balls are fine, but her fingers dancing along my dick makes him perk up. I take her hand to stop her. "We can just sleep."

"You can try to sleep, Elio. But I'm going to suck your dick."

23

PIPER

Life is as it should be. As it should have always been. I want to savor it, Elio's devotion to me and Elysse, Elysse finally having the family she deserves. Even so, I have this fear that it's all going to go away. Something will happen, and I'll lose the peace and love and security I've longed for.

But right now, I push those fears aside and focus on Elio. He's been sweet, patient with me even though I can see that it's hard for him sometimes. I owe him so much, and right now, I want to show my appreciation.

My fingers slide along the hardening dick behind the zipper of his slacks.

"I don't want to hurt you," he says, his voice rough with growing desire.

"So don't. Didn't I say I was going to do all the work?" I undo his belt.

His smile is a quick flash of delight. "I've missed this part of you."

I look up at him, wondering what he means even as I think I know. "What part?"

"Your irreverence. Your snark."

I arch a brow. "Snark? It's snarky to tell you I'm going to suck your dick?"

"I feel like I'm about to fuck this up," he says with amusement in his eyes. "That's the part I miss. You keep me on my toes, keep me wanting that sassy mouth."

"Well, then." I drop to my knees, and as I lower down, I tug his pants and boxer briefs down, freeing his impressive dick. "Let this sassy mouth take care of this."

I swirl my tongue around the tip, licking off the pearl of precum from the tip. He sighs my name, and it does things to my heart. Is it possible to be loved so powerfully? Even back in high school, there were times I wondered what it was he saw in me. He's so handsome and charming, any girl would want him. Yet he wanted me. Only me. Apparently, even after all this time, it's still me. It fills me with awe.

I suck the tip, my lips gripping around the edge.

"Yes... I love your mouth." His fingers thread through my hair. "More. Take more." His hips gently move forward, sliding him deeper into my mouth.

I press my lips as tight as I can around him as he rocks. My fingers massage his balls and the soft, sensitive skin just behind his dick.

"Fuck, baby..." His dick thickens, the ridges more pronounced.

I use my hand to stroke him as I suck on one ball, then the other, and then take him in my mouth again. I move faster, deeper, every now and then stopping and perversely enjoying the groan of frustration from him when I do.

"You're teasing me," he says the third time I do it.

"Do you want me to stop?"

"No fucking chance." He grips my chin, his eyes intense as he looks down on me. "Make me come in your mouth, Piper."

I'm already feeling pretty aroused, but at his words, the way his dark eyes penetrate through me, there's a strong chance that I'll come too.

I focus, using my hand and mouth to stroke and suck him, harder, faster, tighter.

"Yes... fuck, right there. Don't stop, don't stop, don't stop..."

I keep moving, squeezing him as tightly as I can until his hips buck forward and warm liquid fills my mouth. I swallow and continue sucking, working him, doing my best to drink him in.

"Fucking hell..." He lets out a last gasp before he steps back. He grips my arms and hauls me up, kissing me hard. "I may never get hard again after that."

I laugh. "That will be a shame."

"Don't worry, baby." He pushes me back until I fall on the bed. "I can make you happy even without my cock."

"Promises, promises." I grin up at him.

"Now you've asked for it." He crawls on the bed like a wild animal about to pounce on its prey. My body shudders in anticipation. He pushes my legs open, sliding his hands underneath me, lifting me up to his mouth. "Hold on, Piper."

My fingers grip the sheets as his mouth lowers to my pussy and does the most delicious, amazing things. I go from zero to sixty and then soar in a matter of moments. He gives me a moment to catch my breath before he does it again. And again. And again until I'm a whimpering puddle.

"Elio..." I don't think I can take any more.

He slides up my body. "Yes, Piper?" His expression is smug. He knows he rocked my world... more than once.

Deciding I might be able to handle a bit more after all, I respond. "Fuck me."

He thrusts hard, forcing the breath from me. I grip his shoulders, arching my back as my entire body responds to his invasion.

He lets out a feral growl as he moves, fast, hard, like he's not quite in control. But that's okay because I don't feel like I'm in command of my body, either. We move together like we are made for each other. A perfect, wild dance. Loud. Wet. Hot.

The end comes too soon. My entire body goes taut, that sweet moment of exquisite torture right before unbridled pleasure. He's with me.

"Yes, baby... now... fuck, so good... so good." He rocks, driving in and out as our orgasms crash through us. Ultimately, exhaustion takes over. He collapses on me. I'm boneless under him.

A moment later, he lets out a small chuckle.

"What's so funny?" Should I be offended?

"I feel like I did the first time we did this in high school, remember? I had no clue what I was doing, but my body knew exactly what it wanted and how to get it."

I laugh. "It was a bit out of control."

He rolls off me and pulls me close. "When do you think we made Elysse?"

I wasn't expecting the question, but considering how much he missed, I can understand his wanting to know. "About a month before we moved away. I hadn't known." I look into his eyes, needing him to understand the truth I am about to tell him. "I didn't have an inkling. It was my parents who suspected. After that, they called your parents. God, Elio..."

He holds me tighter.

"It happened so fast. One minute, I'm staring at a positive pregnancy test, and the next minute, your parents are in the living room and they're telling my parents to take the money and go away."

"I'm so sorry about that, Piper."

I press my hand to his cheek. "It hurt you too. I'm sorry I didn't realize that sooner."

He gives me a gentle kiss. "Let's just focus on the future, shall we?"

I nod and settle in next to him. I'm still waiting for the shoe to drop, but right now, in Elio's arms, I'm loved and protected. I can't ask for more than that.

I open my eyes, momentarily disoriented by the unfamiliar surroundings. Sunlight filters through heavy curtains, casting a warm glow across the luxurious bedroom. Relief floods through me. Yesterday wasn't a dream. I'm safe with Elio.

The memories of yesterday come flooding back. Gabriel's rage-filled eyes. His hands around my throat. The terror coursing through my veins as I struggled to breathe. Elio bursting through the door, his face a mask of fury as he pulled Gabriel off me. The drive to this house, Elysse clinging to my side.

Sitting up slowly, I take in my surroundings. The decor is masculine, with dark wood furniture and muted colors. A familiar scent lingers in the air—Elio's cologne.

Being here brings a mix of emotions—relief, gratitude, and a twinge of uncertainty about what the future holds. But for now, I'm thankful to be away from the constant fear that defined my life with Gabriel.

Elio isn't here. Instead, I find a note on his pillow.

Good morning, Beautiful,
I hope you slept well. I know I did.

I smile as I remember his touch, the pleasure he brought me.

Sleep as long as you like. I'll take care of Elysse. Rest up, baby. I want a
replay later tonight.
Yours, Elio

I trace my fingertip over that last word. Yours. Could the dream finally be coming true? I spent the last eight years trying to forget Elio D'Amato, trying to convince myself that what we had was just a teenage dream, a fantasy.

But now, here in his house, surrounded by his things, surrounded by him, those feelings are rushing back with a vengeance. The way he looked at me yesterday, the tenderness in his touch as he helped me shower, the fierce protectiveness in his eyes when he saw my bruises.

I'm overwhelmed with gratitude for everything he's done, for the way he swooped in like a knight in shining armor to rescue me and Elysse from Gabriel's brutality.

But at the same time, in the early morning light of a new day, I can't help but feel a flicker of unease. I've just escaped one controlling relationship. Am I ready to dive headfirst into another? Even if it is with the man I've never been able to forget?

I need time. Time to heal, to rediscover who I am without a man defining me. Time to be a mother to Elysse, to create a stable life for her. As much as my heart yearns for Elio, I know I can't rush into anything. I need to be careful, to guard my heart and put my daughter first.

With a sigh, I fold Elio's note and set it on the bedside table. I shower and dress, then make my way downstairs, following the sound of laughter and the enticing aroma of pancakes. As I enter the kitchen, I'm greeted by Elio and Elysse standing side by side at the stove, both wearing aprons and wielding spatulas. Elio flips a pancake with exaggerated flair, making Elysse giggle and clap her hands. In the background, I spot Elio's cook, looking mildly exasperated but also amused by their antics.

"Good morning," I say softly, not wanting to interrupt their fun.

They both turn to me with matching grins, and for a moment, I'm struck by how much Elysse resembles her father. The same dark hair, the same mischievous sparkle in their eyes.

"Mommy, look!" Elysse exclaims. "We're making pancakes!"

"I see that." I walk over to see how well they're managing. "It smells delicious."

Elio hands me a plate stacked high with fluffy pancakes. "Hope you're hungry. We've made enough for an army."

I go to take the plate, but he pulls it back and puckers his lips. At first, I'm not sure if I should kiss him in front of Elysse. And then I wonder why not? I give him a quick kiss and take the plate.

Elysse scrunches her nose. "Kissing is icky."

"Is it?" Elio picks Elysse up and smothers kisses on her cheek.

"Daddy!" She squeals with delight.

· · ·

As we sit down to eat, I have that sense of rightness again, followed by a fear that it will vanish. Watching Elio and Elysse interact, I'm filled with a bittersweet longing. I know I need to be careful, to take things slow and consider Elysse's wellbeing above all else. She's been through so much already, and I don't want to disrupt her life any further.

And yet, I can't deny the joy I feel at seeing her so happy, so at ease with Elio. It's clear that he adores her, that he wants to be a part of her life.

As we finish our pancakes, Elysse looks up at me with a curious expression. "Mommy, am I going to school today?"

My heart clenches with worry. The thought of sending her out into the world, of risking Gabriel finding her, fills me with dread.

Elio must sense my unease because he reaches over and takes my hand. "Don't worry. I have someone keeping an eye on him. He won't come near either of you."

I nod, feeling a wave of relief wash over me. That doesn't mean I'm not still nervous. But if Elysse is to go back to normalcy, she needs to have her routine, and that means school.

"Yes. You'd better run up and finish getting ready." I stand. "We brought her backpack..." But I'm not sure what's in it.

Elio rises and puts his hand on my shoulder. "Whatever she needs, we can get it."

A few minutes later, Elio is driving us to Elysse's school. He pulls into the drop off zone behind the other cars.

"There's my teacher." Elysse points out the window. "Ms. Kramer."

"Is she nice?" Elio asks.

"Mmm... yes. Sometimes, she gets mad when kids don't listen."

"But you listen, right?" Elio asks.

Elysse nods like a bobble head. I scan the area, looking for Gabriel. He doesn't care for Elysse, but he knows she's the key to controlling me. I'm terrified that Gabriel might somehow find her, that he might try to hurt her to get back at me.

We pull to the spot to let her out.

"Ready, kiddo?" Elio asks, turning around to smile at Elysse in the backseat.

"Ready, Daddy!"

The word "Daddy" coming from her lips makes my heart skip a beat. I exit the car and open the door on her side as Ms. Kramer steps up to us.

Elysse jumps out, and I kneel down to give her a hug. "Have a great day, sweetie. Today, I'll pick you up, okay?"

She nods, then turns to Elio. "Bye, Daddy."

Ms. Kramer's brows pull together because clearly, Elio isn't Gabriel.

"Bye, Elysse. Have a good day," he says back to her.

I get back into the car, and Elio and I watch as she disappears into the school. My heart aches with a bittersweet mix of love and fear. When she's out of sight, I feel Elio's hand on mine.

"She's going to be okay. I won't let anything happen to either of you."

I lean into him, drawing strength from his solid presence. For the first time in years, I allow myself to believe that maybe, just maybe, everything will be alright.

We return to Elio's spacious mansion, for lack of a better description. He guides me inside with a gentle hand on the small of my back, his touch both comforting and electric. As we step into the foyer, a distinguished-looking man in a well-tailored suit rises from the couch to greet us.

"Tony, thanks for coming," Elio says to him. He turns to me. "Piper, this is Tony Ferrara, my attorney. He's here to help you draft the divorce papers."

I shake Tony's outstretched hand. "Thank you for coming." I'm really doing this. I'm really going to be free from Gabriel.

We settle in Elio's office. Tony pulls out a notepad and asks me a variety of questions. At first, I insist that I don't want anything from Gabriel. No money, no property, nothing. I just want to be free of him, to never have to see his face again.

But as Tony gently prods me to consider my future, I realize that I have no financial means of my own. For the past four years, I've been entirely dependent on Gabriel, with no access to my own bank account or credit cards. I haven't worked. The work history I have is a few short years as a single mom in England.

The thought of starting over from scratch, with no resources to support myself and Elysse, is daunting. I glance at Elio, knowing in my heart that he would never let us struggle. But at the same time, I don't want to have to rely on, to be at the mercy of, a man. Not even one as kind and generous as Elio.

After much discussion and soul-searching, I finally agree to a fair settlement—enough to cover Elysse's needs and give us a cushion to start our new life, but not so much that I feel like I'm taking advantage.

"What about the child—"

"The child isn't his," Elio says with a growl.

Tony keeps his attention on me. "Even if he isn't the biological father, if he adopted—"

Elio tenses next to me.

I quickly shake my head. "He didn't adopt her. He has no legal claim to her."

Elio lets out a breath of relief.

"I'll get this drawn up and to you ASAP. You'll sign, and I'll arrange for their delivery," Tony says.

By ASAP, he meant it. Within a few hours, he is back with the documents. As I sign my name on the dotted line, a surge of emotions courses through me. I'm finally breaking free from the chains that have held me captive for so long. I feel a sense of empowerment at taking a significant step toward reclaiming my independence and forging a better future for myself and my daughter.

When Tony leaves, my need to be able to care for myself, along with a growing sense of confidence, has me wanting to find my own purpose, my own identity outside of my relationship with Elio.

"You okay?" Elio asks as he takes me in his arms.

I nod. "I'm just thinking about reclaiming my life."

He smiles. "I know I'm reclaiming mine." He means me. It makes me wonder how he'll take my desire to have something more.

"I... ah... being free of Gabriel means I can pursue other things."

His brow furrows. "Like what?"

I shrug because I have no clue. "A job? Or at least something to occupy my time, to give me a sense of purpose beyond just being a mother and a girlfriend."

His jaw tightens for a moment. "You're more than a girlfriend."

"The point is, for four years I've been nothing except what Gabriel wanted. I've lost... me."

His expression softens. "Well, then, we need to find you. I support you in finding a purpose or whatever you need. Just know that you don't have to rush into anything. You've been through so much, and you deserve time to heal."

Gratitude surges through me at his words, for the way he always seems to know exactly what I need to hear.

"Thank you."

He kisses my forehead, his touch gentle and reassuring. "I just want you to be happy, Piper."

I sink into his embrace knowing he means it. He means all of it. The protection. The love. The support. Perhaps it's time to let go of the gnawing fear that something will go wrong and accept that for the first time, everything will go right.

24

ELIO

I lie in bed with Piper nestled against my body. Like all the other nights over the last week, we've had some pretty spectacular sex. It's the icing on the cake that has become my life since Piper and Elysse moved in with me and life has been fucking perfect. Waking up every morning to Piper in my arms and seeing Elysse's bright smile at breakfast fills my heart with a joy I never knew was possible.

I take Elysse to school each day, relishing our talks and her infectious laughter. In the evenings, Piper, Elysse, and I have dinner together, sometimes with Lana and Matteo joining. Afterward, Elysse and I play games or watch movies while snuggled up on the couch with Piper. Then Piper and I tuck Elysse into bed together. Perhaps over time, the novelty of all this will wear off, but what won't change is how grateful I am that despite my parents' attempts to thwart my happiness, I have found true bliss.

The only shitty parts of my life are the usual. Vincenzo's pathetic attempt at revenge by having my men arrested on bogus charges was an annoyance. And while he's acting like a middle school child with his pranks, so far, they're more irritating than a problem.

Then there's Lana who hasn't given up criticizing my leadership.

But none of that puts a damper on my incredible mood. I feel on top of the world and invincible with Piper by my side. I know with absolute certainty that she is the woman I want to spend the rest of my life with. The three of us are meant to be together.

I've hinted at such with Piper, and I think she feels the same. But the words have not been spoken. Each time she says she needs to find herself, I have a mini-panic attack, worried that she'll find herself in a place that doesn't include me.

But as she lies next to me tonight, as she has every night since coming home with me, I savor this life we're building. She nestles her head on my chest, her breathing slowing as sleep starts to claim her. I trail my fingers gently through her silky blonde hair, marveling at how perfectly she fits against me, like she was always meant to be here. I've felt this way about her since the moment I saw her.

"I love you, Piper," I murmur softly, my lips brushing her forehead. "You and Elysse... you're my whole world now."

She hums contentedly, a small smile on her lips even as her eyes remain closed.

I tighten my arms around her. "I'm going to give you and Elysse the life you deserve. And one day soon, I'm going to make you my wife, if you'll have me."

Piper mumbles something unintelligible, snuggling even closer. I know she's barely awake now, likely not registering my words. But that's okay. For now.

With a deep sigh of contentment, I let my own eyes drift shut, joining Piper in slumber.

The next morning, I wake up excited for the day, as always. After the pancake incident the first morning Piper and Elysse were here, my cook has insisted that she make us breakfast. Something about my making too much of a mess and not properly using her pans. I like having a happy cook, so I concede and let her fix us breakfast that we share as a family. Then I take Elysse to school while Piper does whatever she does to find herself.

For most of the week, I've worked at home, but this week, I need to make appearances at the office. Yes, even the Mafia have official offices. Mine are to manage my legit operations. My more unsavory businesses are operated from home or alternative locations, such as the basement of my restaurant. Thinking of which, it's time I take Piper out for a real date at her favorite place.

I have a meeting this afternoon with Vincenzo, that fucker. The guy is like a dog with a bone. He won't give up on the idea that I marry Ava. I wish I had a brother I could offer. Then again, Lazaro was always a bit wild. I'm not sure I'd want to make her endure his brand of crazy.

Midmorning, I'm about ready to take a break from spreadsheets when Tony shows up.

I greet him with a grin. "Tell me something good, Tony." I rub my hands together in anticipation. Perhaps I'll take Piper out tonight to celebrate her divorce. I should buy a ring.

Tony's expression is grim as he slides the folder across my desk to me. Frowning, I flip it open and scan the pages. My blood runs cold. Scrawled on the signature page is a note from Gabriel to Piper.

You think you can get away that easy, you adulterous whore? Just wait until I file a lawsuit against your lover for attacking me in my own home. We'll see if you still want a divorce when they grant me custody of your daughter.

Blinding rage surges through me as I stare at the note from Gabriel "That mother fucker!" I look up at Tony. "What is this?"

Tony sighs heavily. "Gabriel is threatening to take the girl from her mother. He's claiming Piper is with a dangerous man who assaulted him. He's refusing to sign the divorce papers unless Piper agrees to give him full custody of the girl."

White hot rage surges through my veins. I slam my fist down on the desk, making Tony jump. How dare that abusive piece of shit threaten to take my daughter! My daughter!

"He can't do that. I'm her father." I start pacing, hands fisted at my sides. I've half a mind to drive over to his house and end his pathetic life right now. Yes, Piper wants to handle this the legal way, but fuck that. I should have killed Gabriel when I had the chance. It's clear he's not going to stop coming after what's mine until he's six feet under. No one will miss the abusive dick. Piper and Elysse would be safe. They wouldn't ever have to live in fear again…

I realize Tony hasn't said anything. "What? You think he can take Elysse? He's an abusive slime."

Tony nods. "I'm sure he is, but he's been acting as her father for years now. Plus, unless you have a DNA test proving you're the father, you don't have much of a claim."

"He nearly killed her."

"But there is no proof. No photos. No police reports. I've looked. Not just here, but in England too."

Fucking hell. I need to take pictures of Piper's injuries. They're fading, but not gone. I need to have the doctor write up something attesting to her injuries. Plus, Matteo was there. He saw Gabriel with his hands around Piper's neck.

"I can get photos—"

"A week after the fact? His lawyer will argue that you put them there."

"Except she'll say differently."

Tony sighs. "She'll say anything to keep her child."

I scoff. "You haven't met Piper. She's the one trying to do this all the nice way." Ugh! "Son of a bitch!"

Tony lets me vent for a moment. Finally, I turn to him. "So you're telling me that piece of shit has a shot at taking my daughter because Piper was too scared to report what he did to her?"

"I'm saying the courts put weight on documented history and established guardianship. With Piper only recently leaving Gabriel and no concrete proof of long-term abuse… Gabriel could argue she's being vindictive and that you're a dangerous influence. A judge might grant him temporary custody or at least visitation until a full trial sorts it out."

A growl rumbles in my chest. Over my dead body will Gabriel get his hands on my family again. I'll put a bullet between his eyes myself before I let that happen. No. I'll choke the life out of him like he tried to do to Piper.

"Find a way to block his custody claim," I order Tony sharply. "I don't care what it takes. Hire a private investigator to look into that fucker. Bribe the judge if you have to. But that bastard is never getting near Piper or Elysse again. Understand?"

Tony nods solemnly. "I'll do everything in my power. I promise you that. But Elio, you need to keep a clear head here. Don't do anything that will make things worse for you."

He's telling me not to kill Gabriel. I won't promise that.

"You've got your family back. You don't want to have to go to jail—"

"Then you fix this."

He nods and leaves my office.

I grab my gun and put on my coat, heading down to the garage. Gabriel thinks he's won, but he hasn't. I almost feel sorry for him. He doesn't know the heap of hurt he's just brought down on himself.

25

PIPER

I sit at the beautiful mahogany desk in a sitting room Elio said was once his mother's. He's given me a laptop to use so I can figure out who I'll be moving forward. The task is more daunting than I imagined. I can barely remember who I was before I was ripped away from Elio and moved to another country. I had once thought I'd be a journalist, but the media landscape has changed so much that I don't know if it's a good choice now.

Maybe I could do something around domestic violence. Become a counselor or something. But that feels a little disingenuous. Yes, I was a victim, but my escape was easy compared to others'. I didn't go to a shelter. I haven't had to worry about finding a job, a home, and feeding my child.

I don't know where to start as I stare at the search engine with the cursor blinking in the search box. With no new ideas, I type in words related to journalism. Job prospects aren't so bad, but competition is tight and favors those with new media skills. I don't have those.

My eye stops on an ad for an online adult extension course in creative writing that I can do from home. I used to love writing, filling endless notebooks with stories and poems. To be honest, I wanted to be a famous best-selling author, but my parents suggested I pursue something a bit more predictable and stable. That's how I settled on journalism.

I click the creative writing course, reading through the syllabus with growing interest. I can picture myself crafting stories again, pouring my heart onto the page, rediscovering that part of myself that I thought was lost forever. I've often made up stories to tell Elysse. Perhaps I could write children's books. My heart races as I select the registration button. Emotion wells as I take a step toward a new me. For so long, I've let myself be defined by others. My parents. Gabriel. And if I'm not careful, the same could happen with Elio. Enrolling in this course feels like a declaration of independence.

I cross my fingers that Gabriel hasn't cut off my access to the bank yet as I complete the registration process. It's a small step, but it feels monumental. My breath holds as I wait for the payment to go through. Shockingly, it does.

I sit back, smiling and feeling victorious.

"You look satisfied with yourself."

I look up to see Elio entering. I'm giddy with excitement, but that falters as I see the expression on his face belies the lighthearted statement. He's tense. His eyes are dark, making me think of the time he was determined to murder Gabriel.

I glance at the clock, noting it's early for him to be home. "Did something happen with your meeting?"

He shakes his head as he walks toward me. "My meeting is later. Tony stopped by with the divorce papers."

This should be a joyous moment, but it's clearly not. "He didn't sign them?"

Elio hands me the paper, and I scan the scrawled message, my eyes widening in horror as I read Gabriel's threatening words. My hands start to shake, the paper crinkling in my grip.

"No... he can't take her. He's never wanted her, not really."

Elio nods grimly. "Tony says that since you never pressed charges or documented the abuse, Gabriel might be able to make a case that your living with me is a danger to Elysse. Especially with the evidence he has against me."

The room is spinning. It's happening. The shoe is dropping. Just when everything is going right, Gabriel has to take it away again. Just like he always has.

The thought of Gabriel getting custody of Elysse is too horrifying to comprehend. Tears sting my eyes, and I press a hand to my mouth, trying to stifle the sob that rises in my throat.

Elio pulls me into his arms, holding me tightly as I tremble against him. "I won't let him take her." He leans back. "I was on my way to deal with it the way I should have last week. Against my better judgement, I'm here because I know you don't want that, but fucking hell, Piper... I won't let him live if he's going to continue this bullshit."

I take a shuddering breath to steady myself. If I'm going to be strong, I can't let my fear consume me, paralyze me. "He's doing this to hurt me. He knows Elysse is the key to making me do what he wants. He's using her as a pawn to get back at me for leaving."

Elio nods, his eyes hardening.

My hands curl into fists at my sides. "I won't let him use Elysse against me. Not anymore."

Elio takes my hand, his fingers lacing through mine. "Then I'll go."

It takes me a minute to understand what he's saying. I shake my head. "You can't just solve problems with violence. That's what he does."

The minute the words are out of my mouth, I regret them. The look on Elio's face, pain and disappointment, heightens my guilt.

"I'm nothing like him," he says with a clenched jaw.

"Elio, I didn't mean—"

"I'd never put my hands on you or Elysse or anyone in my family to hurt them."

"I know." I reach out to him, but he's offended by my insinuation and steps back.

"But I will protect what's mine. Any man would, Piper. Any man who says they wouldn't kill to protect their family is a liar."

"I'm just tired of the violence—"

"I can make it stop, Piper. If you think he can be negotiated with, you're delusional."

I feel bad for making the comparison because Gabriel and Elio are different men. I don't know Elio's experience with violence, but when I consider how easy it is for him to talk about Gabriel's death, I have to believe he's killed before.

I'm also not too thrilled to have him call me delusional. "Just because I want a peaceful resolution doesn't make me delusional. Is that how you solve all problems?"

"No. If it were, Vincenzo Rinella would be dead. What is delusional is thinking Gabriel will stop. Ever. Do you really want to live the rest of your life with him lurking behind your back? Lurking around Elysse?" He slices his hand through the air. "I won't allow it, Piper. I won't try to control you, but I'll be damned if I'll let Elysse get caught up in all this."

He's threatened that before. It scares me to death, and yet I know he's right. "Elio, please. I know you want to protect us, but there must be another option."

Elio shakes his head, his jaw clenched. "You don't understand, Piper. Men like Gabriel, they don't respond to reason. The only language they understand is force."

I feel a flare of frustration, mixed with a growing sense of desperation. "Let me talk to him."

"What the fuck, Piper? No. Sorry. I put my foot down—"

"Maybe he doesn't know who you are... who you work with."

Elio rolls his eyes. "Who I am is his whole case. It's why I'm 'unsafe'," he says with air quotes around *unsafe*.

"Not necessarily. You beat him up. I can call him, convince him that it's not a wise idea."

Elio lets out a soft laugh. "Baby, he'll use that to say you threatened his life. Don't poke Mafia man Elio D'Amato or you could end up dead."

He's right. Even so, we have to try. I don't know how I'll live knowing Gabriel's death is on my hands. "If there's even a chance we can resolve this without resorting to violence, don't we owe it to ourselves, to Elysse, to try?"

Elio runs a hand through his hair. "Gabriel's not going to listen to reason."

I step closer to him, placing my hand on his chest. "I know it's a long shot, but maybe..." I don't finish. Elio is right. Gabriel won't give in. But I have to try.

"You're not going anywhere near Gabriel. I won't allow it."

I bristle at his commanding tone, a surge of indignation rising in my chest. "I'm not a child, Elio. I can make my own decisions."

Elio's jaw clenches, and he takes a step closer to me. "I know you're not a child, but Gabriel is unpredictable. He's already shown that he's willing to do anything to hurt you. For fuck's sake, he nearly killed you."

I open my mouth to argue, but something in Elio's expression stops me. Beneath the anger and the protectiveness, I see raw, desperate fear. The thought of losing me, of having me slip through his fingers again, is clearly terrifying to him.

I take a deep, calming breath. "I won't see him in person. I'll call him." I pick up my phone from the desk.

"Fine." Elio pulls me into his arms, holding me tightly against his chest. "I can't lose you again, Piper. I won't survive it."

I bury my face in his shoulder, breathing in his familiar scent. "You won't lose me." I dial Gabriel's number.

Elio plants his hip on the corner of the desk. "Put it on speaker."

The phone rings once, twice, three times.

"*Well, well, well.*" Gabriel's voice drips with smug satisfaction. "*If it isn't my dear, devoted wife.*"

I grit my teeth, fighting back the urge to lash out at his mocking tone. "I'm calling about the divorce."

Gabriel chuckles, the sound sending a chill down my spine. "*Oh, I think we're well past the point of talking, sweetheart. Unless, of course, you're ready to beg for our daughter's sake.*"

"She's not your daughter. Don't pretend you ever thought otherwise," I snap. I haven't used this tone with him for years. Not since it resulted in a beating. "I'm not going to beg you for anything."

Elio's brow arches, and I suspect he didn't think I had this fight in me.

"*Then you'll suffer.*"

"Why are you really doing this? Just to hurt me? Because I hurt your feelings? Grow up, Gabriel." It occurs to me that I might be going too far, but all this pent-up anger surging to the surface needs to be expressed.

There's a beat of silence on the other end of the line, and for a moment, I think I've caught him off guard. But then he laughs, the sound cold and cruel. "*Let's cut to the chase, shall we? You're my wife, Piper. Mine. And I don't take kindly to what's mine being stolen from me.*"

"I'm not your property. I'm a human being, with my own thoughts and feelings and choices. And I'm choosing to leave you to build a better life for myself and for Elysse."

Gabriel scoffs. "*You really think you can just walk away from me? From our marriage? There will be consequences. I can make your life a living hell if you don't come back to me.*"

I can't imagine how, except, of course, his threat to report his injuries from Elio to the authorities. But would it stick? Elysse, Matteo, and I would confirm it was in defense of me. But would they be believed? Would they be seen as biased?

I take a deep breath, trying to quell the rising panic. "I'm not coming back. But I don't want this to get ugly. Can't we find a way to resolve this peacefully?" Maybe I should just let him have everything in the divorce. Walk away with nothing but Elysse.

"*You know, it's funny you should mention resolving this peacefully,*" he says, his tone dripping with false sincerity. "*Because I've already taken steps to ensure that things go my way.*"

I feel a sinking sensation in the pit of my stomach. "What are you talking about?"

"*Don't think I don't know who your new boyfriend is. To be honest, I'm surprised I'm not dead yet. Perhaps he's a Mafia pussy.*"

I glance at Elio. His eyes narrow to slits. God, Gabriel, don't be so stupid.

"I've provided my lawyer with some rather incriminating evidence against your new boyfriend. Evidence that could land him in a world of trouble if anything were to happen to me."

His threat terrifies me. I don't want to lose Elio, not even to prison. Elio's brows furrow, as if he's considering what Gabriel is saying.

"What kind of evidence?" I demand, my voice shaking.

"Oh, you know, the usual. Proof of his involvement in certain unsavory activities. Enough to make the authorities very interested in him if I were to suddenly disappear."

He's bluffing, Elio mouths.

"You're bluffing."

Gabriel laughs. *"Are you willing to take that chance? Are you willing to risk your precious Elio's freedom, his very life, on the off chance that I'm lying?"*

My world feels like it's crumbling around me. I know Elio would do anything to protect me and Elysse, even if it meant sacrificing himself. But I can't let it come to that.

"What do you want, Gabriel?" I ask, knowing I don't want to hear the answer.

"I want you and Elysse back where you belong." His tone is cold and unyielding. *"And if you don't come willingly, I'll take you by force. And there's nothing you or your precious Elio can do to stop me."*

With those chilling words, the line goes dead.

I look at Elio. He seems unfazed as his arms wrap around me.

"You can't kill him. He'll send you to prison," I say, feeling hopeless, helpless.

"Maybe. But unlike him, I'm willing to risk anything to keep you and Elysse safe. You have to let me—"

I shake my head. "I can't... I need to think."

"Don't take too long, Piper. My patience with this is nearing the end."

I look up at him. "I can't have his death on my hands."

"It won't be. And if it makes you feel better, it won't be my hands, although I'd sure like it to be."

"What about the threat?"

Elio's smile is like a Cheshire cat. "I'm not worried. No, the only one who should be worried now is Gabriel."

A chill runs down my spine at Elio's deadly tone. There is so much at stake here. Not just lives, but my very soul. How can I be a part of Gabriel's demise? Yes, he's a terrible man. But does he deserve to die? And can I be the one who sets it in motion?

26

ELIO

Piper shakes her head. "You can't. If anything happens to him, you'll be the prime suspect."

I curse under my breath, frustration building that she doesn't see what needs to happen. Why is she giving him so much power? Why is she protecting a man who nearly killed her?

Straightening to my full height, I square my shoulders, my eyes hardening with lethal intent. "I'll handle Gabriel my way." My tone should tell her that there won't be any argument. "He was given his chance and he fucked it up. Now he pays."

Piper's eyes widen with alarm. "Elio, no. You can't. If you hurt him, it will only make things worse."

I cup her face in my hands, my thumbs brushing over her cheekbones. "You have to trust me. I know what I'm doing." God, I don't want to spell it out for her. The underbelly of my work is dark, seedy, and violent. I hide it well. It makes society see me as a legit businessman, doubting the rumors of my less than legal actions. Sometimes, it makes people underestimate me, think I'm a pussy, which I use to my advantage. Right now, I'm hiding the ugly side of me because I don't want Piper to fear me or judge me. Yes, she knows about my ties to organized crime, but like the rest of society, she can ignore it because she hasn't seen the reality of it.

"You're not the only one who doesn't want to lose you again."

Her words help soften the raw edges of my soul. "Piper... he can't hurt me except through you and Elysse. Any accusations, I can likely get out of. And if I go to prison, it will be worth it if you're safe."

"We'll find another way to handle this. Together. We can sit down with your lawyer and develop a solid legal strategy, find a way to protect ourselves and Elysse without resorting to violence."

I grimace at the thought of involving lawyers and the fucking legal system. In my world, disputes are usually settled with fists or bullets, not courtrooms and paperwork.

"And what happens when he makes an attempt to get you or Elysse? The man I heard on the phone will follow through, Piper. Maybe not today, maybe not tomorrow, but someday. He'll be breathing down our backs until he's dead." I don't know how else to put it. "Are you willing to risk that? To risk Elysse's life?"

Her eyes flash with annoyance. "Don't try to guilt me. I know what's at stake. But I can't be a part of murder. And what will Elysse think?"

My own irritation flares. "Am I the only one here who is willing to risk it all—your love and respect, Elysse's love and respect, jail time, my own death—to keep you and Elysse safe?"

She looks at me in confusion. "I..."

I lean close to her, having difficulty reining in my anger at her stance. "Tell me, Piper, would you kill him if he had Elysse in his clutches right now? Or would you be negotiating?"

"I would do anything to protect her."

I shake my head. "No, you wouldn't. You aren't. That man just threatened your child, and you still think you can reason—"

"I'm trying to protect you."

"I don't need your protection, Piper!" I bark the words out.

She flinches.

"Fuck." I run my fingers through my hair, walking away to take a breath. I turn back, and the way she's looking at me makes my heart crack open wide. I wouldn't say it's fear. It's more like she doesn't know me. Or perhaps she's wondering what she doesn't know about me.

My phone rings. I want to ignore it, but I can't. "Yeah."

"Are you on your way to the Rinella meeting?" Matteo asks.

Fuck again. I nearly forgot. For a moment, I consider canceling, blowing Vincenzo off to deal with this family emergency. After all, the Rinellas haven't exactly been playing nice lately, with Vincenzo's petty attempts to mess with my business.

But as much as I'd rather focus solely on protecting my family, I know I can't let things with the Rinellas spiral further out of control. The last thing I need is a full-blown Mafia war on top of everything else.

No, I have to play this smart and meet with Vincenzo and try to smooth things over before they escalate beyond repair. If I can get the Rinellas off my back, I'll have more resources and manpower to devote to handling Gabriel.

"Just about. I'm at home," I tell Matteo.

"I'm near there. I'll swing by and get you."

"Good."

I take a breath trying to hide my frustration, my pain. "I can see you're wondering whether I'm a monster too. I suppose I am. Would you protect me as vehemently as you protect the man who had his hands around your neck?"

"Elio—"

"Perhaps we can table this discussion until later. I really can't miss this meeting."

She nods stiffly. "Of course. I need to pick up Elysse from school, anyway."

I don't want to leave with this tension between us. I want to cup her face and kiss her. But her guard is up, as is mine.

"I won't be long. Danny will drive you," I tell her, my tone brooking no argument. Unable to help myself, I wrap my hand around the back of her neck and pull her toward me, kissing her forehead. Then I reluctantly pull away and head for the door.

Matteo is just pulling up, and I climb into the SUV. My mind is still reeling from Gabriel's threats. My instincts scream to hunt the bastard down right now and make him pay for even thinking of coming after my family. I push the violent urges aside to focus on the task at hand. I need to smooth things over with Vincenzo, to ensure the Rinellas don't become yet another enemy I have to fend off while I'm trying to keep my family safe.

"Everything alright?" Matteo asks with a glance at me.

"Just a bunch of bullshit from Piper's ex."

Matteo shakes his head. "Why he's still breathing, I don't know."

"Yeah, well... he won't be for long."

"Good."

I arch a brow at him. "Why are you so keen to see him dead?"

Matteo's fingers flex and then regrip the wheel. "It's not a good look that he can go around fucking with you, that's all."

"You think it makes me look weak?"

He shrugs. "I know you, Elio. You can be one deadly mother-fucker when you need to be. But to the outside... he nearly killed your woman. He should have been dead the minute you pulled him off Piper."

My jaw clenches because I know he's right.

"And all this with Rinella. Yeah, I know it's a bunch of pussy-ass shit, but he's getting away with it. It's not going unnoticed by the other families. Probably not Caruso, either."

"You sound like Lana." Before he can respond, I run my hand over my face. "I'll take care of it. You don't have to worry that you're working for a pussy."

Matteo rolls his eyes. "I know you're not a pussy. And I know you'll make anyone pay who thinks otherwise."

Matteo parks near the neutral meeting spot Vincenzo and I agreed upon, the back room of a bar located outside both our territories. I stride to the room, working to put on an air of indifference. I don't want Vincenzo getting a whiff of my frustration about this situation.

The minute I lay eyes on Vincenzo, I can tell this isn't going to be a pleasant conversation. His face is pinched with anger, his dark eyes glittering with barely concealed hostility.

"Elio," he greets me tersely, not even bothering to stand up from his seat.

I take a deep breath, forcing myself to remain calm and composed. "Taking time away from your juvenile games, Vinny?" I sit across from him.

His jaw clenches. "Word is you've gone soft."

"And you'd like to test that, would you?"

"What I want is for you to honor our fucking deal, D'Amato. The one where you agreed to marry my daughter, Ava."

I barely resist the urge to roll my eyes. Here we go again, the same fucking broken record Vincenzo's been playing for weeks now.

"You mean the one you made with my father when your daughter was what? Ten years old?" I shudder. "Fucking pedo. Who arranges a marriage for their ten-year-old daughter?" I think of Elysse, only seven now. There's no fucking way I'd make a deal to have her marry someone, let alone when she's ten.

"You didn't seem to have a problem with it. You saw her, Elio. She's eighteen and has all the qualities of a perfect Mafia wife." He leans forward. "Tell me the truth. You rubbed one off thinking about her, didn't you?"

It's all I can do to keep from gaping. I glance at Matteo, who looks like he's ready to throttle Vincenzo.

"I'm going to pretend I just didn't hear you talk about your eighteen-year-old daughter in a sexual way and tell you what I've been telling you for weeks. The deal is off."

Vincenzo's face flushes an alarming shade of red. How convenient it would be if he dropped dead of a stroke or heart attack. "The hell it is! Your father gave me his word, and I expect you to honor it!"

I feel my own temper rising to match his. "I'm not marrying Ava. I'm marrying someone else."

That seems to take Vincenzo by surprise, his eyes widening slightly before narrowing into angry slits. "What the hell are you talking about? Who could possibly be more important than cementing our alliance?"

I meet his gaze head-on, unflinching. "That's none of your fucking business."

"It is my business. We had a deal."

I sigh, ready to be done with this. "Look, I want an alliance with you, but not through a marriage. I'm sure we can—"

"No. A deal is a deal. Who is so important to you that you'd fuck this all up?"

"She's a woman I love. We have a child." I wince, wondering if I should reveal so much.

Vincenzo stares at me in stunned silence. Then he sits back and laughs. "Fucking hell, Elio. Is it that girl from high school?"

I blink, wondering how he knows.

"Your father, he was so fucking pissed that you knocked her up. Jesus, he paid a fortune to make her go away. And now she's back?" He laughs like my heartache is the funniest thing in the world. "Look, keep the high school sweetheart and the kid. She's shown she'll fuck you without marriage. Have them on the side. No big deal. But marry Ava."

Matteo shifts, causing me to look at him. He does a subtle nod, letting me know I need to keep my cool.

"Don't abandon this deal for some whore you knocked up."

I'm on my feet before I even realize I've moved, my hand fisting in the front of Vincenzo's shirt as I yank him halfway across the table. "Watch your fucking mouth."

Matteo pulls me off just as Vincenzo's man pulls out his gun. I release Vincenzo, pushing him into his seat.

He smooths out his shirt as he looks up at me with murder in his eyes. "You can't just walk away from this, Elio. There will be consequences."

"Let me guess, more of your juvenile pranks?" I shake my head. "I'll deal with your consequences. But I'm not abandoning my family. Not for you, not for anyone." I rise from my chair. "You're on the verge of underestimating me, Vincenzo. Perhaps you should consider that we can negotiate a new deal before this escalates into something you don't want."

"You threatening me?" He stands too, as if he can intimidate me.

"Not at all. Think of it as a warning." With that, I turn and stalk out of the room. I know I've just made a powerful enemy, but I can't bring myself to care.

Piper and Elysse are my priority now, and I'll burn the whole fucking city down before I let anyone tear my family apart again.

27

PIPER

I'm still shaking as I climb into the back of Elio's town car, my mind reeling from the argument we just had. I know Elio is furious that I won't let him handle Gabriel his way, but the thought of being responsible for a man's death, even a man as vile as my husband, makes my stomach turn. Why must Gabriel be like this?

As the driver pulls away from the house, I find myself questioning whether I'm being too stubborn. Elio has a point—Gabriel is a threat, not just to me but to Elysse. Can I really put my own moral code above Elysse's safety? The very thought makes me feel like a terrible mother.

I lean my head back against the leather seat, closing my eyes as I try to sort through the tangled web of my thoughts. I've endured so much violence already. It doesn't feel like it should be the answer. But what if, in this case, it's the only way to protect the people I love?

Elio's words echo in my mind, his insistence that we need to prioritize Elysse above all else. As much as I hate to admit it, I know he's right. There's nothing I wouldn't do for my little girl, no line I wouldn't cross to keep her safe. So why am I resisting now? Is it just not wanting to condone murder? To be complicit in it? Or maybe it's because this isn't a side of Elio I've seen before. In high school, I never knew of his involvement, if any, in his family's activities. Until the day he saved me from Gabriel's grip, I hadn't ever seen Elio be anything but charming. Am I afraid to know the other parts of him?

I don't know what the right answer is. All I know is that I can't bear the thought of losing Elysse, of Gabriel getting his hands on her. And if it comes down to a choice between my moral high ground and my daughter's well-being... well, that's not really a choice at all. Elysse's safety trumps everything.

"Should I just pull into the pickup line?" Danny says, looking at me through the rearview mirror.

"Yes." I look out the window for Elysse. She's usually with a group of friends playing patty-cake games.

Danny pulls up to the curb and I open the door.

"Mrs. Collins," the pick-up duty teacher says, looking at me in confusion.

I shudder at the name, hoping to be rid of it soon. "Where's Elysse?"

"Elysse's father already picked her up about fifteen minutes ago."

For a moment, I'm struck with a wave of relief. Elio must have changed his mind about the meeting and decided to get Elysse, wanting to keep her close after the troubling developments with Gabriel.

"Oh, I'm sorry," I say to the teacher, shaking my head. "There must have been a miscommunication. Her father and I are... well, it's a bit complicated at the moment."

"It has been awhile since he's picked her up."

I start to get into the car when her words strike something inside me. "Wait... who picked her up?"

The teacher's brow furrows even deeper at my words. "Mr. Collins. He said you were feeling under the weather and asked him to get her."

The blood drains from my face. My heart stops. It wasn't Elio who picked up Elysse... it was Gabriel.

Panic rises, threatening to choke me. How could I have been so stupid? I should have known Gabriel would try something like this. God, why didn't I say something to the school?

I grab the teacher's arm, my fingers digging into her skin as terror consumes me. "Are you sure it was him? Did he say anything else? Did Elysse seem okay?"

The teacher looks startled by my intensity, but she nods. "Yes, I'm certain it was Mr. Collins. He was very charming, as usual. Elysse... well..." Her face scrunches up as if she's thinking. "She did seem wary, but then he told her you were home and wanted to see her."

I can barely process her words, my mind spinning with horrifying possibilities. What if Gabriel hurts Elysse? What if he takes her somewhere I can't find her? What if I never see my little girl again?

I whirl around, racing back to the car as I call out to Danny. "We need to go to my house." I rattle off the address. "Right now. Hurry."

Danny tenses. "Is something wrong?"

"Hurry!"

He puts the car in gear and peels away from the curb. I dig my phone out of my purse, my hands shaking so badly I can barely dial Gabriel's number.

The phone rings and rings, each unanswered tone ratcheting up my terror. By the time Gabriel's voice comes on the line, I'm nearly hysterical.

"Gabriel, please," I beg, my words tumbling out in a frantic rush. "Please tell me Elysse is safe."

I'm met with a cold, mocking laugh. "*You sound upset, Piper. Is something the matter?*"

I clench my jaw, fighting back the urge to scream at him. I know I need to stay calm, to try to reason with him, but it's so hard when all I can think about is my little girl in his clutches. I can't deny that if Elio were here now, I'd give my consent to end this once and for all.

"Gabriel, please," I say again, my voice breaking. "Just tell me where Elysse is. I'll do anything you want, just don't hurt her."

There's a long pause on the other end of the line. "*Anything, Piper?*"

I swallow hard. "Yes. Anything. Just please, Gabriel, let me talk to Elysse. Let me know she's okay."

Another pause, longer this time. I can hear him breathing on the other end of the line. "*I'll tell you what,*" he says finally. "*I'll let you talk to Elysse. I'll even let you see her. But only if you come home, alone. No Elio, no police, no one but you.*"

My stomach twists at his words. I know what he's doing. It's exactly what he said he would. I just didn't think he would act so quickly. I shouldn't fall for it, but what choice do I have? I can't risk Elysse's safety, no matter what it means for me.

"Okay," I whisper, closing my eyes as defeat washes over me. "I'll come home, Gabriel. Just please, don't hurt Elysse."

"*I knew you'd see reason, Piper. And don't worry about Elysse. As long as you do exactly as I say, she'll be just fine. You know I've never hurt her. And I never will, as long as you behave. If you try anything... well, I can't make any promises about what might happen.*"

The line goes dead, and I'm left staring at my phone, my heart pounding in my ears. With shaking hands, I dial Elio's number, praying that he'll pick up.

"*Piper?*" His voice is warm, even apologetic. "*Listen, how about you and Elysse—*"

"Gabriel has Elysse. He picked her up from school, and he says I have to come home alone or he'll hurt her."

There's a sharp intake of breath on the other end of the line. "*Tell me you're not going home.*"

Danny turns onto Gabriel's street.

"I have to—"

"*Piper, listen to me. You can't go there alone. It's too dangerous. I'm on my way.*"

I close my eyes, tears streaming down my cheeks as I clutch the phone like a lifeline. "I don't have a choice, Elio. He has our daughter. I have to go. I have to make sure she's safe. Even if it means..." I trail off, unable to finish the thought.

"*Piper, no.*" He swears and sucks in a breath. "*Is Danny with you?*"

"He's driving, but Gabriel says I can't bring anyone—"

"Stay with Danny. I'm coming. Fucking hell, Piper... just this once... please... don't walk in there alone."

The desperation in his voice breaks my heart. I wish I could comply. I wish I could ease the terror he's feeling. But my mind is made up. I have to go to Gabriel. I have to do whatever it takes to protect Elysse. She's the one pure and good thing in my life, and I won't let anyone hurt her. Not even if it means sacrificing everything else.

"I'm sorry, Elio," I whisper, my heart breaking with each word. "I have to do this. I have to keep her safe, no matter what it costs me."

"Dammit, Piper."

"It's what you'd do. You told me so. You're right. I'd give anything... everything for her."

"Baby... please... just wait."

Danny pulls the car into the drive.

"Elio, I love you." I realize I haven't said the words to him since I was eighteen years old.

Elio curses. *"I'm on my way, okay? I'm coming to help you. We'll get Elysse back, I promise. I won't let that bastard hurt either of you."*

I close my eyes, my heart clenching at the desperation in his voice. "We're here. I love you." I end the call. There's no time to waste.

Danny goes to get out of the car.

"Wait here. Don't let him see you—"

"The boss wouldn't like that," Danny says.

"You'll only make it worse. He'll hurt Elysse if he sees you."

Danny doesn't like it, but he nods in understanding.

I steel myself for what lies ahead. The punches. The kicking. Maybe he'll kill me. I hope I can get Elysse out before any of that happens. As I step up to the door, I pull together my resolve and I take solace in knowing Elio will save Elysse and raise her in a loving home.

28

ELIO

I sit in the SUV as Matteo drives through the city. I'm pissed at Vincenzo and loaded with guilt about my behavior toward Piper today.

"Problem?" Matteo asks.

"It's time to put Vincenzo in his place. I've been patient and trying to work this out for long enough."

"No fucking doubt about that. What do you have in mind?"

I scan my brain for ideas that don't include murder. "I don't want to do the same petty shit he's doing."

Matteo laughs. "It's petty because he's too afraid to do more."

I nod, although I'm thinking his fear is of Caruso, not me. "What do we know about ships on the lake?" I ask of Vincenzo's smuggling operation.

"Rumor he's got a drug haul going out."

"Sink it."

Matteo's eyes widen in shock and admiration. "Damn. That's a bold move."

"I've done my best to make things right with him, and he continues this bullshit. He called Piper a whore. No one does that without severe consequences. He's lucky I didn't put a bullet in his head right then and there."

Matteo nods slowly, a grin spreading across his face. "Lana will be thrilled."

I laugh, knowing no doubt, she will.

Matteo's expression turns serious. "What about Caruso? Should you check—"

I wave off his concern, my confidence unwavering. "I'll handle Caruso." With that decided, my next problem is Piper. I shouldn't have been so terse with her. When we talk later, I'll need to do better at managing my frustration. Still, I need her to understand that as long as Gabriel is walking this earth, he'll be a threat to her and Elysse. But I need to do it in a way that absolves her from guilt.

Perhaps I should take her for dinner and we can talk there. I haven't taken her on a real date since our reunion.

My phone rings, interrupting my problem solving. I see it's Piper and my heart fills with emotion. God, I have to make this work.

"Piper?" I'm glad to have the opportunity to start making amends. "Listen, how about you and Elysse—"

"Gabriel has Elysse. He picked her up from school and he says I have to come home alone or he'll hurt her."

My world stops. "Tell me you're not going home."

"I have to—"

"Piper, listen to me. You can't go there alone. It's too dangerous. I'm on my way." I turn to Matteo. "Get to Gabriel's. Fast."

"I don't have a choice, Elio. He has our daughter. I have to go, I have to make sure she's safe. Even if it means..." She trails off. I know what's she saying, and it feels like my fucking life is ending.

"Piper, no. Is Danny with you?" I'm sure he's supposed to be driving her.

"He's driving, but Gabriel says I can't bring anyone—"

"Stay with Danny. I'm coming. Fucking hell, Piper... just this once... please... don't walk in there alone." I want to reach through the phone and make her obey me.

"I'm sorry, Elio. I have to do this. I have to keep her safe, no matter what it costs me."

Fucking hell. I slam the side of my fist into my door. "Dammit, Piper."

"It's what you'd do. You told me so. You're right. I'd give anything... everything for her."

"Baby... please... just wait."

"Elio, I love you."

Fuck. Now she says the words I've been desperate to hear? Now? "I'm on my way, okay? I'm coming to help you. We'll get Elysse back, I promise. I won't let that bastard hurt either of you, no matter what it takes."

She hangs up.

"Fuck! Fuck! Fuck!"

"I'm going as fast as I can. I take it Gabe's got the kid?"

"Yes." The weight of the world crashes down. I should have dealt with him when I had the chance, should have made sure he could never hurt Piper or Elysse again. I fucked up.

I immediately call Danny. "What the fuck?"

"We just got here. I was about to call."

"And you let her walk in?"

"She said it would be worse if I went in with her. The guy told her no one should be with her, or the kid would suffer."

I acknowledge he's in a tough position. If he goes in and Piper and Elysse die, I'll blame him. But right now, he's her only hope.

"Can you tell what's going on?"

"Things are quiet."

"I'm on my way. If something starts to go down, you save them, Danny..." Fuck! Why aren't we there yet?

"Will do."

I hang up and take a deep breath, trying to calm the storm raging inside me. I can't let my emotions cloud my judgment, not now. Piper needs me to be strong, to think rationally. We have to approach this situation carefully, or I risk losing both of them forever.

I close my eyes, my mind racing with possibilities.

As the car speeds through the city streets, Matteo's knuckles white on the steering wheel, he glances over at me. "Can we end this asshole once and for all this time? I'll do it if Piper doesn't want you to."

"We end him." I'm not afraid to go to jail. But if there is a way to do this without being arrested, I want to try it. Finally, an idea hits me. I'll pull out my phone and call Jones, one of the policemen on my payroll.

After a few rings, his gruff voice comes on the line. "D'Amato. What can I do for you?"

"Jones, I need a favor."

A few minutes later, I hang up. I glance outside, wondering how much longer until we get there. It feels like a fucking lifetime.

"So you're going to have him arrested?" Matteo sounds disappointed.

"I'm protecting our asses."

Matteo nods, his expression grim. "And what about Gabriel? What happens to him when they bring him in?"

I clench my jaw. "Hopefully, when they bring him in, he'll be in a body bag."

Matteo pulls up to the curb outside Gabriel's house, my heart pounding in my chest. The street is eerily quiet. The house more so. I don't hear crying or screaming or yelling. I don't like it. It feels like I'm too late.

Danny meets us as we exit the car.

"Okay, here's the plan. I'm going to go in through the front, confront Gabriel directly. Matteo, you sneak around back, see if you can find a way in without being seen."

Matteo nods. "Got it."

I turn to Danny. "You're backup. If this goes tits up, I want you to kill Gabriel."

He nods.

"Promise me that motherfucker won't survive this."

"I promise." Danny glances at Matteo. He probably wonders

about my sanity, losing my mind like this over a woman. But Piper isn't any woman. She and Elysse are my life.

I grab my gun, checking the magazine. I hold it out for any nosy neighbor to see.

Danny's eyes widen. "You're going to draw unnecessary attention."

I nod, a grim smile on my face. "That's the point."

29

PIPER

I pour Gabriel another whiskey, my hands shaking as I add a few ice cubes to the glass. The sharp scent of alcohol stings my nostrils, but I don't dare show my revulsion. Not when Elysse is sitting next to Gabriel at the kitchen table, her eyes wide and frightened as she watches him.

Gabriel's face is a mess of purple bruises, his nose encased in a protective plastic cast. Elio did a number on him, and I can't help the small thrill of satisfaction that zings through me at the sight. But it's quickly replaced by dread as Gabriel takes a long sip of his drink, his cold eyes finding mine over the rim of the glass.

"Is dinner almost ready?" His words are slightly slurred, a testament to how much he's already had to drink.

I nod, turning back to the stove. "Five more minutes."

The chicken sizzles in the pan, and I stir the sautéed vegetables, trying to ignore the way my stomach churns with nerves.

Elysse shifts, her movement drawing Gabriel's attention. He sets his glass down on the coffee table with a thunk, leaning forward to pin her with a hard stare.

"And what about you, princess? Are you happy to be home with me?"

I tense, my grip tightening on the wooden spoon. Elysse mumbles something I can't quite hear, but it seems to satisfy Gabriel. He leans back, picking up his drink once more.

My heart pounds as I wait for the food to finish. Gabriel watches my every move, his eyes dark and glittering with a dangerous light. The knife I used to chop the vegetables now sits on the table next to him, too close to Elysse.

"Just in case you get any ideas," he'd said when he took it and sat next to her.

I told Danny not to help me. Gabriel said he'd hurt Elysse if any help arrived. Yet I stand here, hoping that Elio will save us yet again. That he'll find a way to get us out of this nightmare once and for all. Until then, I have to play the dutiful wife. I have to keep Gabriel calm and placated.

"Come sit," he commands. I'm about to tell him the dinner might burn, but that will likely inflame him. As will a burnt dinner. I can't win.

I comply, sinking into the chair across from him. Elysse is next to him, her small body rigid with tension.

Gabriel's hand snakes out, gripping Elysse's arm in a bruising hold. She whimpers, and I lurch forward, ready to intervene. But the look he shoots me freezes me in place, a silent warning.

"Not a word from you," he hisses at me, his fingers tightening on Elysse's arm. "Or I'll make sure she regrets it."

I swallow hard, my eyes burning with unshed tears. I've never felt so helpless, so utterly powerless to protect my daughter.

"My real daddy will come for us. He won't let you hurt us anymore." Elysse's voice is trembling but clear.

Gabriel's face contorts with rage, his grip on her arm turning brutal. "Your real daddy?" His eyes blaze with a terrifying madness I've never seen before. His fingers dig deeper into Elysse's arm, and she cries out in pain.

"You turned her against me," he snarls at me, spittle flying from his lips. "Filled her head with lies about her 'real daddy'. This is all your fault, you fucking whore!"

I flinch at the accusation, my heart racing. "Gabriel, please. Let her go. She didn't do anything wrong."

But he ignores me, his attention fixed solely on Elysse. "I'm your father. Not that Mafioso piece of shit. Me!"

Elysse whimpers, tears streaming down her face. I can't take it anymore. I lunge forward, grabbing Gabriel's wrist, trying to pry his fingers loose.

"Stop it!" Desperation claws at my throat. "You're hurting her!"

Gabriel backhands me with his free hand, sending me reeling backward. Pain explodes across my cheekbone as I hit the floor, stars dancing in my vision.

"You did this," he slurs, staggering to his feet. He sways drunkenly, his eyes unfocused and wild. "I've got a fucking broken nose from your murderous lover. You got me fired. Turned my own daughter against me. It's all your fault, you bitch!"

I taste blood in my mouth. Gabriel advances on me, his fists clenched at his sides. I scramble backward, my heart in my throat.

"I'm sorry." I hold up a hand to ward him off. "Please, Gabriel. Don't do this."

But he's beyond reason, lost in a haze of alcohol and rage. He reaches down, grabbing a fistful of my hair and yanking me to my feet. I cry out, my scalp burning as he drags me up. "I'll show you. I'll show you what happens when you cross me."

Terror seizes me, cold and paralyzing. I know what he's capable of, the brutality he can inflict. And Elysse is watching, helpless and afraid...

I take a shaky breath, trying to calm my racing heart. "Gabriel, please," I say softly. "I know you're upset. I'm sorry."

He blinks down at me, his eyes still glazed with alcohol and anger, but there's a flicker of uncertainty there too.

I press on, choosing my words carefully. "I'm sorry things have been so hard lately. I never meant to hurt you or turn Elysse against you."

Gabriel's jaw clenches, but he doesn't lash out.

I take it as a sign to continue. "I know you love her in your own way. And I know you want what's best for her."

He nods slowly, his grip on my hair loosening further. "I do. I just want us to be a family again."

My heart twists at the misplaced regret in his voice. I know it's a lie, a manipulation tactic he's used countless times before. But I have to play along.

"I want that too." I force a small smile. "I want us to be happy."

Gabriel's brow furrows, and for a moment I think he might argue. But then he sighs, his shoulders slumping in defeat as he lets go of me. "I know. I fucked up. I hurt you and Elysse. I'm sorry."

The words ring hollow, but I nod anyway. "I appreciate your saying that." I move closer to Elysse, hoping to be in a better position to protect her.

He nods, a glimmer of hope in his eyes. "I will. I'll do better, I promise. Just come back home, and we can start over."

I hesitate, knowing it's a trap. But I need to keep him talking, to buy more time for Elio to get here.

"Maybe we can just forget about everything that's happened with Elio. We can start over."

Elysse looks at me like I've betrayed her. I hate that she's too young to understand what I'm doing.

Gabriel's face darkens, and for a moment I think he might lash out again. But then he looks away, his expression almost sheepish. "I never actually contacted a lawyer. I was just trying to scare you into coming back."

Relief washes over me. He was bluffing. Just like Elio said. It means there is no threat of Elio going to prison for beating up Gabriel. It also means that I've fallen for Gabriel's plan. Because I didn't listen to Elio, Elysse is in danger again. Guilt and regret grow.

I can't think about that. I need to keep a level head until I can get Elysse safe. Now that things are calm, I keep talking, keeping Gabriel calm, keeping him distracted.

Until help arrives.

"Let me serve us dinner." I turn back to the stove when there's a knock on the door. I freeze, my heart leaping into my throat. Gabriel's head snaps up, his eyes narrowing.

"Who the fuck is that?" he growls, his hand inching toward the knife on the table.

I shake my head. "I don't know. I swear." I turn off the stove hoping it looks normal, nonchalant.

Gabriel stalks over to Elysse, grabbing her roughly by the arm and hauling her to her feet. She cries out in pain and fear, but he ignores her as he stands in the opening of the kitchen, looking toward the front door.

"Open it," he orders me, his voice low and dangerous. He positions Elysse in front of him like a human shield. "And if you try anything stupid, I'll snap her neck like a twig."

I nod frantically. "I won't. I promise."

With shaking hands, I reach for the doorknob, my heart pounding so hard I'm sure Gabriel can hear it. I pray that it's Elio on the other side, that he's found a way to save us.

I pull open the door with trembling hands. There stands Elio, his face a mask of barely contained fury. A gun is clutched in his hand, the metal gleaming dully in the dim light of the entryway.

For a moment, hope surges through me. Elio is here. He'll save us, just like he promised.

"Stand aside, Piper." Elio raises the gun, pointing it at Gabriel.

Gabriel wraps an arm around Elysse's waist, lifting her and holding her in front of him. "Go ahead. Shoot me. But the only way you'll kill me is if you kill the kid."

30

ELIO

I see red as Gabriel pulls my daughter in front of him, using her as a human shield against my rage. The fucking coward.

"You spineless piece of shit," I snarl, keeping my gun trained on him even as I'm terrified I might accidentally hit Elysse. "Hiding behind a child? What a fucking pussy of a man."

Gabriel just laughs, and there's a note of hysteria in it that sends a chill down my spine. "You call it cowardice. I call it intelligence. I know my limits against a brute like you."

My grip tightens on the gun as I imagine a hundred ways to end this bastard. But with Elysse in the line of fire, I can't risk it. I'd never forgive myself if I hurt her. I just have to hope this plan works. In the meantime, I need to get Elysse safe and keep Gabriel distracted a little longer.

"Brute?" I scoff, noting a knife on the table not far from him. It's way too close to my daughter for my liking. "Says the man who beats his wife and terrorizes a little girl. You're not intelligent, Gabriel. You're pathetic. No wonder your life is shit."

I sense more than see Matteo's dark form slipping into the dining room from the far doorway, moving with the stealth and grace of a panther. My cousin is damn good at what he does. If anyone can get to Gabriel before he hurts Elysse, it's him.

I keep my eyes locked on Gabriel, not daring to so much as glance at Matteo and risk giving away his position. But in my periphery, I track Matteo's careful progress across the room, drawing steadily closer to the bastard holding my daughter hostage.

Just a moment longer. Gabriel will be neutralized, and Elysse and Piper will be safe.

Matteo is mere feet away when Gabriel seems to sense the danger at his back. He starts to turn, to pivot and face the threat. But I can't let him see Matteo.

I raise my gun and pull the trigger twice in rapid succession, sending two bullets straight into the ceiling above us. The shots are ear-splittingly loud in the close confines of the house, and the acrid scent of gunpowder fills the air. These are not new sensations for me, but I hate that Piper, and especially Elysse, have to experience it.

Gabriel flinches violently and jerks his head up to stare at me with wild eyes. "What the fuck are you doing?" he shouts, his grip on Elysse tightening until she cries out in pain.

It's physically painful to restrain myself from rushing him, from tearing my daughter out of his arms and putting a bullet in his brain. But I need to trust Matteo. I need to buy him the time to get into position. I give a slight nod toward the knife. Matteo glances in the direction, nodding back that he sees the potential weapon within Gabriel's reach.

I force a cold smile, keeping my gun pointed at Gabriel's face. "Just reminding you who's in charge here. I've got a bullet with your name on it, you worthless fuck. The only question is, will you let Elysse go before or after I pull the trigger?"

Gabriel's eyes go wide as he spots Matteo diving for the knife on the table. He lunges for it at the same time. The movement frees Elysse, who charges toward Matteo, the closest safe person to her.

My heart stops as Gabriel's fingers close around the handle a split second before Matteo's while he also grabs Elysse, yanking her back to him, pressing the blade of the knife to Elysse's throat.

"Oh, God, Gabriel, no!" Piper drops to her knees. Her agony mirrors my own. But I can't let it distract me. I need to focus to save my little girl.

"Back off!" Gabriel's voice shakes with a mixture of fear and adrenaline. "Both of you, or I swear to God I'll slit her fucking throat!" He picks Elysse up with one arm, holding her in front of him again with the knife in his other hand at her neck.

Elysse whimpers, tears streaming down her face as she stares at me with terrified eyes. "Daddy."

Fuck. Rage and terror war within me, and it takes every ounce of self-control I possess not to pull the trigger and put a bullet right between Gabriel's eyes. But with that knife against my daughter's throat, I can't risk it.

"Okay," I say through gritted teeth. "Okay, just take it easy, Gabriel. Don't do anything stupid."

Matteo backs away while his eyes dart around the room, searching for an opening.

Gabriel lets out a harsh laugh, tightening his grip on Elysse. "Stupid? You're the one who's stupid, Elio. Thinking you could just take my wife and kid and I'd let you get away with it? I don't think so."

I suck a breath, wondering where my backup is. "Your wife? She stopped being your wife the second you laid a hand on her, you abusive fuck. And Elysse was never your kid. She's mine. Always has been."

"Please Gabriel, don't hurt her," Piper pleads. "She's innocent in all of this. Just let her go. Take me. I'll do whatever you want."

No. I can't let that happen, either.

"Will you take your lover's gun and kill him?" Gabriel asks.

Piper's eyes close tight.

"It won't come to that," I tell them both. I decide to go with a different tactic. "Listen to me, Gabriel. No one needs to get hurt here. Just put the knife down and we can talk about this like civilized men."

Gabriel lets out a harsh bark of laughter. "Civilized? That's rich coming from you, D'Amato. You and your fucking cousin barged into my home with guns and threats, and you expect me to be civilized?"

I grit my teeth, biting back the urge to tell him exactly what I think of his version of civilized behavior. But I need to keep him talking, need to buy more time.

"You're right." I force the words out through clenched teeth. "We shouldn't have come in here like this. But we were just trying to protect Piper and Elysse."

Gabriel's face twists into an ugly sneer. "They're not yours to protect. They're mine. My wife, my kid. And if you don't want to see just how far I'm willing to go to keep them, you'd better get the fuck out of my house right now."

I exchange a quick glance with Matteo, seeing the same helpless frustration in his eyes that I'm feeling. We're backed into a corner here.

"How about I lower my gun and you lower the knife?"

"How about you leave?"

I nod. "Sure. I'll leave, but you need to lower the knife. Let Elysse go. Then I'll be gone." I wait a moment, then slowly, carefully, lower my gun, holding my other hand up in a gesture of surrender. "I'm putting my gun down. Now how about you lower that knife and we can end this peacefully?"

Gabriel's grip on the knife loosens slightly, the blade shifting away from Elysse's throat.

Elysse cries out, driving her heel back into Gabriel's groin. Gabriel howls in pain, releasing Elysse as he doubles over, covering his dick.

Elysse drops to the floor. Matteo is there in an instant, reaching her for her. But again, Gabriel lunges, grabbing her arm, wrenching her back toward him even as he's still doubled over in pain.

"You little brat," he snarls as he raises the knife. "You're going to pay for that." The knife flashes in the light as Gabriel raises it over Elysse, murder in his eyes. Terror fills me.

Piper screams in horror, the sound tearing through me like a physical blow. My heart stops in my chest as I realize I'm about to watch my daughter die right in front of me.

A gunshot suddenly echoes through the house, the sound deafening in the enclosed space. Another two follow. Time stops. Have I just lost everything?

31

PIPER

A loud bang echoes through the house. I'm paralyzed with fear and confusion. We're all looking around, even Gabriel. The two more shots ring, and Gabriel drops to the floor.

My ears are ringing from the sound. I can't wrap my brain around what's happening, but all I can think about is my daughter. I whip my head around, searching for her frantically.

I spot Elysse clinging to Matteo, her arms wrapped tightly around his waist as she buries her face against his stomach. He cradles her head protectively, shielding her eyes from the grisly sight of Gabriel's body.

I rush over to them, desperate to hold my daughter and know she's safe. I reach for her as two other men enter the house. They must be Elio's men. I don't care who they are or that they've killed Gabriel. Elysse is all that matters. Elysse and Elio.

I look for him. His eyes are on me and Elysse as he talks to one of the men while the other checks Gabriel.

It's then I notice he has a police uniform on. He's taking his mic and talking into it. "Dispatch, we have a hostage situation with shots fired. One suspect down. Need medical on scene ASAP."

The cop's gaze falls to Gabriel's lifeless body and the growing pool of blood surrounding his head. He approaches, leaning down to check for a pulse.

After a moment, he shakes his head and speaks into the radio again. "Suspect is deceased. Cancel medical."

I'm still reeling from the shock of everything that's happened when I feel strong arms wrap around me from behind. I tense for a split second before Elio's familiar scent envelops me and I relax into his embrace.

"Are you okay? Did he hurt you?" Elio's deep voice is laced with concern as he turns me to face him, his eyes scanning my body for any sign of injury.

I shake my head, my voice trembling as I respond. "No, I'm okay."

His gaze drops to my cheek where Gabriel hit me earlier.

"Daddy." Elysse's little arms reach up to him.

He picks her up, holding her close. "You're safe now. You both are. He's never going to threaten you again." I hear the quaver in his voice. I imagine he's thinking about how he nearly lost everything, just as I'd been thinking.

After a moment, Elysse pulls back slightly, her tearful gaze finding Elio's. "I knew you'd come and save us. Just like you did before."

"I'll always come for you and your mom. No matter what."

Tears fill my eyes as the reality of his words sinks in. After years of living in fear, of enduring abuse and torment from the man who was supposed to love and protect us... it's finally over.

I bury my face against Elio's chest as sobs rack my body. His arm tightens around me, and he presses a kiss to the top of my head and then to Elysse's. "Shh, it's okay. I've got you. I'm never letting anyone hurt either of you ever again."

"We need statements," one of the men says.

"Let me take them away from him." Elio nods toward Gabriel.

Elio leads us to the living area.

"How'd the police know to come?" I ask. It seems odd that Elio would call them considering his line of work.

He takes a deep breath, glancing around to make sure no one is within earshot before he continues. "I know them." His eyes are intent, telling me there's more to the relationship. Finally, it dawns on me that they're on Elio's payroll. I suppose that should bother me, but I'm aware that no business, organization, or political group is free of corruption.

"I didn't order him to be killed, if you're worried—"

"I didn't think of that." In my mind, I'm thinking thank God they got there when they did.

"I wanted Gabriel on police body cam. That way, if he survived, we had proof of his violent tendencies."

I'm impressed. "You thought of that?"

He arches a brow, and his lips twitch up slightly. "Why does it sound like you're shocked I could think of it?"

I smile. "I'm not. I just... well, I am impressed."

"You don't have to worry about my getting in trouble. They have him on body cam, and Jones pulled the trigger." He rubs Elysse's back as she continues to cling to him in his embrace.

I glance at the police. "It doesn't look like I would have worried even if you did kill him. If they work for you."

"Having cops working for me helps, but it's not foolproof. This was better."

I swallow hard, trying to process everything he's telling me. I'm sad that it had to come to this, that Gabriel couldn't be a better man. But I'm relieved that he won't be threatening us again.

"And if the police hadn't shown up in time?" I ask, almost afraid to hear his answer. "What would you have done then?"

Elio's gaze hardens. "I would have killed him myself. I told you, Piper. I'll do whatever it takes to keep you and Elysse safe. No matter the cost."

I nod, knowing he's earnest in his commitment to our safety. The fact that I'm the cause of today's terror fills me with guilt. If Gabriel's demise was going to be the outcome anyway, I shouldn't have tried so hard to be diplomatic.

There are so many things I've done wrong, starting with not telling Elysse's school not to let her go with Gabriel. It never occurred to me that he'd get her now that he didn't have to. Calling Gabriel probably motivated him to take action. I should have listened to Elio and just not done anything. Instead, I butted heads with Elio and brought us to near destruction.

"We need to give statements," Elio says as one of the policemen steps up to us. "It's best if we do it at the station. You and Elysse don't need to be here now, and we shouldn't do it at my place. It might raise questions."

I nod. "Will it take long? I'd like to get Elysse home."

"We'll do our best to accommodate you," the policeman says.

"I'll drive them over," Elio tells him. He leads us to the car, carrying Elysse. He puts her in the back as Matteo climbs into the driver seat.

Before I slip in next to her, I press my hand to Elio's chest. "It's all over?"

His eyes are soft. "Yes, baby. It's all over."

I give him a quick kiss, only later wondering if I shouldn't have in front of the law enforcement men. Would that raise questions?

Then I climb into the backseat, taking Elysse's hand.

We're free.

32

ELIO

I'm no stranger to police interrogations, but this time, I'm antsy, irritated. I should take my family home so they can begin to recover from the horror of the day.

Finally, after hours of questioning, I'm able to drive Piper and Elysse home. Matteo stays behind a little longer to make sure he and I are in the clear of any wrongdoing.

The night has been long and emotionally draining for all of us, but especially for Elysse. She's been through a traumatic ordeal no child should ever have to face. I grew up in a family that wasn't beyond using violence, but I'd never seen it until I was a teenager. Elysse is only seven!

I glance over at Piper in the passenger seat beside me. She looks exhausted, her face drawn and pale. But there's a fierce protectiveness in the way she holds Elysse close. I'm breaking the law driving them with Elysse in Piper's lap, but there was no way Piper was going to stop holding Elysse.

I roll my shoulders, feeling unsettled, although I can't pinpoint why. Piper and Elysse are safe from Gabriel forever. Perhaps that's it. They don't need me to protect them anymore. Piper is free to pursue her goals and dreams, find herself without me. After everything that's happened, I wouldn't blame her if she wanted nothing more to do with me or the violence that follows me.

When we arrive back at the house, I carry Elysse as Piper and I walk through the front door.

Lana greets us. "Thank God you're safe."

"Is there anything for them to eat?" It's way past dinnertime. In fact, it's past Elysse's bedtime. But I want normalcy for them before they go to bed.

"I'll check." Lana leaves us to check the kitchen.

"Daddy?" Elysse whispers. "I was so scared."

I smooth her hair back from her face. "I know, baby girl. But you were so brave. I'm so proud of you."

Elysse's bottom lip trembles as tears fill her eyes. "He said he was going to hurt Mommy if I didn't behave. That it would be all my fault."

White hot rage fills me at Gabriel's cruel manipulation. But I push it down. He's dead, and Elysse needs me to be calm, steady.

"He was wrong. Nothing he did was your fault. And Mommy and I will always protect you, no matter what." I carry her to the family room and sit on the couch with her on my lap. I desperately need a shot of something one-hundred proof.

"He said you weren't my real daddy. That you stole me and Mommy from him and he was going to make you pay."

I exchange a pained look with Piper over our daughter's head.

"That's not true. Remember, I knew your daddy a long time ago. We're his family," Piper says, resting her hand on Elysse's.

Her words fill me with hope that Piper isn't going to decide she needs independence from me.

Elysse curls into my body. "I tried to tell him I wanted to go back to school and wait for Mommy to pick me up. But he got really mad." A shudder racks her small frame. "He grabbed my arm really hard and said if I didn't do what he said, he'd hurt Mommy."

Piper makes a choked sound, tears spilling down her cheeks. I feel sick to my stomach. I want to resurrect Gabriel just so I can kill him again, slowly and painfully.

But I focus on my little girl. "You listen to me, Elysse. You did nothing wrong. What Gabriel did, the things he said, he was wrong. You were so brave today. So strong. Mommy and I are so proud of you."

"That's right, baby," Piper says tearfully.

"Just remember, you should only leave school with Mommy or me. Maybe Matteo or Lana." Perhaps I should discuss that with Piper first. In fact, I should discuss private school with her. I have no problem with public school, but private establishments are easier to assert my control over. With a few bucks, I can make sure Elysse has a guard with her.

Elysse nods solemnly. "Okay." She snuggles against me again, her little body growing heavy, her breathing evening out as she succumbs to exhaustion.

"She's asleep." Piper brushes Elysse's hair away from her face. "We should put her to bed."

"Shouldn't she eat?"

"I think she'll be okay. I was able to give her a snack when I got to... well..."

I take Piper's hand and squeeze it. "Let's put her to bed."

I carry Elysse upstairs to her bedroom, using my elbow to flick on the lights. She stirs slightly as I lower her to the bed but doesn't fully wake. I tuck the covers around her, making sure her favorite stuffed bunny is nestled in the crook of her arm.

For a long moment, I simply stand there, my arm around Piper as we watch Elysse looking peaceful in sleep. The events of the day replay in my mind. I came so close to losing her, losing both of them.

I lean down to press a kiss to Elysse's forehead. "I love you, baby girl."

I make sure to turn on the nightlight before quietly slipping out of the room with Piper, leaving the door cracked so the hall light filters in.

"How are you?" I ask, taking Piper into my arms. "Hungry?"

She shakes her head and lets out a laugh. "I left dinner on the stove."

"Don't worry about that. Let's go down—"

"I'm tired too. I want to go to bed."

I lead her back to our bedroom. When I close the door, Piper presses herself into me.

"Thank you. For protecting Elysse. For keeping her safe."

I tighten my arms around her. "I'll always protect her, Piper. Her and you." Will she let me keep protecting them?

She pulls back to look at me, tears spilling down her cheeks. "I was so scared, Elio. When I realized Gabriel had taken her from school, I thought..." She chokes on a sob, unable to finish.

I cup her face in my hands, brushing away her tears with my thumbs. "I know. But she's safe now. We all are."

I lean in to capture her lips in a soft, tender kiss. It's not about passion or desire, but rather a reaffirmation of love and my commitment to her.

When she breaks away, she presses her head against my chest. "I'm sorry for putting you and Elysse through all that fear today. You were right about Gabriel. I should have listened to you from the start."

My instinct is to tell her it's alright, but I don't. I want her to trust me, trust me to honor her need to make her own choices, but also to trust my advice.

"I understand why you wanted to handle things your way. You've had so much taken out of your control. It's natural to want to take some of that back. But sometimes, you need to heed warnings and advice."

She nods, sniffling softly. "I'm still struggling with finding my center, my sense of self again."

I tense, worried this is where she's going to tell me she needs time away to find herself. "I get that, Piper. I do. I'm always going to support you in finding your way. But I need you to know that you can lean on me, too. That accepting help and support doesn't mean you're giving up a piece of yourself."

She gives me a wobbly smile. "I know. I'm working on trusting that you have my best interests at heart."

I swallow hard, steeling myself to ask the question I'm afraid to find out the answer to. "Is that what your resistance has been about? Not wanting to need a man? Or do you equate Gabriel's behaviors with my work?"

Piper's eyes widen. "What? Elio, no. I know I said that, but you're not like him."

"It's okay if it is," I assure her, even as my heart clenches at the thought. "I know my life isn't easy, that loving me comes with a price, a risk. And after everything you've been through, I wouldn't blame you for being uncertain. You said since you were forced to move to England, you haven't been in charge of your own life. Maybe that's what you want. Without me." My breath stalls in my chest as I wait, wondering what she wants.

She shakes her head vehemently, reaching out to cradle my face in her hands. "Elio, I meant what I said earlier when I thought I might not make it out of that house. I love you. I've always loved you. It won't ever change."

Relief crashes through me, but I have to be sure. "Even if loving me means dealing with the darker parts of my world?"

Piper holds my gaze, her blue eyes fierce and unwavering. "Even then. I'm not going to pretend it doesn't scare me sometimes. But I know the man you are, Elio. The father you are. And that's the man I love, the man I choose."

I capture her lips with mine. I pour every ounce of my love, my devotion, into the kiss. Piper responds with equal fervor, her hands sliding into my hair to hold me close.

When we finally break apart, I rest my forehead against hers, breathing heavily. "I love you, Piper. You and Elysse are my entire world."

She smiles. "I trust you, Elio. With my life, with our daughter's life. With my heart."

I pull her into my arms, holding her close as we sink back down onto the bed. "I can't tell you how much I needed to hear that."

"Maybe you can show me."

I smile as my heart, on the verge of cracking apart since the moment I heard Gabriel had Elysse, begins to mend. "I'll do my best."

I take my time touching her, exposing and caressing her soft skin as I undress her. I kiss her languidly, wanting to draw this moment out forever.

She pushes me back, her own hands sliding over me, touching me like she's wanting to reacquaint herself with me. She settles over my thighs, and I lever up, cupping her tits, rubbing my thumbs over the hard, pink nipples.

She gasps, and it's beautiful.

"I'm sorry I didn't come looking for you eight years ago," I say. The guilt of that mistake will haunt me forever. To think of all I've missed. To think if I'd hunted her down, she'd never have been subjected to Gabriel's battery.

"Like you said. That's the past. Let's just move forward, Elio. Can we?"

I nod as I guide her hips over me. "We can. We will." I ease her down, her body surrounding my dick, embracing it.

She lets out a sigh as she wraps her arms around me. "Starting now."

"Starting now," I agree.

Words are lost as we give in to sensation. The pure love radiating between us. The glorious sensations of my body joined with hers. It's beyond perfection.

I roll her under me, pushing her knees up so she can open more, so I can sink in deeper. I want to be a part of her. Not just her body, but her very soul.

Her legs hook around me. Her body moves with mine. I take her hands, gripping them in mine as I dip down and kiss her. We are connected deeper than ever before. My heart has always been hers, but now I'm sure hers is mine too.

"Elio." She arches back, exposing her long, graceful neck. I lean over, gently sucking, not caring if I leave a mark.

"Yes, baby. What do you need?" I shift, wanting to make sure I'm reaching all her most erotic parts.

"Oh!" Her body goes taut. "I love you... I love you." She comes apart chanting the words I've always wanted to hear.

"I love you..." I want to say more. To ask for a lifetime. But my orgasm crashes into me, consuming me. I hold on, hoping she can feel my love, my intention to love her forever.

33

PIPER

Two weeks after Gabriel's death, I move through Elysse's room at our old home, gathering her favorite toys, books, and clothes. My mind wanders as I pack, the events of the past few weeks still raw and surreal. It's hard to believe that Gabriel is gone, just as it's amazing that Elio came back into my life and we're finally getting the chance at the future he promised me so long ago.

My gaze drifts to the window, taking in the well-manicured lawn and the grand exterior of the house I once shared with Gabriel. It's a beautiful home, but it holds so many painful memories. The bruises may have faded, but the emotional scars remain.

As I tape up another box, I wonder what I should do with this place and all of Gabriel's assets he's left me. I've arranged to have most of his things shipped to his parents in New York. They didn't seem shocked to hear about his demise. It makes me wonder if he'd been mercurial and volatile as a child. How had he hidden it from me until after we married? Why hadn't they warned me?

As far as the house and his other assets, a part of me wants to sell everything, to rid myself of any reminder of the man who made my life a living hell. But another part of me hesitates, knowing that the money from the sale could provide a solid foundation for Elysse's future.

Elio has assured me that money isn't an issue. Considering the house he lives in, I'm sure he's telling the truth. But I have some reservations about being completely dependent on him. It has nothing to do with not trusting him. I need the security of knowing I can take care of myself.

I sigh, pushing a strand of hair behind my ear. The decision about Gabriel's home and assets is a decision I'll have to make soon, but for now, my focus is on getting Elysse settled into our new life with Elio. I want her to feel safe, loved, and cherished—everything I never had with Gabriel.

As I carry the boxes downstairs, I can still feel remnants of the negative energy. I can't wait to be rid of this chapter in my life. It makes me realize that the answer I see is clear. Selling the house is the fastest way to end the past and focus on the future. I'll put a portion of the money into a trust fund for Elysse's education, a nest egg that will grow over the years until she's ready to pursue her dreams.

But the rest? I'll donate it to domestic violence charities, to organizations that help women and children escape the same hell I endured for so long. It's a way to turn my pain into something positive, something that could change lives.

I'm about to head out when I decide to go to my bedroom, the one I'd shared with Gabriel. There's nothing there for me but bad memories. Well, not all bad. Elio made love to me here. I open the jewelry box on my dresser. I dig down to a hidden compartment and pull out the only item I want to take with me, leaving behind my engagement and wedding rings from Gabriel.

I return downstairs, carrying the last boxes to the car Elio provided for me. I get into the passenger seat, thinking about the last time I drove. Admittedly, it had been some time. Gabriel had slowly made my world so small, and I hadn't realized it was happening until it was too late.

But now my world is opening up. I'm free. Free to build a new life with Elio and Elysse, free to heal and grow and love without fear. I drive to his home and am met by a few of his men who help me carry the boxes to Elysse's room. I leave them there thinking she and I can deal with them together when she's home from school and her dance class.

I move back down to the sitting room, opening up the computer to work on my homework for the creative writing class. I love it. The creativity, the connection to my professor and other writers even though it's only online. For the first time in years, I feel like I'm finally finding my footing.

I pull out my notebook, flipping through the pages filled with scribbled notes and half-formed story ideas. There's something magical about the process of creation, of taking a spark of inspiration and nurturing it into a living, breathing story.

Later that evening, Elio comes home, spinning Elysse around and giving me a big kiss as he does every evening.

"Dress up, ladies. We're going to dinner."

"Yay!" Elysse jumps up and down, then zooms up to her room to change.

"What's all this about?" I ask.

"I haven't taken my ladies on a real date yet. We're going to your favorite place. It's not easy to get reservations there, but I have an in with the owner." He winks at me.

I change into a nice dress and help Elysse with hers. Elio beams at us when he sees us descend the stairs. "I'll be the envy of every man tonight."

It's silly, but I love how romantic he is. I'd nearly forgotten that part of him.

We're led to a private table in the back, candles flickering on the white linen tablecloth. Elio pulls out my chair, his hand brushing against the small of my back as he helps me sit.

"Help me, Daddy."

"Of course." He pulls out her chair and scoots her in. "I hope you don't mind, but I took the liberty of ordering for us."

"Is it spaghetti? 'Cause I like spaghetti."

"Yes. Plus a few other items I know your mother will enjoy." He sits down, reaching his hands out so he's able to hold mine and Elysse's hands. "I love you both."

"I love you too, Daddy."

I smile. "I love you too."

Wine is served, as is our dinner. It's even more delicious than I remembered from when I was in high school.

When we finish and our dishes are taken away, Elio sips his wine and clears his throat.

"Are you okay?" I ask.

"Yes... well... a little nervous, maybe."

"Why?" Elysse asks.

He leans close to her like he wants to tell her a secret. "Well, I'm about to ask your mom to marry me."

Her eyes widen, as do mine.

"Yes, ask her. You'll say yes, right, Mommy?"

I lean to her, my gaze on Elio's. "Yes."

His grin is a mile wide as he reaches into his pocket, pulling out a small velvet box. He opens it, revealing a stunning diamond ring.

"I've known since the first day I saw you in the hall at school that you were the one for me. I love you so fuc—ah." He glances at Elysse. "So very much. Will you marry me?"

"Yes, yes, yes."

He slips the ring onto my finger, and I marvel at the way it looks, like it was always meant to be there. Elysse squeals with delight, clapping her hands together.

"I have something for you too, sweetie," Elio says, reaching into his pocket once more. He pulls out another box, opening it to show a delicate gold necklace, a tiny lion pendant. "This is for you, my brave little lion, to remind you of how strong and courageous you are."

Elysse's eyes widen as he fastens the necklace around her neck, her fingers tracing the intricate details of the pendant. "Thank you, Daddy." She throws her arms around his neck.

He sits back and wipes his brow. "Whew. That went well."

I laugh. "Did you think it wouldn't?"

"I wasn't sure if it was too much, too soon."

"Elio." I arch a brow. "It's been eight years. I think it's about time."

He lets out a lovely laugh. "You're right."

Later that night, we put Elysse to bed and return to our room.

"I finished at the house today," I say, going to my dresser to retrieve the item I'd pulled from my jewelry box.

"Did you decide what you wanted to do?" He begins to undress from his suit and put on lounge pants.

"I'm going to sell it and everything left inside it. I'd like to put some of the proceeds into a trust for Elysse. Everything else, including his financial assets, I want to donate to domestic violence organizations."

He looks at me with awe in his eyes.

"Why does it seem like you're shocked?"

"I'm impressed," he says, echoing the words I'd said to him before.

"I found something today. It's the only thing I'm taking for me."

"Oh?"

I sit down on the edge of the bed, patting the space beside me. Elio joins me, his brow furrowed with curiosity.

I hold up the item.

It takes a moment, but then his gaze jerks to mine. It's filled with surprise, but more than that, so much emotion.

"I gave you that eight years ago."

"You made me a promise with this ring. And finally, you get to fulfill it."

"You kept it," he whispers, his voice thick with emotion. "All these years, you kept it."

"I couldn't bear to let it go," I confess. "Even when I thought you didn't want me, even when I thought you'd abandoned us. Perhaps deep down, I knew the truth but hid it away like I'd hidden so much of myself away."

Elio takes the ring from my hand, turning it over in his fingers. I can see the emotions playing across his face, the love, the regret, the hope for the future.

"I never stopped loving you," he says softly, his eyes meeting mine. "Not for a single moment. And I'll spend the rest of my life making sure you never doubt that again."

He slips the ring onto my finger, next to the engagement ring. We've come full circle, like a piece of my heart that's been missing has finally been returned.

I lean in, capturing his lips in a soft, sweet kiss.

"Finally, the dream is coming true," he murmurs.

I tug him with me as I lie back on the bed. "It's about damn time."

EPILOGUE: PIPER

The day of our wedding arrives just a few weeks later, and not a moment too soon. After eight years, both Elio and I are ready to fulfill the promise.

I stand in front of the mirror, smoothing my hands over the delicate lace of my dress. It's simple, elegant, and perfect for the intimate ceremony we've planned.

Lana appears behind me, a soft smile on her face. "You look beautiful. Elio is a lucky man."

I turn to face her, tears pricking at the corners of my eyes. "Thank you. I can't believe it's finally happening."

"Well, you'd better believe it. Elio is about to spontaneously combust, he's so ready for this." She pulls me into a hug. "Come on. Any minute, he's going to show up here and drag you down."

We make our way downstairs, where Elysse is waiting, bouncing on her toes with excitement. She looks adorable in her little white dress and a pillow with our rings.

"Mommy, you look like a princess!" she exclaims.

I crouch down to her level, brushing a stray curl from her face. "And you, my darling, look like the most beautiful ring bearer in the world."

She grins. "Daddy says I'm a princess too."

"Yes, that too."

As we step out into the garden, I'm struck by the beauty of it all. The sun is shining, the flowers are in full bloom, and the air is filled with the soft strains of music. It's almost as if the world is finally with us.

My parents are there, looking proud and a little nervous. Things have been tense between us since they arrived, the guilt of their actions weighing heavily on their shoulders. But as I walk toward them, my father takes my hand, his eyes misty with emotion.

"I'm proud of you, Piper." He clears his throat. "Your mom and I regret that we didn't do more to help you, but look at you. You're strong and radiant."

"Thank you, Dad."

With my arm hooked with my father's, I walk down the aisle. My eyes lock with Elio's. He looks devastatingly handsome in his suit, his dark hair slicked back, his eyes shining with love and adoration.

Elysse skips ahead of me toward her father. Elio grins with pride at her. Matteo stands beside Elio, looking proud and a little emotional.

Finally, I'm by Elio's side. The day we've always dreamed of having is finally here. To be honest, I don't hear much of the ceremony. I'm too lost in Elio's eyes, the way he looks at me like I'm his world.

Finally, the priest announces us husband and wife, then we kiss, sealing our union. Our happily ever after is finally here.

As we move into the reception, I can't stop smiling, my hand clasped tightly in Elio's.

"Whose idea was it that there should be receptions?" he whispers to me. "I'm ready for the honeymoon."

"Soon," I promise him.

We mingle with our guests, accepting congratulations and well wishes. Most of the people there for Elio, I've met. He only has Lana and Matteo as family, but it's clear that he values his friendships and that they respect him.

During a quiet moment, Lana pulls Elio aside, her brow furrowed with concern. I can't hear what they're saying, but I catch the name "Rinella". I'm vaguely aware that Elio is having business difficulties with this man. At this point, I don't ask about his business, and I think he senses that I don't want to know the details. Not yet, anyway.

"It's all good, Lana. Taken care of," he assures her with confidence. "Today is my wedding day, so can we please focus on that?"

She acquiesces, clicking her champagne glass with his.

He returns to me, pulling me into his arms. "I love you, Mrs. D'Amato. How about a dance?"

"I love you, Mr. D'Amato, and I'd love to dance."

As we dance, I catch sight of Elysse twirling with Matteo, her little face alight with joy. My parents are chatting with Lana. They hadn't been too thrilled about my dating Elio in high school, knowing his family. But now, I think they're grateful to him for saving me and Elysse.

The celebrations are still going, but like Elio, I'm ready to start the honeymoon, a week of uninterrupted time just for us. We change to get ready for the short trip to the airport hotel for our wedding night, and then we fly tomorrow to some surprise Elio has set up.

I check in with my parents who will be staying with Elysse for the week. As difficult as it had been without their support during my marriage to Gabriel, I'm happy to see Elysse and my parents together again.

I help Elysse get her little suitcase, making sure she has all her favorite toys and blankets. She's bouncing with excitement, chattering away about all the fun things she's going to do with Grandma and Grandpa.

As I zip up her bag, I feel a lump form in my throat. It's the first time I'll be away from her for more than a night. I know she'll be in good hands, but it's still hard to let go.

My mom appears in the doorway, a knowing smile on her face. "Your dad and I are grateful that you're letting us take care of her. Considering how we behaved, you'd be within your right to deny us."

I hug my mother. "I just want to move forward."

She nods. "You and Elio deserve this time together. Don't worry about a thing."

We make our way downstairs, where Elio and my dad are chatting quietly. Elio takes my hand, his thumb brushing over my wedding band. "Ready to go, Mrs. D'Amato?"

I grin, leaning in to kiss him softly. "More than ready, Mr. D'Amato."

We say our goodbyes, hugging Elysse tightly and promising to call every day. I slide into the passenger seat of the car while Elio gets behind the wheel. "We did it. We really did it."

"No regrets?"

"Not one."

He lifts my fingers to his lips, pressing a soft kiss against my skin. "I love you, Piper."

And with that, we pull out of the driveway, ready to start our new life together.

We arrive at the hotel and are shown to the wedding suite. I'm giddy with excitement. I'm finally married to the man who stole my heart in high school. We're a family with our beautiful daughter.

He scoops me into his arms, carrying me over the threshold. "Time for a honeymoon. How about some champagne?"

I loop my arms around his neck. "Not for me."

He frowns. "Are you sick? You didn't have any at the reception either."

"I'm not sick." My smile is so wide I can barely contain it. "I'm pregnant."

For a moment, he's silent, his eyes widening with shock. But then, a grin spreads across his face, his joy palpable as he kisses me. "I... I'm so fucking happy, I don't know what to say."

"And you'll be here for all of it." I know it pains him to have missed so much of Elysse's life.

He sets me down, his hands cradling my face. "You amaze me. You've given me life, Piper. I don't deserve all this happiness."

"You do. We both do." I give him a kiss. "Now, Mr. D'Amato, I think it's time we consummate this marriage."

His grin is wolfish. "Whatever my beautiful bride wants."

We tumble back onto the bed, lost in each other. I hold on to him, pouring all my love into him. As he rises over me, joins with me, I feel so happy, so grateful. I have the love of my life, the love I thought I'd lost but who is now mine, heart and soul, forever.

EXTENDED EPILOGUE

Lana

I stare at the computer screen, a satisfied smile playing on my lips as I read the news article about one of Rinella's boats mysteriously sinking in Lake Michigan.

"Good job, Elio," I murmur to myself, pride swelling at my brother's handiwork. Here I thought he was being wishy-washy with Rinella. Turns out he's been plotting his retaliation. Smart of him to arrange it while he's on his honeymoon.

A knock sounds at my office door at our downtown office building. I glance up, my smile fading as two men in suits stride in. They look official. One of them, the older one, is attractive enough, with a rugged, world-weary look about him. Normally, I don't respond to men I've never met, handsome or otherwise. But there is something in his gray eyes that I find intriguing.

He steps forward, flashing a badge. "Detective Henry Lutz," he introduces himself before gesturing to his partner. "This is Detective Peter Hartley. We'd like to ask you a few questions, Miss D'Amato."

What a disappointment. He's a cop. I make it my mission in life to stay away from them.

"It's just Lana," I reply coolly, leaning back in my chair. "And I'm a little busy at the moment." It's no lie. Elio has been giving me more responsibility, and I want to prove to him that he can trust me in the business.

The detective gives me a tight smile. "I'm afraid this can't wait. We have some questions about your family's whereabouts and activities on a few specific nights recently."

I arch an eyebrow, keeping my expression neutral despite the flare of unease. Elio always says it's best to appear cooperative with cops. Appearing being the operative word.

"I suppose I can spare a few minutes." I gesture to the chairs in front of my desk. "Please, have a seat."

The detectives sit, and Lutz pulls out a small notebook, flipping it open. "Have you heard about the boat owned by Vincenzo Rinella sinking on Lake Michigan the other day?"

"It was in the news."

"What do you know about it?" Hartley barks at me.

I frown. "Nothing. Why would you think I would?" That's the truth too. Until I read the news article, I had no idea it sank. While I feel certain it's Elio's doing, I have no direct knowledge of it.

Hartley sneers. "Everyone knows you have a beef with the Rinellas."

I shake my head. "I have no issue with them."

Lutz gives his partner a look, then turns back to me. "Where were you the night it sank?"

I pretend to think for a moment before shrugging. "I was likely here at the office, working late, as usual. I'd have to check my calendar to be certain, though."

Lutz makes a note, his pen scratching across the paper. "And your brother, Elio? Do you know where he was that night?"

"I'm not my brother's keeper, Detective," I reply with a hint of annoyance. "But I do know he's on his honeymoon."

"That doesn't absolve you or him," Hartley says.

"Then why ask for alibis if you're not going to accept them?"

Lutz's lips twitch up slightly. I think he's amused by me. Interesting.

He holds up a placating hand. "We're not accusing you of anything, Miss D'Amato. We're just trying to get a clear picture of events. Anything we could learn about your business... your relationship with the Rinellas... could help."

I narrow my eyes, studying him intently. There's something in his tone that sets my instincts on high alert. Like his true intention isn't the Rinella boat, but that's the excuse that brought them here. He's fishing for information. What's his real agenda?

"I already told you, I was likely here working," I reply tersely. "As for the Rinellas, whatever misfortune may have befallen them is not my concern. Now if that's all..." I start to rise, signaling the end of this little interrogation.

"What about Gabriel Collins?"

Now I know there's something else up. I sit back down. "If I'm not mistaken, one of your own shot him as he held a knife to his step-daughter's throat."

Once again, Lutz eyes his partner with a short, curt shake of his head. I want to tell Lutz to keep Hartley on a tighter leash.

"Your brother was there," Hartley says, ignoring his partner.

I do an exaggerated eye roll to annoy him. "Yes. Gabriel was planning to kill the woman Elio loves and his daughter. It's clear that you've never loved anyone, so perhaps you don't know the lengths people will go to protect their loved ones. More importantly, I fail to see what it has to do with my family and the Rinellas."

Hartley's eyes glint with something ugly and accusatory. "Maybe nothing. Or maybe your brother had a hand in setting that little scene up, to get rid of his girlfriend's inconvenient husband."

Annoyance and a little worry mix. Could Elio orchestrate a murder? Sure. Were the police he has on his payroll involved? Yep. But Gabriel really was threatening Piper and Elysse. The guy was a menace and had to go. The question is, are Lutz and Hartley really here about that?

I level a cold, assessing stare at the two detectives, my voice dripping with disdain. "It's interesting, the things that capture your attention. A boat sinks, a woman's abusive husband turns up dead after
terrorizing her and her child, and suddenly, you're on my family's
doorstep, looking for a connection. I should be flattered that you
think we're so powerful."

Hartley's face twists into an ugly sneer. "Don't play dumb."

"Tone it down, Pete," Lutz tells his partner. He turns to me. "We're
just doing our job."

"You're doing your job?" I laugh derisively. "How noble of you. It's
just a shame you couldn't have put this much effort into finding my
brother Lazaro when he went missing."

Hartley opens his mouth, no doubt ready to spit some vitriol, but
Lutz puts a hand on his arm, holding him back. "Let's keep this
professional." He turns to me. "Miss D'Amato, we're not here to
accuse you or your family of anything. We're simply trying to gather
all the facts."

I lean back in my chair, crossing my arms over my chest. "The
facts about what? Unless you think Gabriel sank the Rinellas' boat.
But I have no information about that. I don't have information about
any of it. Maybe it was human error. Maybe Vincenzo doesn't keep up
the boat. Accidents happen. And as your own colleague's report
shows, one of *your* men shot Gabriel when he tried to kill my niece."

Lutz studies me intently, his eyes searching my face for any hint of
deception. But I've been playing this game far too long to let anything
slip. My mask stays firmly in place, cool and unruffled.

"I think we're done here," I say after a long moment, rising from
my chair. "Unless you have any actual evidence of wrongdoing, I
suggest you stop wasting my time and go back to writing parking
tickets or whatever it is you do."

Hartley looks ready to argue, but Lutz puts a restraining hand on
his shoulder. "We'll be in touch if we have any further questions."

"Hmm... I suppose you'll be back, then." To be honest, I wouldn't
mind another visit from Lutz. He's older than me by a decade, at least.

But as much as I don't like the police, there's something about him that radiates authenticity. Like he sincerely believes in his work.

"I imagine we will," he says.

I walk around my desk toward the two men now standing and ready to leave. A sly smile plays on my lips as I tilt my head, studying Detective Lutz. "It sounds almost as if you're stalking me."

Lutz's jaw tightens imperceptibly, but he keeps his cool, professional mask in place. "Just doing my job, Miss D'Amato. It pays to be thorough in my line of work."

"Lana," I purr, my voice honey-sweet with just a hint of mockery. "And I have to wonder, is this level of thoroughness reserved for all your cases, or just the ones involving women?"

Hartley scowls at me, clearly not appreciating the sudden shift in tone, but Lutz doesn't even blink. He leans forward as he fixes me with an intense, unwavering stare.

"I can assure you, my interest in this case is purely professional," he says, his voice low and even. But there's a flicker of something in his eyes, a heat that belies his cool exterior. He's interested.

I feel it too, the electric crackle of tension between us, and I can't help but lean in. "Is that so?" My gaze drops deliberately to his lips before flicking back up to meet his eyes. "And here I thought we were starting to have a connection."

Lutz's eyes narrow, but he doesn't pull back, doesn't break the charged eye contact. "I think you're mistaking professional curiosity for something else, Miss D'Amato."

"Lana," I correct him again. "And I don't think I'm mistaking anything, Detective."

We're close now, so close I can feel the heat of him. The air between us is thick with tension, a heady mix of suspicion and attraction. I know I'm playing with fire, but I can't seem to stop myself. There's something about this man that draws me in even as it sets off all my warning bells.

Hartley clears his throat awkwardly, breaking the spell, and Lutz blinks, pulling back abruptly. He stands, straightening his jacket with a sharp tug. "We'll be in touch, Miss D'Amato." He hands me his business card.

I take the card from Lutz, our fingers brushing lightly in the exchange. A spark of electricity zings through me at the contact, and I fight the urge for more contact. It's one thing to use my wiles to manipulate men, but this isn't that. Or not only that. What is wrong with me? The man is a cop, for Christ's sake.

"If you think of anything else that might be relevant to our investigation, please don't hesitate to call," Lutz says.

I glance down at the card, running my thumb over the embossed letters of his name. "Detective Henry Lutz," I read aloud. "Do you go by Henry or Hank?"

"Detective Lutz."

I sigh. "Shame. This would have been an interesting meet cute, although asking me out for coffee or a drink would work better than accusing my family of nefarious activities."

Lutz's eyes widen slightly, and for a moment I think I've managed to catch him off guard. But then he throws his head back and laughs, a deep, rich sound that sends a shiver down my spine.

"I'll keep that in mind for next time," he says, his eyes twinkling with amusement.

Beside him, Hartley shifts impatiently, his face set in a scowl. "If you're quite finished flirting with the suspect," he grumbles, shooting me a venomous look.

I arch an eyebrow at him, unimpressed. "Suspect? I thought this was just a friendly chat."

Lutz clears his throat, the laughter fading from his eyes as he steps back, putting some distance between us. "We should be going. Thank you for your time, Miss D'Amato."

"It's Lana, Hank," I correct him again, just to see the flicker of annoyance in Hartley's eyes.

Lutz nods, a ghost of a smile playing at the corners of his mouth. "Lana," he repeats, like he's testing out the feel of my name on his tongue.

Then he turns and strides out of my office, Hartley trailing behind him like a sullen child. I watch them go, my gaze lingering on the broad expanse of Lutz's shoulders beneath his well-tailored suit. Can he afford that on a cop's salary? Maybe he's on someone else's payroll. Rinella, maybe?

As the door clicks shut behind them, I sit in my chair, leaning back. I turn Lutz's card over in my fingers. I have a feeling this isn't the last I'll be seeing of Detective Henry Lutz. And despite my better judgment, I find myself looking forward to our next little tête-à-tête.

Dear Fabulous Readers,

*I hope Elio and Piper's explosive reunion left you breathless and craving more. This is the first book in the thrilling **Dynasty of Deception series**, where passion, power, and family secrets collide in Chicago's dangerous underworld.*

*Hungry for your next dose of mafia romance? The journey continues with **Ice Princess**, available now on Amazon. Keep the intrigue and desire burning!*

Your incredible support breathes life into this world of shattered alliances, hidden children, and forbidden love. From the depths of my heart, thank you!

Until we meet again in the shadows of the Windy City...

Keep turning those pages, and remember – in the Dynasty of Deception, loyalty is a double-edged sword, and love is the most dangerous game of all!

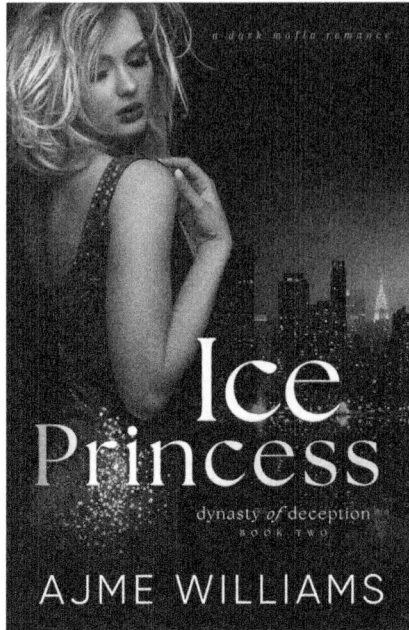

Ice Princess (Henry and Lana)

WANT MORE AJME WILLIAMS?

Join my no spam mailing list here.

You'll only be sent emails about my new releases, extended epilogues, deleted scenes and occasional FREE books.

Printed in Great Britain
by Amazon